Esme's Wish

elizabeth foster

ODYSSEY
BOOKS

Published by Odyssey Books in 2017
www.odysseybooks.com.au

Copyright © Elizabeth Foster 2017

The moral right of Elizabeth Foster to be identified as the author
of this work has been asserted.

A Cataloguing-in-Publication entry is available from the
National Library of Australia

Series: Foster, Elizabeth. Esme Series; book 1
ISBN: 978-1-925652-24-6 (pbk)
ISBN: 978-1-925652-25-3 (ebook)
Keywords: Young adults, Fantasy, Mystery

Cover artwork by Furea (www.fureadesigns.com)
Map artwork by Christopher Foster

To Chris

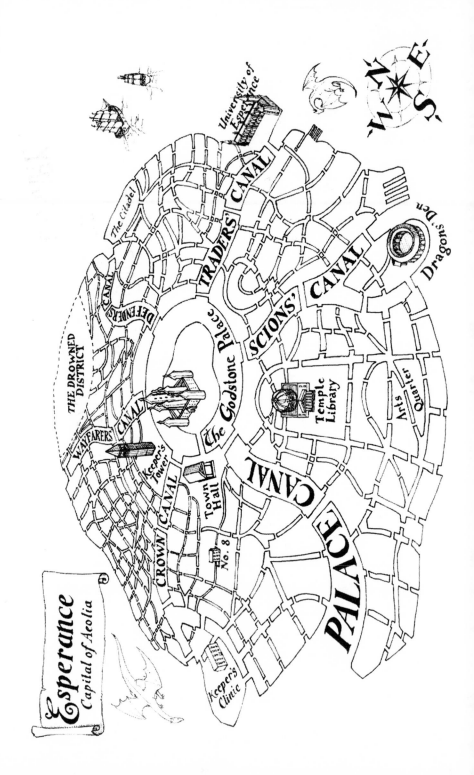

Esperance
Capital of Aeolia

THE DROWNED DISTRICT

The Citadel

DEFENDERS CANAL

TRADERS CANAL

University of Esperance

SCIONS' CANAL

Dragons' Den

WAYFARERS CANAL

The Godstone Palace

Keeper's Tower

Town Hall

No. 8

CROWN CANAL

PALACE CANAL

Temple Library

Arts Quarter

Keeper's Clinic

The sea, once it casts its spell,
holds one in its net of wonder forever.

—Jacques-Yves Cousteau

Chapter One

'If any of you can show just cause as to why these two should not be lawfully wed, speak now, or forever hold your peace.'

Fifteen-year-old Esme was seated in the front row, only a bouquet's throw away from her father and his bride at the altar. The events of the last few months flashed before her, and the years before them. This was her last chance.

Her hand twisted high in the air. 'I object.'

Somebody tittered behind her, but covered it quickly with a cough. Whispers and murmurs spread from pew to pew. The groom swung around toward his daughter, the colour draining from his face, before his bride steered him back to the altar. The vicar merely sighed, ignored Esme's objection, and carried on with the ceremony.

Esme lowered her hand and shrank back in her seat, her cheeks burning as if she'd just been slapped. The rest of the service passed in a blur: the vicar inviting the bride and groom to exchange vows; his pronouncement of them as man and wife; the church organ, wheezing out a hymn as the newlyweds signed the wedding register.

All Esme heard was static.

'I'm sorry, Mum,' she whispered, as the organ breathed its final note.

⚘

Outside, confetti clouded the air, sticking to skin damp from the summer heat. Children, dizzy with joy at being released from the confines of the church, chased each other round and round in circles. Esme's father, Aaron, and his bride, Penelope, lingered by the entrance of the church, greeting the slipstream of guests that issued from within.

Penelope, swathed in white, glittered and shone like the brightest star in a constellation. Aaron stood stiffly by her side, tugging awkwardly at the cuffs of his suit. He spotted Esme and started toward her, but a glacial stare from Penelope pulled him back to her side.

Desperate to avoid Penelope's gaze, Esme glanced skyward, and was struck by an unusual sight. Perched on the bell tower above her, looking very out of place, was a sea eagle: its broad white wings peppered with countless black specks. It cocked its head and stared directly at her. She recognised it as one of the birds that hung around at home; she'd never seen it down here in the village. The wedding bells began to sound, and the majestic creature took off, winging its way toward the harbour.

Esme threaded her way through the crowded courtyard, heading to the one place she knew she would be left alone. The guests' animated conversations stopped abruptly as she passed by, but every frozen smile and stifled sentence spoke volumes.

We've all moved on, they seemed to say. *Why can't you?*

The peal of bells followed Esme to the far end of the church grounds, where lichen-licked tombstones leaned in toward the earth. A row of cenotaphs stood beneath a sprawling oak tree, commemorating those whose bodies had never been found. The leaves shivered in the breeze, casting a mosaic of shifting light over the stones below. Esme paused by the last tablet, dated seven years ago.

In Memory of
ARIANE MAY SILVER
Beloved Wife of Aaron and Mother to Esme
1950—1981
Lost at Sea

Tears pricked behind Esme's eyes. The words blurred. Her mother had vanished, without trace, when she was eight. No one knew what had really happened to her—or so they said.

Esme didn't believe that her mother had drowned—she *couldn't* believe it. Ariane had always been a strong swimmer, careful and responsible around the ocean. But some nights, fear got the better of her. Some nights, Esme would wake with a scream, haunted by an image of her mother sinking beneath the waves.

She slid down to the ground, and leaned back against the oak, ignoring the bark digging into her back. Her heart felt bruised and battered, like someone had thrown it in the air and missed the catch. Each moment replayed over and over: the guests' titters, her father's bloodless face, the vicar's condescension. Objecting had made no difference, in the end.

Why did I even bother?

Deep down, she knew why. Because sitting there and saying nothing had felt too much like betrayal, like she had given up on Ariane, just like everyone else.

The bark jabbed into her back like an accusatory finger.

So instead, you let them all down.

As she made her way into the reception hall, the rest of the guests eyed her like an unwanted wedding gift. Her paternal grandparents, who had never approved of her mother, beckoned her toward their table. Esme cringed inwardly before taking the empty seat beside them.

Aaron's mother arched her finely pencilled eyebrows up toward the heights of her heavily coiffured hairdo, taking in Esme's untidy hair and wrinkled dress with a scathing glance.

'Aren't you a bit old to be playing in the dirt?'

Esme bit back a retort.

As the reception wore on and wineglasses emptied, talk turned to Ariane. Despite their hushed tones, Esme could hear every word of the conversation her grandmother was having with a guest.

'I *told* him he was making the wrong choice,' her grandmother opined, 'but of course, he wouldn't listen.' She popped a grape into her mouth. 'Pick someone more—more—'

'Normal?' the guest suggested.

'Exactly. Pick someone more *normal*, I said, or else things won't end well. And just look what happened!'

Esme's fists were clenched so hard that they were shaking. She desperately resisted the urge to empty the bowl of grapes over her grandmother's head.

'You don't know anything about my mother,' she said in a low voice. 'You don't know her like I do.'

Her grandmother tilted her chin up, exposing her ropey neck, and swallowed another grape. Then she leaned in close, delivering her next words with a side of wine fumes and minty lamb breath.

'We know more about your mother than you *ever* will.'

As Esme opened her mouth to reply, the band struck up the bridal waltz.

The sight of Penelope leading her father to the dance floor was a painful one, but it also provided an opportunity for escape. She slipped away from the table. On her way out, she stopped by the wedding cake and cast a glance back at her father.

Her eyes flickered between the plastic miniatures of the bride and groom atop the cake, and the flesh and blood versions entwined on the dance floor. The cloying aroma of rose petals, scattered around the cake, clung to her as she passed through the doors. The future stretched out before her, and it smelled sickly sweet.

The strains of music faded as Esme climbed up through Picton Village, past shops and houses and the school she attended each day, now closed for the summer. At the sight of the dingy grey signboard, Esme couldn't help but laugh. Her mood lifted for the first time that day. During the wedding reception, somebody had scratched out the 'Z' in 'Penzance':

PEN ANCE HIGH SCHOOL

She resumed her trudge up the hill. *Rachel would have laughed at that too*, she thought with a pang. Rachel, her only close friend from school, had left Picton Island a few months earlier. Now Esme was floating between groups, on the edge of things. Friendships had been few and far between since her mother's disappearance, although it wasn't for want of trying.

The villagers had never liked Ariane, and their antipathy extended to Esme, too. It was bad enough that her mother wasn't Picton born and bred, but something else drove the islanders' prejudice—something Esme could never quite put her finger on. '*Stay away from that Silver girl*,' the villagers would warn their children. '*There's something wrong with the women in that family.*'

Sometimes, in her lowest moments, she wondered if that was true.

At the crest of the village she stopped to catch her breath. Picton Island formed part of an archipelago, and hills rose up on every side of it. On approach from the water, it bore a faint resemblance to a permanently beached whale.

She cinched her long, ill-fitting dress up over her belt and began the long trek home. Her heart lifted at the sight of the lighthouse beam, sweeping across the northern end of the island. Her father had been employed as lighthouse keeper and ranger, here at Splinter Bay, for as long as she could remember. He and Esme lived in the lighthouse keeper's cottage, mere steps from the tower.

The sun had set by the time she reached the whitewashed gate of the cottage. The gate was shabby and in need of repair. The garden, too, had been neglected in recent months. But home still smelled like home. The tang of the sea mingled with the heady rush of lavender—her mother's favourite—coming from the bushes nearby.

A dark shadow swooped overhead. Esme ducked, feeling the wind brush over her. It was only the sea eagle from earlier that day, the largest of the birds that frequented these cliffs.

You again?

It flew off toward the tower, its proud bearing briefly illuminated in the roving lighthouse beam.

Esme was no stranger to the local wildlife. Her father's duties often involved rescuing injured animals from precarious situations, and from time to time, he enlisted her help in delivering them to the vet. The veterinary hospital was the one place in the village she *did* feel welcome. She watched as the sea eagle circled the lighthouse, its wings dipping in and out of the beam.

What were you doing down at the church today?

Birds such as this one often used the blue dome of the tower to rest, settle their interminable squabbles, and spy out food in the ocean below. Her mother had been especially fond of this particular sea eagle, and had even included it in one of her paintings.

You miss her too, don't you?

Inside the cottage, she stopped in the hallway, before a dramatic painting of Poseidon, holding his trident up in triumph over a boiling ocean. Her finger traced the initials in the corner: 'A S'. Ariane's art covered the walls, her signature in every room.

Something brushed against her leg, and Esme automatically bent to scoop up her ageing cat, Reuben. He purred as she cradled him in her arms, warm against her breast. His once pure black velvet coat was starting to grey, but his green eyes held the same knowing look they always did. He had turned up on their doorstep one stormy day, a sodden mess, bloody and mewling for help after a fight with the village strays, and had never left.

Up in her room, Esme deposited Reuben on the end of the bed, where he curled up on the covers. She slouched her way out of her borrowed dress and tossed it in the corner. The only thing she liked about it was the colour: aquamarine, the same as her eyes. The taffeta dress, two sizes too big, had been thrust at her at the last second, after Penelope found out that Esme had been planning to wear something more suited to a funeral.

After changing into khaki shorts and a worn t-shirt, she slumped down on the bed. Her room was in its usual chaos, crowded with her own things and a few of her mother's. Ariane's wooden easel stood unused in the corner, crusted with dried paint, draped with clothes Esme couldn't be bothered putting away. Paints and pencils lay forlornly in the corner. She had brought them up here with the vague idea that she might use them herself, but had never been able to sketch more than a couple of lines without scrunching it up and throwing it away.

She picked up one of her mother's books from the bedside table and flicked through it. It was full of richly illustrated legends: stories of Greek gods shifting their forms to trick humans, and chasing sailors across the waves. She grimaced at the sight of Orpheus's sorrowful face as Eurydice was carried away from him, ensnared in dark tendrils from the Underworld.

'Maybe I really am stuck in the past,' she muttered to Reuben, who fixed her with his inscrutable stare, his eyes green pools of light.

On another page, she caught a glimpse of Narcissus, staring at his own reflection in a pool. Mired in her own pool of misery, Esme shut the book and noticed something poking out the back of it. She pulled out the dun-coloured envelope and stared at it glumly.

Her end of year report card. She must have forgotten to give it to her father, although she couldn't remember whether she'd forgotten on purpose. Either way, he'd been too busy trailing around after Penelope to ask for it. As usual, she had scraped through in every subject, just enough to avoid having to repeat. Except in art and history. Even with minimal effort, she still came close to top of the class in those.

On her dressing table, sketches of creatures, both real and make-believe, dotted the mirror's border—a summer project from long ago. Esme let her hair out of its elastic prison and it fell in tangled disarray over her shoulders. It needed another comb and a tidy-up; but then, it always did.

'Found you on the beach one day. Washed up on shore,' her mother used to say, as she coaxed endless knots out of Esme's hair, hair as stringy as seagrass matting, and the same colour: a washed-out brown. Esme had seen dried-out kelp on the beach that was better behaved.

A snow globe at the back of the dresser glinted up at her. She tilted it, and watched white flakes drift over a miniature city of canals. Her mother had often held exhibitions elsewhere, on other islands—places where her art was more appreciated. From time to time, she would bring home gifts like this, as well as stories, both real and imagined.

She peered into the globe. It seemed, in the corner of her eye, that the city's liquid streets were moving, too; but when she looked closer, saw they were nothing more than paint and glue.

The night her mother had given her this snow globe, Esme had pestered her with endless questions about the city contained within. She had beguiled Esme with stories of a place where waterways shone, boats moved of their own accord, and people made magic with music.

'*The boats really move on their own?*' Esme had asked. '*With dragons on them? But don't they burn the boats?*'

'*No, silly,*' her mother had laughed.

An image of Ariane's dark, glossy hair floated back—as did her laugh, low and gentle. Her heart-shaped face and dimpled chin, reflected in Esme's own features, were easy to recall.

'*Every boat has a dragon on the prow, but it's only a wooden one,*' she had said. '*But there are real dragons, sea-dragons, high up in the sky. And there are people who can make the water move, the way it does in Splinter Bay.*'

Beside the globe lay another of Ariane's gifts: a bell with a brass fishtail wound around its handle. It, too, often whispered of enchantment, but for now it only reminded Esme of the peal of the church bells, ringing out the successful nuptials.

Her stomach growled, reminding her of how little she had eaten at the reception. She headed downstairs to fossick for food, Reuben swishing his tail beside her. After feeding him, she ate too, watching the pale moonlight stream into the kitchen. It glanced off the lighthouse key that hung on the rack by the door.

On impulse, she grabbed the key and left the cottage. Reuben was too fixated on the remains of his meal to follow.

Outside, the clouds had blown away, and the moon was at its zenith, cloaking everything in a soft, unearthly glow. The lighthouse stood twenty yards away, anchored on the edge of the cliff. On the leadlight panel set into the top of the door, a blue whale swam beneath the words: '*Olim Periculum Nunc Salus*'.

Once perilous, now safe.

She jiggled the key in the lock, and it gave way.

Moonlight bathed the steps, filtering in through narrow window slits cut into the thick stone walls. At the top, Esme flicked on the light to the service room.

Neglect hung in the air. A layer of dust covered the logbooks on the desk, and the clock was stuck on half past the hour. A large storage cupboard, behind the ladder to the lantern room, caught her eye. The door, usually locked, was ajar.

She opened the cupboard door wide and stepped back in shock. The past came rushing back. The air hummed with loss. The cupboard was full of her mother's paintings, ones she hadn't seen for years.

Esme pulled out the canvases and propped them up against the round walls of the service room, immersing herself in her mother's world: oceans and lakes, beaches and caves, rivers and waterfalls; dolphins, whales, and ancient deities of the sea, with the power to call forth raging storms and split ships in two.

Ariane's presence filled the space. Each painting shimmered with a life of its own. In one, a golden-scaled dragon emerged from the ocean, spraying drops of water high into the air. Another depicted an elusive finned creature, swimming by a rocky cave.

Footsteps on the stairs broke into her reverie.

'Esme?'

Her father entered the room, still dressed in his wedding suit. Aaron's face had furrowed in recent years, and his black hair was shot with grey. The pink rose in his lapel had browned around the edges. Esme's eyebrows rose a fraction when she noticed that he had added a sprig of lavender beside it.

She braced herself for a blast. He must have walked all the way up here from the village, getting angrier and angrier with every step.

Instead, he wrapped his arms around her in a hug. 'I'm glad you're okay. I've been worried about you ever since the ceremony.'

Esme flushed. 'Back at the church—I'm not sure what I was thinking. It's just ... it felt like the right thing to do at the time.'

He didn't meet her eye-to-eye, something she was grateful for. He merely nodded, while taking in the art strewn around the room. 'I see you've found your mother's paintings. There wasn't enough space at home, so I stored some of them up here.'

Esme joined him in front of a canvas depicting dolphins riding the waves—silver-grey streaks amongst the white.

'It's good to see them again,' she said. 'I helped her with this one ... or at least, I tried. That swirl was mine. The brush slipped and made a mark right across it. Mum just laughed, said to leave it. She thought it made the painting more interesting.'

His face relaxed. 'She was right.'

Aaron paced around the room, reminiscing about when and where each artwork had been painted. After a while, though, his manner began to irritate her. He sounded so distant, like a museum curator talking about a long-dead artist.

'How come you can remember all this, when you don't even think about her these days?'

Aaron flinched. 'Of course I think about her.'

His face crumpled and he stepped away, opening the door to the balcony that ringed the lighthouse. The sounds of Splinter Bay flooded in. Esme followed him outside. The moon and the sweeping lighthouse beam lit up the ocean; the skies crowned the vista with stars. Her father was cradling the sprig of lavender in his hand, his face ashen.

The sight was heart-wrenching. Years back, she had sometimes found him like this, late at night, sitting alone at the kitchen table, walled over with grief. The strain of the past seven years was etched permanently on his face.

'I was up here last night, looking at the paintings. I guess it was my way of saying goodbye.' His voice was almost inaudible over the crash of the waves below. 'I know how much you idolised her,' he continued. 'How much you still do. We both do. But we have to move on.'

He gripped the railing, and the purple sprig of lavender fell into the darkness.

Her shoulders slumped. Maybe it *was* too late. Maybe she had missed her chance. Maybe she should just accept the words on the cenotaph as the closest approximation of the truth. Her father patted her arm but she shook him off with an irritated shrug.

'No,' she said, more to herself than him.

I have to find out the truth for myself.

She turned to face him square on. 'I haven't had the chance to move on,' she said firmly. 'I haven't been able to go look for her, the way you have.'

His face tightened. 'I don't want you going anywhere near Spindrift.'

'Why *not*?'

He said nothing, then changed the topic—the way he always did. The way he had for years. 'Penelope will be good for us,' he said. 'She's got plenty of family and friends and she's nothing like—' He stopped, mid-sentence, with a slight shake of his head.

'Nothing like what? Like *who*?'

Her words didn't reach him. He had already disappeared back into the lighthouse. Esme remained outside, staring out to sea. For once, she found no solace in the sights and sounds of the night:

the crash of waves against the cliffs below, the circling lighthouse beam, the stars of the night sky scattered carelessly across its inky face.

A rush of wings, close by, made her jump. The sea eagle had returned. It landed noiselessly on the railing, and inclined its beak toward her.

Esme blinked at the bird. Her mouth fell open.

A sprig of lavender hung from the eagle's beak. The same sprig that had just fallen from her father's hand.

How …?

The bird dropped it on the deck before her, and flew off into the night. Stunned by its strange gesture, Esme froze for a moment. Then her heart, and mind, started to race.

Is this some sort of sign?

As she picked up the stalk of lavender, a current ran through her, crackling like an electric storm. The night pulsed, charged with possibility. For almost half her life, people had been keeping things from her—her father, especially. She couldn't take it anymore, and now she didn't have to. She no longer needed protecting from whatever unpalatable truth was out there.

'I'm going to find out what happened to you, Mum,' she said out loud. 'No matter what.'

The wind carried her words across the water, where the lighthouse beam lingered over the wine-dark sea. As the searching beam swung back round, it seemed to wink at her, like a secret conspirator, before flying out of sight once more.

Chapter Two

The day had dawned a sullen grey, and the sun hid behind a bank of cloud. Pelicans strutted around Picton Harbour's foreshore, scouring it for scraps. The air was laden with the smell of impending rain, mingling with the wharf's usual odours: fish and old rope and greasy diesel.

None of the vessels from the fishing fleet had yet returned from their daily run. The wharf's jetties were a skeletal sight, stripped of the boats that usually bobbed on either side. A large launch was moored at the end of one of the jetties. People clustered beside it, orbiting around Penelope and her large yellow hat as if she were the sun.

Esme's father broke off from the group, and enveloped her in a goodbye hug. Her nose twitched unpleasantly. He reeked of something strange: as though Penelope had drowned him in a bottle of her perfume.

He loosened his hold on her, but she stayed pressed against him a little while longer. When she stepped away, he forced a smile, his eyes moist.

'Thanks for coming down to say goodbye.'

Her own eyes brimmed over, too. She wanted what she couldn't have. She wanted her old father back—the one that stunk of fish and grime and the salty sea, not this one. She wanted to say the right words, but they wouldn't come. She tried to wish him a safe, happy trip, but all she managed to blurt out was: 'I hope everything goes okay.'

Penelope advanced toward them, her lips pursed as if she had just tasted a sour lemon. She spoke through gritted teeth. 'Let's not be late, *dearest*.'

The launch soon slipped its moorings and motored off. Birds swooped behind it, searching for scraps, before heading to better pickings back on shore.

A hollow feeling spread inside Esme, relieved only by the prospect of having the cottage to herself for a while. The honeymooners would be away, and out of contact, for the next few weeks. Aaron had agreed that Esme could stay there on her own, on the proviso that her new in-laws check on her every so often. This was her chance to go through her mother's things once more, search for clues. She'd looked over them a hundred times, but *surely* there was something she'd missed.

'Es-may!'

Mavis, Penelope's older sister, strode up to her. Dressed perpetually in brown, she reminded Esme of a moth, one that clung to people and was impossible to get rid of. Though she lived alone in the village, the two sisters were rarely apart.

'Hello, Mavis. And it's pronounced Es-mee, not Es-may.'

Mavis huffed. 'Well, *I'd* appreciate it if you'd call me aunt, dear. I just wanted to let you know I'll be a little late this afternoon.'

'Late for what?'

'Your father didn't tell you? Arrangements have changed. I'm to stay with you while they're away.'

Esme stiffened. 'What are you talking about? No one's said anything.'

Mavis pursed her lips and pulled a key out of her pocket, waving it at her. 'Don't look so put out. Penelope had a word with me last night, at the reception. We both agreed that you're far too young to stay on your own while your mother and father are away—'

'She's my stepmother, not my mother. And I'm almost sixteen. I'm perfectly capable of looking after myself.'

Mavis snorted. 'Not after yesterday's performance.' She pocketed the key. 'By the way, Penelope's asked me to do some sorting out while I'm there.'

'Why? Our house is fine the way it is.'

'I'm sure it is. But you may need some help getting the cottage ready for the move to the village.'

The words didn't stick.

Is this some sort of joke?

Esme's mouth went dry. A buzzing started up in her ears. 'What did you just say?'

'The move to the village.'

'What are you talking about?' she cried. 'We're not moving anywhere!'

'It's not up to you. What *you* need is company.' Mavis flicked at an imaginary speck of dust on her skirt. 'Strange girl. I thought you'd be pleased to get away from that isolated place. Children your age need to be around good influences, like me. Anyway, it wasn't my idea. It was Penelope's. Aaron has no idea—but I'm sure by the end of the honeymoon, she'll have convinced him …'

Mavis prattled on and on, but Esme didn't hear a word she said. She couldn't listen anymore. It felt like her heart had dropped through the jetty and impaled itself on the rocky seabed. She had lived in the lighthouse keeper's cottage her whole life. It was home, and her last link with her mother. The village was Penelope's domain, where she reigned with her family and friends.

After Mavis left, Esme stood on the empty wharf for a while, gazing up at the village. Each house stared down at her like an eye, ready to track her every move.

The clouds finally broke, pelting her with fat raindrops all the way home.

It was still storming when Mavis moved in that afternoon. Esme's new step-aunt immediately embarked on a cleaning frenzy, attacking every surface until the cottage smelled like a hospital ward. While Penelope acted as if Esme didn't exist, and as if Ariane never had, Mavis latched on to Esme and wouldn't let go.

The rain stopped eventually, but the running war of words between them continued unabated. Even Reuben got caught up in the fray. One day, Esme found her step-aunt backed into a corner with Reuben hissing at her. After that, Mavis resorted to keeping a large broomstick nearby, and tried to whack the cat with it whenever he came into sight.

As the days progressed in painful succession, the uneasy thought that Penelope had made some sort of deal with Aaron's parents—a deal to bring him back into the village community—crossed Esme's mind more than once.

Aaron's parents had been so eager to pay for the wedding, and the honeymoon, and even the enormous ring on Penelope's finger. Aaron and Ariane had moved to Splinter Bay soon after their marriage, angering Aaron's parents. The senior Silvers ran the island's fishing fleet, and the move had thwarted their plans to train him in the family business.

From time to time, Esme looked out for the sea eagle that had acted so strangely on the day of the wedding, but it was nowhere to be seen. The bird, along with the beleaguered cat, had made itself scarce.

One afternoon, she entered the living room, and for a brief moment, thought that she was in the wrong house. The mementos that had always decorated the mantelpiece—small picture frames, a piece of driftwood, and a cornflower-blue vase—were gone. In their stead stood oversized photographs of Penelope and her extended family. Mavis was attempting to remove the painting that usually hung above the mantelpiece: a depiction of the sea eagle flying above the lighthouse, underneath a full moon.

'Here, Es-may, help me get this down. There's an awful lot of clutter on these walls. It's like a shrine in here.'

Esme stopped dead. Red spots ran riot in front of her eyes. 'What do you think you're doing?' she yelled.

'Getting this place ready for my sister, of course. Once we've finished here, we'll get started on your room.'

Esme glowered. At that moment, if Mavis had been struck by lightning and rent in two, she wouldn't have cared. She blazed at her.

'Hasn't Penelope been married twice before—*briefly*? How long do you think she'll stick around this time?'

The only sound in the room was a sharp intake of breath. Mavis's lip curled. She stalked over and leaned into Esme's face. 'If there are any problems with my sister's marital choices, it's that the men she marries are never *good enough.*'

Esme backed away, but Mavis bore down on her again, so close that Esme could see the perspiration beading on her upper lip.

'Don't you *dare* criticise my sister. Instead of sticking your nose into other people's business, why don't you concentrate on making yourself useful?'

A manic laugh escaped Esme. 'You think *I'm* the one sticking my nose into other people's business?'

Mavis's lips twisted into an unexpected smile. Her voice softened unnaturally. 'I wonder what Aaron might say to you coming to live with me for a year? Give the lovebirds some space.'

Esme stepped back. 'You wouldn't dare—'

'Wouldn't I?'

Esme stalked off into the kitchen and filled the sink up with soapy water. Mavis had unearthed every vase in the house, including the cornflower-blue vase from the mantelpiece. She dipped it in the water and scrubbed at it, Mavis's face taunting her from every soap bubble, until she wanted to scream.

A throbbing started on the side of her head, a familiar pounding that signalled one of her headaches was coming on. Esme had suffered from them for as long as she could remember, but this time, the pain was worse than ever. She decided to leave the kitchen and escape to her room.

Or at least—she tried to.

Her hands wouldn't budge. She couldn't move a muscle.

Her first panicked thought was that she was having some sort of seizure. The pressure on her head grew worse, a cap of pain squeezing at her skull. Her eyes closed of their own accord, and a roaring sound engulfed her.

She fell into a trance.

When the roaring sound subsided, Esme, in her mind's eye, was no longer in the kitchen. She was standing in the living room of her own house, pressed up against the wall behind the sofa. The blue vase stood on the mantelpiece, filled with lavender. The painting of the sea eagle hung above it. The wallpaper was fresh and new; Esme had always known it to be cracked and peeling in places. A fire blazed in the hearth below.

What's happening to me?

Rooted to the spot, she spied Reuben curled up by the fire. Others were in the room, too. A man and a woman on the sofa, facing each other. They were deep in conversation and didn't seem to notice that Esme had materialised right behind them.

Reuben, his coat black and sleek, his gait unhindered by age, stirred. He padded over and stared up at Esme inquisitively, before slinking back to his post by the fire.

The man was her father, his face younger, his hair showing no signs of grey. She couldn't see the woman's face, but it didn't matter. There was a map of this person within her, one that she had folded and unfolded countless times. The fall of her hair, the slope of her shoulders, the shape of her, was more than enough. Esme's heart was close to bursting.

Mum.

The conversation grew heated. Her father's voice was edged with frustration. Ariane was sitting very still.

'I got a letter from Dr Wright,' he said. 'You missed your last appointment.'

'I'm not going back. I'm fine. I told you,' Ariane murmured.

Aaron shook his head. 'You're not fine. You need help, Ari. You've been acting the way Lucinda did, before she passed. Making up strange stories. Sleepwalking. I'm worried that one night, you're just going to get up and walk right out of the door.'

What on earth are they talking about?

Her mother flinched. 'I just *might*, if you keep talking like this!'

Aaron stood up and stormed out of the room, but Ariane called him back.

'Wait, I'm just a bit worn out, that's all. Just tired.' She rose up off the sofa. 'Come back. I don't want to fight.'

The scene started to fade, and Esme cried out. 'Mum!'

Her mother twisted round toward her, a strange glimmer in her eye. Her face was taut and tired, but lovely as ever. She only looked for an instant, seeming to see right through Esme, before turning back to Aaron.

The room vanished. Esme was back in the kitchen—no longer frozen in place.

She dropped the vase in the soapy water and fled the room.

Esme slumped down on her bed and buried her face in her hands, desperately trying to make sense of what had just happened.

With no warning, apart from the onset of a headache, she had somehow borne witness to a scene from the distant past. It wasn't a memory of her own, or at least she didn't think it was. Maybe it was all just her imagination.

She massaged her temples, trying to ease the headache, which had returned with a vengeance. Her hands were still white from soaking in the tub, the lines on her palms distended like a river swollen in flood.

It had all been so vivid.

Mum. I just saw Mum.

She was right there, looking at me.

Her heart stung, cut by the serrated edge of memory. Painful recollections rose in her mind—real ones, this time, not strange visions. Her younger self was perched on the front steps of the cottage, squishing tiny buds of lavender between her fingers, the scent of it on her hands and in the air around her. A bee buzzed nearby, feeding on the purple blooms. Silently she sat, swamped with a loneliness her small frame couldn't contain. Any moment now her missing mother would walk through the gate. Tell her it had all been a mistake. Just a mean trick on her part.

The memory lingered a while, like part of her was still waiting on those steps.

Reuben, who had followed her upstairs, jumped into her lap, jolting Esme back into the present. She had no idea what to do about her vision, or who to tell. Certainly not Mavis. The headache began to ease, and she decided to tell no one—for now. When her father returned, she would ask him about it. Surely, he would reassure her, tell her that everything was okay. After all, her mother had experienced the same headaches, and nothing like this had ever happened to her.

At least, as far as she knew.

Mavis appeared downstairs the next morning, a large bag on her arm and a sour expression on her face. Stopping at the front door, she threw Esme a piercing glance.

'I'll be over at my cousins' all day. I expect you to be on your best behaviour while I'm gone. No snooping around.'

'If anyone's been snooping around, it's you,' muttered Esme.

'What was that?' Mavis called back from halfway down the path.

Esme beamed at her. 'I said you're in for a sunny afternoon.'

Mavis banged the gate shut and stalked off toward the village. Esme retreated to her bedroom and extracted a box from underneath her bed; Mavis had tossed it on a pile of things to throw away, and she had saved it just in time. It was full of letters to her mother from friends on other islands, whom she had met while exhibiting her artwork. In amongst them was an old envelope with the name 'Lucinda' on it.

Esme was reminded of her father's words, in her strange vision. *'You've been acting the way Lucinda did, before she passed.'*

Downstairs, a row of old photographs hung along the wall. Lucinda, Esme's great-grandmother, regarded her from a gilded oval frame. Her face was shrivelled with age, but a fierce light shone in her eyes.

Lucinda had taken in her granddaughter after Ariane's parents, who had lived on another island, perished in a boating accident. Esme's strongest memories of Lucinda were of her final days, and of Ariane's grief as she held Lucinda's hand. Esme could vividly recall her great-grandmother's papery, yellowed skin.

'Her skin, it's a funny colour. Is that why she's sick?' she had asked.

'No, little one,' her mother had said, eyes bright with tears. *'It's just all worn out. She won't need it much longer.'*

Inside the envelope were a number of faded, yellow letters, one of which included a sketch. Tiny fish, urchins, periwinkles, and starfish swirled around a teardrop-shaped rock pool. The lines wavered a little, and the letter itself was written in a spindly hand.

Dearest Caspian,

I am dreadfully sorry for my long absence. It is my greatest desire to visit you all again, but my constitution has taken a turn for the worse. My memory, thankfully, remains as strong as ever. These days, I must make do listening to Ariane's accounts of her visits to you, and content myself with the small pleasures of this world, while I am still able. Esme, my great-granddaughter, is a source of endless delight. Perhaps she, too, will visit you one day.

I still enjoy the occasional trip to Spindrift, and have enclosed a small sketch of the rock pools for you.

Fond regards, Lucinda

Letter in hand, Esme walked outside to the garden, her eyes drawn to the north, where Spindrift lay. The smallest of the islands in the archipelago, Spindrift was renowned for its winter fishing, and Esme had often holidayed there with her family, in a cottage bequeathed to them by Lucinda. Her mother had used the cottage from time to time to prepare for upcoming exhibitions. It was on one of these solo trips that she had disappeared.

The breeze grew stronger, swirling Esme's hair around her face. She tied it back with a hairband from her wrist.

For years, she had been locked out of the search for her mother. Now, everyone was moving on, and dragging her along with them. Her father had warned her to stay away from Spindrift, but for all she knew, Penelope's next plan would be to sell Lucinda's cottage, and any clues as to what might have happened would be lost.

A plan of her own rapidly formed in her mind.

If she left now, she could be at Spindrift by nightfall, search the cottage, and be back here the next day. Her father was gone. Mavis was gone. There was no one around to stop her.

Time to find out what you've all been hiding.

Esme ran inside and crammed a bag full of clothes and food, before scribbling a brief note to Mavis. As she filled bowls with food and water for Reuben, he wound himself around her legs, and cast her a mournful glance.

'Don't look so sad, Reuben. I'll see you tomorrow, for sure.'

Esme cast one last look around the cottage, and hurried out the door.

The thought of how much trouble she would be in briefly crossed her mind, but she let it slide. There was only one ferry each day to the outlying islands, and it left the wharf at noon.

Chapter Three

The ferry hugged the western side of the island, passing by the northern cliffs before peeling off into the open ocean. Picton Island receded in the distance, the lighthouse shrinking in size from a pencil to a pin. Ahead, sea and sky merged together, broken up only by long lines of white cirrus clouds. Esme leaned over the side to watch the water swirling by, intoxicated by the salt and spray, savouring the taste of her temporary respite from Mavis.

With a shiver, she suddenly recalled what the police inspector had told her father, a few days after Ariane had vanished.

They never find the bodies out there at Spindrift. Currents are too strong.

Esme knew very little about the circumstances of her mother's disappearance. What she did know was that her mother had been staying in Lucinda's cottage, finishing up the last few paintings for an exhibition. She was often late home from these trips, so at first, the alarm hadn't been raised. When two days passed with no sign of her, and then three, worry turned to panic. A thorough search of Spindrift had turned up nothing, or so they had said.

She was a strange one, that Ariane Silver, she overheard someone say once. *Like she painted herself into one of those legends of hers, and then she was gone.*

By mid-afternoon, the scribbled grey outline of Spindrift appeared on the horizon. The island was smaller than she remembered, but nothing had really changed, only her perception. Now that she was older, it was like looking at the island through a different-sized lens. Everything had shrunk, even the bay on the left that had once seemed to go on forever.

Out of habit, she found herself scanning the waters around the island, the way her father used to. He would often point out where the shelf fell steeply into the abyss, or seamounts rose up from the ocean floor, creating hidden ridges and valleys, invisible folds where fish lurked in abundance. Now, instead of fish, a chilling picture flashed into her mind's eye, of a body wedged between the rocks, nibbled away at until there was nothing left but bleached bones.

She sucked in a breath and swallowed hard.

The ferry made land and Esme stepped onto the worn wooden treads of the pier. At the pier's end, a wide, sandy path served as the island's main thoroughfare. The general store was closed, shuttered up until the next fishing season; the slate hanging by the door was blank, chalked only with the salt of the sea. The wind and the slap of the water against the jetty, as well as the ghosts of fishermen past, were her sole companions.

She shivered, reminding herself that it was only for one night.

Wispy trees and bushes strayed on to the path that wound up the hill, and branches whipped at her all the way up. At the top, she caught her first glimpse of the other side of the island.

The weather was changing for the worse, and a jittery charge filled the air. Clouds bolted across the steely grey sea, waves bucking beneath them like stirred-up steers at a rodeo. Closer in, a bay stretched from one headland to the next. At the bottom of the hill, behind the pebbled beach, stood the holiday cottage, alongside other weathered fishing shacks.

The garden around Lucinda's cottage was overgrown, a snarl of grass and ancient bushes gone to seed. Esme peered through one of the grimy glass windows, but could only make out shapes and colours—vague outlines of familiar objects. She ran her hand along the windowsill, and flakes of wood broke off beneath her fingers.

The key was tucked away in its usual hiding place. She pulled at a vine that had wrapped itself around the handle, pushed open the door, and walked inside.

Seven years fell away. The past rose up to greet her. It was as if her mother had just gone for a stroll and would be back soon. Tubes of paint and brushes covered a trestle table in one corner of the room; in another, a stack of fishing rods leaned against the wall, beside toys piled up in a basket. Everything was covered in dust, so she opened up the doors and windows, letting the cottage breathe for the first time in years.

A set of double glass doors led out to the veranda. In the bay beyond, the wind slashed the water with a thousand cuts. The breeze brought with it sounds, unearthly music that pricked at her memory. She followed the music around to the side of the house, where a wooden wind harp played to its first audience in years: an audience of one. Esme had helped her parents build this harp only a short while before Ariane had vanished.

This music never had a real melody. Its only instrumentalist was the wind itself. But it still spoke the way music did, expressing what words could not. The harp's lost and discordant notes wailed like a widow's lament. They reached right inside her, as if they were keening for her, too. Its plaintive notes followed her back inside.

The light was fading now, the bay dark and formless at the end of the day. Wind rattled at windows and doors, so Esme shut them, and searched for something with which to light the cottage.

On the mantelpiece, between a pile of shells and a mug straggled with red and blue stripes, stood two pale green candlesticks, their bases puddled with wax. After lighting the candles, she bent down to retrieve some of the shells that had fallen to the floor.

Ash had spilt from the fireplace, and Esme waved one of the candles around its dark interior. Several scraps of paper were scattered in amongst the blackened logs. After piecing them together as best she could, she read them by flickering candlelight:

Dear Mr Silver,
*   ... consider your wife's admittance as an inpatient for an extended period ...*

> *... headaches, delusions, fragmented mind ...*
> *... talk of other worlds ... ... medication ...*

> *... condition worsening rapidly ...*
> *... danger to herself ...*

Dr Charles Wright
Director, Garson Sanatorium

Esme stared blankly at the letter. It was dated only a few months before her mother went missing.

The words, a terrible portent of what was to come, pressed down like a dead weight on her chest. The letter was incomplete, but its contents were clear. Her mother had been ill—seriously ill.

Rain drummed overhead. A window banged open, and Esme dragged herself up to latch it against the battering storm. Back at the table she read the letter over and over again, reliving the past seven years: the whispers and stares, the conversations cut short, the murmured remarks about her mother that she could never quite hear.

A ball of cold, hard fear grew inside her.

She and her mother had always suffered from headaches, but Esme had always dismissed them as nothing more than annoying interruptions to daily life. In recent years, her father had acted overly concerned whenever she developed one. Esme, however, had never seen his concern as anything more than usual parental worry.

Now it all seemed more sinister.

Headaches, delusions, fragmented mind.

She pressed her fingers to her temples and slumped onto the couch.

The timpani of rain subsided, and exhaustion overtook her. This was what her father had stopped short of telling her all these years. He had been trying to protect her from the truth, from the real reason he had given up the search.

Shadows danced around her as she fell into a fitful sleep.

The morning chill woke Esme early. She sat up, blinking in the first light of day, wrung out from worry and broken sleep. Her mind was crowded with questions to which there were no answers, just grim possibilities.

She flung open the doors that led to the deck. Outside, the storm of the previous night had moved on, and the day was brimming with life. Birds peeped in the nearby trees and the waves of the bay made a gentle landing on the pebbled beach.

Back in the cottage, something caught her eye: a few torn pieces of art paper, scattered on the floor beneath an empty easel. She patched the pieces of paper together and propped them up on the wooden stand.

It was a drawing of the city in the snow globe back home: the city full of spires and domes, where ribboned waterways ran with enchanted boats, and magic was a part of everyday existence.

The name *Esperance* was scribbled faintly in the corner.

The words of the doctor came back to her in painful clarity. *Talk of other worlds. Delusions.* Her heart raw, she pictured her father tearing up the sketch in grief and throwing the letter in the fire, before locking up the cottage for the last time.

Everyone must have known—or suspected.

Everyone except me.

The injustice of it all raged through her, anger leaping from limb to limb like branches caught in a wildfire. Her eyes raked the room and fixed on the fireplace. With one swift motion, she swept everything off the mantelpiece. The shells crashed to the floor first, followed by the mug and candlesticks.

Her fingers were still trembling when she restored the battered items to their home. Eventually, the last dregs of anger drained away, leaving her with nothing but a merciful numbness. She moved around the cottage as if in a dream, mechanically opening drawers and searching through cupboards, not sure what she was even looking for anymore.

Some of her own drawings were in them: sketches of shells, one of the wind harp. A set of drawers by the easel yielded more of her mother's sketches, as well as a thick black art diary, dated only a couple of months before Ariane's disappearance. She took the book outside to the small table on the deck, slumped onto one of the slatted chairs, and leafed through it.

Pages and pages were devoted to drawings of the rock pools and objects from beachcombing expeditions: sponges, seashells, and gnarled pieces of driftwood, sculpted into shamanic shapes by the sea. One gleaming shell, titled 'Triton Dreaming', took up a whole page, its shimmering surface a rainbow of colour.

The contents of the book seemed at odds with the diagnosis that she had read in the doctor's letter. From what she could gather, her mother had been as productive as ever in those last few months. There was nothing ominous in these pages, nothing that might indicate a deteriorating state of mind.

At the diary's end were a series of sketches: some of a place called the 'Singing Sands', and another of a fearsome claw, its talons spiking at the air. The final entry was written in a hasty, almost illegible hand.

Returning to Esperance tomorrow, when the tide is right.
Slept badly—dreamt of Nathan.

Esme—Aaron—I'll be back soon.

Next to their names, Ariane had drawn some hearts.

The words had an icy ring to them. *When the tide is right.* Images of her mother, wading into the ocean and disappearing beneath it, assailed her.

Esme flung the book down on the table.

She shook her head. She didn't want to know. The truth was flat and unforgiving. This enchanted city that Ariane had described and depicted so lovingly must have been part of her illness. Esme had known, when she became old enough, that these stories were just that—stories. But her mother, at some point, had lost the ability to distinguish truth from reality. She had lost herself in another world, and lost everything.

A loud cry derailed Esme's train of thought. Her head whipped up. A rush of feathers filled her vision. The sea eagle from home was streaking down toward her, its sharp talons poised, ready to strike.

Chapter Four

Esme leaped out of the way, but the bird ignored her, swooping down on to the deck—and seizing Ariane's notebook. It soared off along the bay, the black diary suspended between its claws.

'Wait! Give that back!'

Dark specks peppered the white bird's wings. This was the same bird that had acted so strangely on the day of her father's wedding. Now it was headed toward the point, stealing away the last words her mother may have ever written.

She set off after it, racing along the sand, arms, legs, heart pumping, sure the bird would drop the book once it realised it wasn't prey.

The sea eagle alighted on a mass of boulders far in the distance, atop the next headland. It poised there, motionless, a furled white flag against the charcoal cliffs. Esme huffed her way up the rocks, but by the time she reached the top, both bird and book were gone.

The headland afforded an unbroken view of the forbidding southern coastline of Spindrift. No beaches bordered this unprotected stretch of land, only miles of rock, shearing into turbulent sea. The Spindrift rock pools lay below, adjacent to the point. Limpid pools of green dotted the fissured face of a rocky platform, which extended from the base of the cliffs to the water's edge.

Shading her eyes from the sun, she scanned for the bird along the cliffs. A flash of white—the ruffle of a wing in a rocky crevice at the back of the pools—caught her eye. She scrambled down and across the platform, picking her way through the watery hollows left by the last tide. By the time she arrived, the bird was gone again, soaring high above the cliffs. Esme kicked at a loose rock in frustration.

Lucinda's pool lay nearby: the teardrop-shaped pool that Esme's great-grandmother had drawn in her letter. Esme had whiled away many hours here as a child, spellbound by the miniature worlds within each pool. She would sit here and sketch them, sometimes with her mother, sometimes with Lucinda, while her father fished off the rocks nearby.

Bronze pearls of seaweed and bright green sea lettuce dotted this pool's perimeter; bright-eyed black crabs crept in and out of crevices between barnacle-covered rocks. A few feet further in, an electric-blue starfish lay spread-eagled on the sea-worn floor.

The steady reverberation of the ocean rose a fraction. Waves were cresting over the rock platform. Esme groaned. The tide was turning—she was out of time. She would have to give up the book for lost.

A cry came from above.

The sea eagle hovered over her, the notebook still dangling from its talons. Folding back its wings, it dove headfirst into Lucinda's pool.

What's it doing?

The tide was coming in fast. The first wave sloshed around her ankles, soaking her sandals. She waited impatiently for the bird to resurface, but it didn't. Her frustration turned to concern. Maybe it was lying injured at the bottom.

Esme quickly waded in, shivering as the water closed around her. She took a deep breath and dove down. With a tentative gesture, she parted the ink-coloured reeds that carpeted the rocky floor. To her astonishment, the bird had vanished. Just as she was about to swim back up, she caught a glimpse of something else.

Hidden amongst the reeds was a lustrous shell. Vivid greens, purples, and blues flickered across its shining surface. She reached out to touch its smooth curves, marvelling at its beauty.

I've seen this somewhere before, she realised.

Triton Dreaming.

Just as her fingers brushed against the shell, the water surged around her. Esme stroked up, but the water twisted with sudden force, flinging her back down. She braced for a collision, terrified of being thrown against the floor of the pool and losing consciousness.

The floor of the pool vanished.

Esme plummeted into the endless black of an underwater abyss. The water relentlessly bore her down. Daylight was shrinking rapidly above her, like an aperture closing in a camera. First it was a fist of light, then a pinhole, then it was gone. Her world had gone pitch black, as if the door on a tomb had closed.

Down here there was no light, no life, no sound—except the rushing of water all around her. Her lungs screamed for air. Then, all at once, the current reversed, propelling her upward, freeing her from its grip.

Light poured in from above. She stroked up, windmilling furiously, one thought pounding in her brain:

I can make it.

Close to the top, her world turned grey. Her eyes fluttered shut. Her body, out of oxygen for too long, took charge. It forced her to inhale, unwittingly dooming her when she was so close to a reprieve.

Her father had been right. She should have listened to him. She should have stayed away from this place. Now her name would be inscribed on a cenotaph beside her mother's.

Lost at Sea.

Esme slid into oblivion.

Chapter Five

Esme hung by a thread, suspended on the very edge of consciousness.

Life rushed back into her. Her eyes flew open. She was still under the water's surface, the current propelling her up, but now air was flowing into her lungs. Somehow, she was breathing in air—sweet, precious air—underwater.

Seconds later, she broke through the surface.

Esme staggered out of the pool and collapsed onto a rock, wrung out and wretched, as limp and sodden as flotsam washed up on shore. She retched, sure she had swallowed half the sea, but nothing came up.

The pool settled back into peaceful somnolence, winking at her in the sunlight. Esme gaped at it. She had just been under that water—*drowning* under that water.

Hadn't she?

Had she?

Her mind spun uselessly, stuck between gears. She scrabbled for something, anything, to orient herself. Around her lay a ledge strewn with rocks, water filling the gaps between the stones. The sea pulsed close by. Wisps of cloud threaded through cyan skies, mirrored in the pools below. Unfamiliar pools.

This isn't Spindrift.

An ice-cold thought slid into her mind.

I'm making this all up.

Her breath came short and sharp. The letter—the one Aaron had thrown into the fireplace—flashed before her.

Headaches, delusions, fragmented mind …

Her mind worked itself into frantic knots, while her body registered a new world that, at first glance, seemed little different to her own. Her clammy shorts stuck to the rock beneath her; the leather straps of her sodden sandals pressed against her feet. Water dripped from her hair onto her face. She put her hand to her chest, and felt it rise and fall.

A shadow passed overhead. The sea eagle was back, the purloined notebook still between its talons.

Esme leaped to her feet. 'Hey! Come back here!'

She sprinted after the bird, almost tripping on the uneven ground. Beyond the rocks, a faint path came into sight, lined with thick foliage.

The bird had vanished once more, but this time it had left the notebook behind. It lay there on the ground, flecked with grime, but somehow still intact. She picked up the notebook, sure it would be ruined, but the pages were completely dry, her mother's drawings perfectly preserved. Ariane's sketch of the rainbow-hued shell shimmered up at her: 'Triton Dreaming'.

A cold shiver ran through her. The rules by which she navigated the world no longer seemed to apply. She hugged the notebook to herself and looked around wildly. Surely there was someone here who could tell her what was going on. She began to walk, and then run, down the narrow path.

Around the next corner, Esme barrelled into a boy. He stumbled and fell back. A spyglass flew out of his hand, spun high in the air, and thwacked him on the side of his head on its way down.

'I'm so sorry! Are you okay?' Esme cried out.

'I think so,' he said, rubbing his head ruefully. 'Except there seem to be two of you.' He swiped a hand in the air next to Esme.

'Maybe you should sit down for a bit,' said Esme, grabbing his hand as it groped at nothing. Feeling something solid sent a wave of relief through her. The boy was real; he hadn't vanished into vapour.

As he picked up his spyglass, Esme took in his appearance

properly for the first time. A sweaty shirt outlined a slight, athletic build. He was of medium height, like her, with dark skin and spiky brown hair, and looked about the same age. A band of distinctive blue markings ran down one side of his face, a series of lines that resembled an endless roll of waves, like the sea had left its imprint on him. He spoke with a slight accent, one she couldn't place.

She swayed a little, and he reached out a hand to steady her.

'Maybe *you* should sit down.'

She put her hand to her head, checking for bumps. Her fingers met only a tangle of stringy, salty hair. Blood had congealed over a cut on her leg, and she was sure her hair and eyes were as wild as Medusa's. The enormity of what had happened was beginning to register. She struggled to speak, in a voice thick with emotion and hoarse with dehydration.

'I'm so glad I found you,' she said. 'One minute I was in the rock pool back home, next thing … I was here. I held my breath as long as I could. I thought I was going to drown. But I didn't, did I?'

The boy shook his head. He was rubbing at his tattooed temple, looking puzzled.

'You couldn't have drowned,' he said. 'Don't you know that?'

She stared at him blankly.

'Oh!' Something dawned in his eyes. 'I get it. You're an otherworlder.' He waved a hand in the direction of the pool. 'I've heard you need masks and things to breathe underwater over there. You don't need anything here. The water's enchanted.'

Otherworlder? Enchanted?

Esme's vision blurred. Everything seemed too close, and too far away, all at the same time. Her head was thick with fog. The ground came up toward her. Something pressed against her lips—the edge of a water bottle.

'Here,' said the boy.

She opened her eyes to see his liquid brown ones regarding her with concern. With a muttered thanks, she took the bottle. He helped steady her on her feet.

'You're taking it better than most,' he said. 'Most otherworlders who stumble across a portal go into complete shock—can't speak for days, afterwards. At least, that's what I've heard. I've never met one. Till now. I'm Daniel, by the way.'

Esme gulped down some more water before returning the bottle. 'I—I'm Esme.'

He grinned. 'Want to see where you are?'

Daniel started up the narrow path before Esme could answer. She hurried to catch him. The path soon ended, revealing a sandy beach fringing a wide lagoon.

Esme stopped in her tracks, her knees threatening to give way again.

A shining island city floated on the surface of the lagoon. Domes and towers rose above timeworn dwellings in pale pinks, creams and ambers. Glistening waterways snaked between them. Spires pierced the skies, and high above them, golden streaks flashed across the firmament.

'Is this ... Esperance?'

She sank down on to the sand. Her stomach fluttered, like someone was playing panpipes inside her.

'I thought you didn't know where you were,' said Daniel.

'I don't. This place isn't meant to exist.'

And neither are you.

Esme removed her sandals and burrowed her feet into the sand. It was warm and gritty between her toes—reassuringly familiar. Her eyes kept being drawn back to the city across the water, tracing the strange ribbons of golden light as they danced across the sky.

Daniel was frowning at her.

'Sorry, I didn't mean it that way, ah ...' She tried to put together a more coherent sentence. 'I've seen this city before. In one of my mother's drawings. It's like she drew it from this very spot.'

He shrugged. 'Maybe she did.'

'She used to tell me stories about a place like this. When I was almost asleep. Like she wanted me to remember, but forget at the same time.'

'So how come she hasn't brought you here herself?'

'I ... I don't know. She disappeared when I was young. They searched for her everywhere.'

Except here. Nobody's looked here.

She stood up abruptly, scattering sand everywhere. 'I have to go there,' she declared. 'To Esperance.'

'Er, your notebook.' Daniel bent down and picked up the book, dusting the sand off it. 'I can give you a ride over if you want,' he said, handing it back to her. 'I was about to leave anyway.'

The stranger's easy manner both disarmed and disconcerted her. Her eyes wandered from him to the city and back again.

'My boat's here—well, my father's boat,' continued Daniel.

She gnawed at her lip. 'I ... I don't know. Maybe I should be heading back.' She glanced behind her, in the direction of the rock pools. 'I *can* go back, can't I?'

'Whenever you want.'

The thought of revisiting the rock pool again, so soon, sent a shudder through her. And if she went home, she realised, she might never make it back here again. Mavis—and her father— would probably never let her out of their sight. Or worse ... send her to the Garson Sanatorium for treatment.

She drew a deep breath and nodded. Hugging the notebook to herself, she accompanied Daniel down the beach.

A wooden boat, with faded blue trim, rocked in the water. The name *Talia* was lettered on its side in a graceful blue flourish, and a carved dragon decorated its prow, projecting out over the water, as if ready to take flight.

'Every boat has a dragon on the prow, but it's only a wooden one,' her mother had whispered.

Doubt tugged at her once more. Was this how delusions worked, by reaching into the past and twisting old memories? She eyed Daniel warily. Her mother had once painted the crossing of the Styx, depicting the foul ferryman Charon with fiery eyes and a greasy waist-length beard. If this *was* the afterlife, Daniel was a much more agreeable guide than the one in Ariane's painting. His eyes weren't on fire, although there was a hint of red in his brown irises.

Esme clambered into the boat and noticed the oars tucked into the side. 'I can help row, if you'd like.'

'No need.' Daniel spoke aloud to the wooden figurehead. 'To the Lake, *Talia*.'

The boat glided off without any visible means of assistance. As they left the shore behind, fragments of old conversations with Ariane came back to her, scraps of information about this world, disguised as make-believe. Her mother couldn't have told her about Esperance outright—of course she couldn't have. Not with the way that everyone would react—with the way they *had* reacted. So she had dropped hints, told stories, drawn pictures, instead.

Unless … I'm making everything up, too.

Esme stared ahead at the city, desperately hoping it wasn't just a mirage.

From a distance, Esperance appeared to be drifting on the lagoon's surface, as if its hold on existence was so tenuous that it could slip back into the depths at any moment. High above the city, sinuous shapes pinwheeled across the sky. Daniel trained his spyglass on them.

'What are those things?' she asked him.

'You mean the dragons?'

'*Dragons*?' she spluttered. She rubbed at her eyes before staring skyward again. As she rose unsteadily to her feet, the boat rocked violently beneath her.

'Here.' He passed her the spyglass. 'Have a closer look.'

Through the lens, she could see the sun refracting off the golden wings of dozens of creatures, gliding effortlessly through the clouds: scaled beasts, with crested heads and long snouts.

'That's what I was doing over at Laertes,' Daniel went on, seemingly oblivious to Esme's disbelief. 'Dragon-spotting. A wild mother and her brood are supposed to have settled down there. But I'd just about given up looking when you ran into me.'

'They're really ... real?' Esme stuttered, as she retook her seat.

Daniel laughed. 'Of course they're real. As real as anything else here.'

Wow, that's reassuring.

But it all *felt* real enough. The boat rocked in the wash of other vessels that passed by. The air was saturated with salt, just the way it was back home. Gulls scoured the shores for food, scattering when pedestrians displaced them. Columned mansions with arched windows and ornate balconies lined the shores; squares and fountains filled the gaps between the blocks of buildings. Winding streets of water curled up into the city and disappeared out of sight.

'We're coming up to the Palace Canal,' said Daniel, as they neared a pale stone bridge spanning the entrance to a wide waterway. The stone flickered and danced in the light, seeming to animate the figures that had been sculpted on it. Breaching whales and slender dolphins swam amongst creatures of myth: gorgons, leviathans, and colossal beasts with countless tentacles. Florid script wound along the bridge's side:

Ephyra, Capital of Aeolia

'Ephyra?' Esme asked. 'I thought this place was called Esperance.'

'That's the old name. It was changed after the wars, centuries ago.'

Talia's bow moved into the shadow cast by the bridge. Esme's skin prickled as they glided underneath, and a strange sensation came over her, as if she had travelled these waters before.

A flotilla of craft plied the canals: flat-bottomed boats, black ferries with gold trim, gondolas in rich jewel-box colours, and other small vessels like *Talia*. Slender waterways meandered off from the larger canal, giving tantalising glimpses of other parts of the city. The banks thronged with people of all sorts, in an eclectic mix of dress.

Further along, a woman garbed in long-sleeved robes, decorated with red-and-pink blooms, approached the edge of one of the narrow waterways that intersected the Palace Canal. The woman stepped directly onto the water, and crossed the canal with ease.

Esme stared, speechless, at the patch of water that the woman had traversed. By the time she found her voice again, the woman was long gone.

Doubts assailed her once more.

Go back now, while you have the chance. People don't walk on water—or breathe underneath it. And everyone knows dragons don't exist.

Soon, *Talia* passed into a shining lake with an island at its centre. Esme drew in a long, shaky breath, and then exhaled slowly. Her mind had been conjuring up fiery pits; Daniel had guided her someplace the complete opposite.

A vast ivory palace stood on one side of the island, surrounded by manicured grounds. A cathedral of towers rose like stalagmites beyond its smooth round walls, their beauty reflected in the lake below. The whole palace was made of the same pale luminous stone as the bridge they had passed under earlier.

'That's the Godstone Palace,' said Daniel. 'It's been here forever—or at least, as long as Esperance has. But the monarchy died out long ago. The mayor lives there, now. It's the seat of the city council.'

Another bridge connected the island to the city proper. As soon as they had passed underneath, the little boat came to a stop. When Esme made a move to climb out, Daniel stayed in and waved her off.

'I can't leave *Talia* here. I'll be back soon.'

Esme stepped out into a wide, circular plaza that curved around the lake as far as the eye could see. In the distance, the gilded roof of a bell tower glinted in the sun. Fountains were scattered throughout the plaza, and Esme stopped to admire the nearest one. Marble sea nymphs cavorted amongst sculpted waves, while real water roiled beneath them, its movement reminding her of the churning rock pool.

Feeling slightly sick, she was about to step back, when a pair of silvery shapes leaped up from the water, taking her breath away. The sylphlike figures hung in the air for a moment, long and graceful shapes composed entirely of glittering drops of water, before splashing back in, their forms twisting beneath the surface.

Her wonder at the sight was interrupted by a familiar sound, carried by the breeze: the same haunting tones she had heard only the night before, at Spindrift. Esme followed the sounds across the plaza to their source: an enormous wind harp.

Twin marble plinths, situated on opposite sides of the harp's neck, bore the faces of a man and woman. Their names were etched on a plaque below:

Michail and Sofia Agapios, Founders of Aeolia
Unde Origo Inde Salus

The wind harp stood at the back of the plaza, in the shadow of a long, domed building. The doors opened, and the sound of the harp was lost in a babble of voices as the hall emptied out into the plaza. A sea of anxious faces passed by.

Last to emerge were a group of men and women robed in royal blue, followed by others uniformed in scarlet tunics, which were clipped at the side. The crowd had almost dispersed when Esme heard a voice call out.

'Ariane! Ariane, is that you?

Chapter Six

A russet-haired lady hurried toward Esme, wearing a scarlet uniform with the words 'City of Esperance' embroidered on the lapel. Accompanying her was a girl around Esme's age. Upon drawing closer, the woman's face clouded with confusion.

'Oh, I'm sorry, I ... I thought you were someone else. An old friend.' She trailed off uncertainly. 'You look so alike ...'

Seized with hope, Esme fastened on the woman's face. 'My mother's name is Ariane,' she blurted out.

'Ariane Silver?' The stranger smiled, her olive eyes crinkling around the edges. 'Then ... you must be Esme? Of course, there's such a likeness.' Her eyes roamed around the plaza. 'So where is Ariane? It's been so long ... at least seven years now.'

Seven years?

Esme's excitement came to an abrupt halt, like a ship suddenly grounded on a reef. She bit down her disappointment.

'I'm Miranda,' said the woman. 'Miranda Lovell, and this is my daughter—'

'Lillian. Hi.'

Miranda's daughter was a head taller than her mother, with a curvy, statuesque figure and long auburn hair that spilled over her shoulders. She had the air of someone who knew that everything had its place, but wasn't completely sure of her own yet.

'Wait. Mum's not with me,' said Esme.

'She's not?'

'She's ... missing. It's been several years, now. I was hoping she might be here.'

'How—what?'

Miranda's eyes glazed over. Esme knew that look well; she had seen it whenever people back home had heard the news. The concept of someone going missing was strangely foreign. People met with accidents, or fell ill—they didn't just disappear.

'Mum went on a trip, and never came back. We searched everywhere ... Most people think she was lost at sea.'

Miranda looked mystified.

'Like, drowned.'

'Drowned?' Miranda put her hand to her heart, reacting as though drowning was some sort of rare disease. Esme had forgotten, momentarily, that people could breathe underwater here. Feeling very out of place, she dropped her gaze, just as Daniel arrived.

'Hey, Esme. I ...' He paused and took in the scene, his tone uncertain. 'Ms Lovell?'

Miranda waved at him in vague acknowledgment. 'Oh, Daniel, hello. Wait, you two know each other?'

'Esme came through the portal on Laertes Island. I was there dragon-spotting when she ran in to me. Literally.' He rubbed his head.

Esme winced at the memory of the pool that had swallowed her and then promptly spat her out again. 'I—I found it by accident. I got pulled under, and ended up here.'

Miranda's eyes fixed on Esme's clothes and hair, as if registering her dishevelled state for the first time. 'Poor Ariane. She never got a chance to tell you about us?'

'In a way ... in stories.'

'Of course. She said her grandmother did the same for her. I never met Lucinda, but Ariane often talked about her ... and you, of course. She was planning to bring you over when you were older.'

Lucinda.

Ever since the pool had dragged her down into its depths, Esme's mind had been working in fits and starts, as it tried—and failed—to make sense of things. Now, the doubting voices in her head were momentarily silenced. Not just one, but two of her family members had been here. The Spindrift rock pools were more than just a way to while away an afternoon. They were the way to Esperance.

'If you don't have anywhere to stay tonight,' said Lillian, 'you can stay with us.'

'Of course,' said Miranda. 'You'd be more than welcome. It's the least we can do.'

Esme hesitated, but her aching muscles begged her to accept the offer, even though she had brought nothing with her, apart from her soggy clothes and her mother's notebook. Miranda and Lillian seemed genuine enough.

She glanced around. The afternoon was wearing on, and much of the city was now in shadow. A surge of notes spilled through the plaza. The wind had picked up, and the harp's soliloquy reminded her of Spindrift—and her mother. If her mother really had been here, then how could she leave without finding out more?

'Thanks … I guess I could …' She glanced at Daniel. 'You said I can go back anytime I want, right?'

'Sure,' said Daniel.

'I have to get back to the palace for another meeting,' said Miranda. 'But Lillian can show you the way home.'

It was only after Miranda left that Esme noticed the uncomfortable silence between Daniel and Lillian. Lillian had taken to examining the pavement, and Daniel was shifting from foot to foot.

'I should go,' he said. 'I'll come by tomorrow, check on how you're doing. If it's all right with you, Lillian.'

Lillian continued to ignore him.

'Or, if it isn't,' he muttered.

He turned on his heel and marched off. Esme wondered what had happened between him and Lillian, but her companion said nothing about it as they made their way out of the plaza.

As they plunged into the maze of alleys and laneways that made up Esperance, Esme questioned the wisdom of her decision to stay.

Away from its prosperous heart, the city appeared to be in dire straits. Rubble was piled up at intervals, rooftops looked close to caving in, and shattered windows had been boarded up instead of repaired. In one street, a row of dwellings leaned drunkenly to one side.

'What's happened here?'

'Earthquakes,' said Lillian. 'That's what the meeting in the plaza was about.'

'Is the city on a fault line or something?'

'No. The quakes have been going on for years. People keep predicting they'll stop soon, but they haven't. It's not just here, other regions are suffering as well, but Esperance always seems to bear the brunt of them. There's talk of evacuating the city, going to other places.' Lillian sighed. 'But nobody wants to leave Esperance.'

Ahead, a group of children laughed as they launched makeshift toy boats into the canal. As the paper ships foundered in the waves of passing traffic, the children sang a song, over and over:

'Pearl of the ocean, pearl of the sea,
No more pearls for you or me.
Take a boat, load it well,
Watch it sinking in the swell ...'

Esme and Lillian stopped on a latticed bridge that spanned a small canal. Beneath them, a slender green twist of water wound off out of sight.

'This is home,' said Lillian, gesturing toward the front door of a house adjacent to the canal. No. 8 Nestor Street was a tall terrace of peeling terracotta stucco, patched up in places like the other houses along the street. A golden sea goddess adorned the knocker. At a touch of Lillian's hand on the deity's wave-swept tresses, the door swung open.

Lillian's house had a cluttered yet comfortable feel to it, reminiscent of home, but without the painful adornments of Penelope and her extended family. A huge gilded mirror hung on the wall to the right, above a long hall table crammed with photos and curios. As her eyes ran over them, she was astonished to see something she recognised: a bell with a fishtail wound around its handle.

'Oh! Mum gave me one of these,' she exclaimed, taking it up in her hand.

'Ring it,' said Lillian, laughing.

At the tinkle of the bell, a rush of glorious sounds filled the hallway, pouring over her and through her, whisking away much of her tiredness, before fading away.

'I—what was that?'

'Just a songspell, threaded into the bell,' said Lillian.

'A *what*?'

The room was spinning. So much had happened in a few short hours. Too much.

'What's the matter? Are you okay?' asked Lillian, peering at her.

Esme grabbed the edge of the table to steady herself. 'It's ... just a lot to take in.' *Magic. Dragons. Breathing underwater. Walking on top of it.* 'I'll be fine.'

Lillian's mother arrived home shortly afterwards. Over a dinner of spicy fish, Esme finally got the chance to quiz her about Ariane. When she asked how they had met, Miranda smiled.

'I used to host visitors to Aeolia from far-flung regions. As part of my job with the council.'

'Far-flung regions ... like, other worlds?'

'No, just different parts of Aeolia. Yours is the only other world we know of, and visitors are quite uncommon. There are only about half a dozen portals between your world and ours. And you've seen how well they're hidden. People rarely stumble upon them by accident. Was the tide turning when you found the shell?'

Esme nodded.

'Aeolia was originally founded as a place of refuge—only those invited here were meant to pass through.' She sighed and took a sip of water. 'Your mother stayed with me whenever she was over here.

The last time I saw her, she'd just finished preparing for an exhibition.'

Esme's fork hovered in mid-air. 'An exhibition?'

Mum painted over here?

'She looked tired,' Miranda went on, 'but I didn't think anything of it. I just assumed she was exhausted from the effort of getting everything ready.'

Miranda sat back in her seat and massaged her forehead.

'She left Esperance the next day. We never saw her again. But I thought nothing of it. Ariane had always said that after the exhibition was done, she would go home for good, so she could spend more time with you ... before bringing you here, when you were older.'

She gave Esme a sad smile.

'It was a bit strange, though ... that she never said a proper goodbye. I always wanted to check up on her, but with the separation and everything—as well as working full time on the council— I just never got around to it.'

'More than full time,' Lillian interjected. 'You practically live at the palace.'

Miranda gave a nod of vague acknowledgement, her mind clearly still on the past. 'I sent letters with the sea eagle,' she continued, 'but never heard anything back. Now I know why.'

'The sea eagle?'

'Yes, a messenger bird that was very attached to Ariane ... one with speckled wings.'

The sea eagle.

More pieces fell into place.

Over the rest of the meal, Miranda's eyes flickered to Esme more than once, but not in the same way that the villagers of Picton would react when they saw her. To the people back home, Esme was an unpleasant reminder of the past, a link to tragic events best left forgotten. Instead, Miranda's eyes held a fond regard. Even though Esme knew she was probably thinking of Ariane, it was a welcome change.

'I'll go sort out somewhere for you to sleep. Maybe not the guest room. It needs a clear-out. That would take days ...'

'What about Finn's room?' asked Lillian.

'I was just thinking that.'

Some time later, Miranda called out for Esme to come upstairs. The walls of the stairwell were covered with artworks and framed photographs, but Esme was too bleary-eyed to take much notice of them—except for one. A small painting of Miranda's house, from the viewpoint of the little bridge outside.

She recognised the style at once: confident brush strokes in a palette of colours she'd seen many times before. Esme knew her mother had painted it even before she saw the initials 'A S' in the bottom corner.

She ran her hand over the edge of the canvas, feeling the bobbled weave of linen. Then she unhooked the canvas and flipped it over, looking for a date. There it was, in Ariane's hand. Her mother had painted it the year before she disappeared.

The surety that her mother had been here settled in her like a pebble dropped into a pond. All that had happened that day—the sea eagle's strange behaviour, the trip through the rock pool, and her arrival in the city—had seemed so surreal, like a dream from which she would wake in the morning. Until now. The knot of fear lodged in the pit of her stomach began to dissolve. She rehung the picture and climbed the stairs, her heart lifting with every step.

Chapter Seven

Unfamiliar sounds filtered into Esme's bedroom the next morning. The pounding waves of Splinter Bay had been replaced by more subdued noises: the lap of water in the wake of passing boats, a child's laugh from the nearby bridge, the muffled toll of distant bells. A melodious voice rose up from the ground floor, floating effortlessly over scales and runs. It was Lillian, practising her singing; she had mentioned Esme might hear her in the morning.

She hardly dared open her eyes. What if these sounds were merely the last remnants of a dream, one that would disappear with the daylight? Esme opened one eye and then the other. The hope and wonder she had felt the night before returned in a rush. Her skin tingled with exhilaration.

I'm here. I'm really here.

She had found her way to the place her mother had whispered of, the place sewn into the fabric of her dreams.

Esperance.

It would take more than one day to adjust to a place where people could breathe beneath the water's surface, and walk on top of it, but her remaining doubts were receding fast. *Mum told me about this place*, she told herself. *She's been here. Her painting's on the wall. And not just her—Lucinda, too.*

Esme sprung out of bed. Her sleeping quarters, located on the uppermost floor of Lillian's house, were sparsely furnished: the room contained only a bed, a desk, and chest of drawers. All traces of the room's former occupant had been packed away, but motes of dust circulated in the air, like old particles of someone else's life still hung there. Full-length shutters at the room's end opened up on to a small, narrow balcony, half of its width taken up by a curved wrought-iron balustrade.

On the balcony, she searched eagerly for signs of dragons overhead. Finn's room was at the rear of the house, and the terrace opposite was patched with scaffolding, as were other houses further along. Lillian's neighbourhood appeared to fall somewhere between the rich heights of the Palace Canal, and the straitened circumstances of streets where citizens couldn't afford to rebuild over and over again.

The back half of the Lovells' paved courtyard, directly below her, was piled high with dusty bricks and broken roof tiles. A mosaic table and a claw-footed bath, packed with pot plants, took up the rest of the space. On the left, a low stone wall marked the border of the property. The little canal she had crossed the day before streamed beside it, perpetually in motion.

An electric thrill ran through her as a glimmer of gold appeared over the rooftops. Two serpentine shapes twisted in and out of view, before pinwheeling away to another part of the city. *Dragons.* Dragons belonged in storybooks and children's games, not in everyday life. Yet here in Esperance, they were a living, breathing presence, riding the winds with consummate ease.

A voice floated out to her. 'I hope my singing didn't wake you.'

Inside, Lillian was depositing a pile of clothes on the bed. Esme's new acquaintance had already changed for the day. Lillian's long legs peeked out from underneath a red flowing kaftan top, while Esme was still dressed in the oversized t-shirt she had borrowed the night before. The wrinkled, salt-stained clothes she had worn the previous day littered the floor beside her.

'Take what you like,' said Lillian, gesturing to the clothes on the bed. 'I'm a bit taller than you, but you might find something in there. I never wear half of them.' Her eyes skimmed the room. 'It's good to see someone up here. This was Finn's room—my brother. We don't see much of him these days. And this house is way too big for two.'

Lillian's face fell while she talked about her brother, but it just as quickly lit up again.

When Esme entered the kitchen a short while later, Lillian was busy whisking eggs together in a bowl. She tilted her chin toward a large leather bag at the other end of the bench.

'That's for you. It belonged to your mum—my mum found it for you last night.'

Esme took the bag over to the little kitchen table where they had eaten dinner the night before. She eagerly undid the drawstring, only to find that the bag was empty. She jiggled it up and down.

'That's weird. It feels full, but there's nothing in there.'

'I noticed the weight, too,' said Lillian, while setting down the meal. 'Must be some trick to it.'

Lillian had cooked scrambled eggs, and served them with bread rolls flecked with some sort of seaweed, along with tangy breyberries: small dark morsels of sweetness, harvested from a nearby island.

'Mum said she was hoping you'd stay a little longer.'

The possibility of staying had already crossed Esme's mind. Her father would be out of contact for a month. He wouldn't even know she was gone.

Her main concern was leaving Reuben alone with Mavis. She would be furious, and Esme was sure she would take it out on him. But Esme had seen him brawling with the other village cats. Reuben could handle himself; in fact, he'd probably end up terrorising Mavis more than she him.

'I'd like to,' she said. 'But what about you? You probably have plans.'

'Not really, apart from avoiding Mum's plans for me,' said Lillian, busy spooning what looked like tealeaves into a pot of water on the stove. 'School holidays have just started here and the dragon festival's coming up. Mum's in charge of all the festivals in Esperance. And she'll drag me in to help if I'm here on my own. But if you stay, I'll have the perfect excuse. It's not every day an other-worlder comes to visit.'

A voice hailed through the kitchen window. 'Hello?'

The warmth on Lillian's face evaporated.

The two of them entered the courtyard to find Daniel bobbing up and down on the other side of the wall. At first Esme started—thinking that he was walking on water like the woman she had seen yesterday—but he was just standing in *Talia*, swaying with the motions of the boat.

'Hi, Esme. Need a lift back to Laertes?'

Esme shook her head. 'Thanks, but I think I'll stay a bit longer … Try and find out more about what Mum was up to while she was here.'

'Great,' said Daniel, studiously ignoring Lillian.

The resentment now radiating from Lillian was just as fierce as it had been back in the plaza.

'Something smells good,' said Daniel.

A spicy aroma floated toward them from the kitchen window. It was the forgotten tea.

'I'll get it!' Esme cried.

She hurried toward the kitchen, but Lillian bounded past her, panting. 'No, I will.'

While Lillian was inside, Daniel took the opportunity to unlatch the gate and seat himself at the mosaic table. 'Is that yours?' he asked, eyeing Ariane's bag with considerable interest.

'It's my mum's,' said Esme. 'She left it here. But there's something odd about it. It feels full, but it isn't.'

'Really? I wonder … can I see?'

Daniel examined the bag and fiddled with the drawstring. He was still inspecting it when Lillian returned with a tray of mugs—three, to Esme's surprise. He rolled the hem of the bag back, exposing the lining, and ran his fingers over the cloth.

'I thought so. Look at the fabric closely. See how it moves?'

Esme squinted at it. The pattern on the lining was swirling around, expanding and receding before her eyes.

'You don't see these around much anymore. My grandmother had one. I was always trying to guess the password.'

'Password?'

He handed the bag back to Esme.

Lillian was riveted. 'Can you think of a word your mother might have used?'

Esme racked her brain. 'Uh … Picton? Spindrift?'

The bag didn't budge.

'What about names?' Lillian suggested.

'Esme!' said Daniel triumphantly, to no effect.

'Lucinda?' Esme tried. 'Aaron?'

At the mention of 'Aaron', the bag came to life. It quivered, then puffed in and out like a pair of bellows, before stretching out to more than twice its original size. Esme watched the bag's contortions in awed silence. When it had stopped expanding, she fumbled with the drawstring and peered inside.

'*Now* I see something!'

She spread the contents out on the table: a small sleeve for photographs and a coin purse—both of which she vaguely recalled from home—as well as a jewellery fold and a shell.

Esme flipped through the photos first, stopping at a black-and-white photograph of herself with her parents, beside the wind harp at Spindrift. Tools were strewn on the ground around them. They must have just finished building it. Ariane stood next to Esme and Aaron, a delighted smile on her face.

She passed it around. 'That's Lucinda's cottage—well, more of a shack, really.'

'Wow, you and your mum do look alike,' said Lillian. 'And that's … your dad?'

In the photo, Aaron's face was open and relaxed. There was no trace of grey in his hair, and his shoulders were straighter, less weighed down than in recent years.

'That's him.' Esme replied pensively. 'He remarried recently. I think one of the reasons Dad gave up on searching for Mum was because she told him about Esperance. There's a letter—I found it just before I came here—a letter from a doctor, questioning Mum's state of mind. Now I know why the villagers were always avoiding me, or giving me odd looks. They must have thought I was going to end up like her.'

Lillian put the photo down. 'That's awful. But what about your friends? They must have stuck by you.'

'Yeah. That's what friends are for,' said Daniel sarcastically. 'Aren't they?'

Lillian's face turned as crimson as her top.

Having little advice, herself, to offer about friendship, Esme scrutinised her mother's possessions. The shell was as big as her palm, and indigo in colour, its smooth surface speckled with dozens of tiny, milky-white dots, like a constellation of stars. It wasn't a surprise to find it in amongst her mother's things; Ariane was an avid collector of shells, and had often used them as subjects in her paintings.

Inside the jewellery fold lay an amethyst ring, a gold chain, and a couple of silver bracelets. She wrapped them up again. It felt strange, looking through her mother's jewellery without her there.

Now only the purse remained. The wad of notes tucked into the bottom weren't ones she recognised. She peeled off a note. A wind harp adorned one side of the yellow paper. Pictured on the reverse was the face of one of the founders of Esperance. It was Michail Agapios, whose statue Esme had seen in the plaza.

'Is this much?' she asked, passing some of the crinkled notes to Lillian.

Lillian held up the yellow note. 'That's ten merles. And this,' Lillian held up a pink one, 'this one's worth twenty. This, and the rest, should last you weeks. Months, even.'

'Longer than that,' said Daniel.

Esme piled everything back into the bag, and pulled the string tight. 'Now what?'

'Same password,' said Daniel.

Saying Aaron's name again tugged at Esme's heart. Even while Ariane had been here, Aaron's name had still been on her lips, Esme's father uppermost in her mind.

The sun was almost perpendicular now, baking the courtyard in its rays. The atmosphere between Daniel and Lillian remained strained as ever. Daniel pushed aside the tea tray to reveal a reclining mermaid, pieced out in shimmering silver tesserae. A number of the tiles were missing, and he rested his hand over the squares where the stone lay bare.

'I remember this from years back. Needs a patch up, don't you think?'

Esme caught the plea for reconciliation in his words, but if Lillian had, she ignored it.

Esme had no idea what their ongoing quarrel was about, but felt pressure to try to say something—anything—to defuse the tension. If it weren't for Daniel, she might still be wandering around Laertes Island, even blundering into a furious nesting dragon's den. And if it weren't for Lillian, she would have nowhere to stay, and no offer to stay longer.

'She's a mermaid, right?' Esme asked uncertainly, touching the mosaic.

Lillian answered. 'No. That's a siren. The sirens guard the songspells of Aeolia. And she's not really a she. Their sex is … indeterminate.'

Intrigued, Esme examined the fishtailed creature more closely. The siren wore a circlet of silver, but was missing the traditional long tresses of a mermaid. The face was fierce, with high cheekbones carved beneath icy eyes.

'Well, I'm off,' said Daniel, pushing back his chair.

'Finally,' said Lillian, under her breath.

'What was that?'

'She said it's hot,' Esme cut in hastily. 'We should go for a swim, or something.'

Lillian gaped at her, but Daniel looked appeased.

'Good idea. I could take us in *Talia*, to the lagoon.'

Lillian shook her head and picked up the tray. The tension in the air was more palpable than ever.

'Well, at least Esme and I are making an effort,' said Daniel.

Lillian dropped the tray back on to the table. The cups rattled perilously. 'Don't put it all on me. This is all your fault in the first place!'

'Look. It grew back, didn't it?'

Things had taken a very strange turn.

'What grew back?' Esme asked.

'He set me on fire!' Lillian cried.

'*What?*' Esme eyed Daniel warily.

He snorted. 'She forgot to mention it was an *accident*. When she was *eight*. We were best friends, up until then.'

'Were the burns bad?' asked Esme, appalled. 'How long did it take to heal?'

'It was only the end of her plait,' said Daniel.

'It was worse than that,' Lillian spluttered. 'It was half my hair. And my back was totally fried, covered in blisters. I was off school for ages.'

'A week,' he muttered.

'Well, it *felt* like ages. I'm sure there's still a scar somewhere.'

'Come on, Lillian,' he protested. 'I was just going through a phase.'

'A phase? I'm surprised you didn't burn our house down—and yours. You were obsessed with fire. I bet you still are.'

'How would you know? You've ignored me for years! It's not like I haven't tried to apologise. More than once. Honestly, Lillian, you must hold the world record for holding a grudge.'

Lillian's eyes were edged with tears, but her face still wore a mutinous expression.

Daniel retreated to the gate, where he turned back around, his hands clenched into fists. He wasn't exactly shouting, but frustration pitched his words high and loud. 'So that's it? We'll just let another seven years pass by. Is that the plan?' Daniel pushed the gate open.

'Wait! There's a problem,' Esme cried out. 'With this plan.'

'What?' Daniel and Lillian said simultaneously.

'This swim plan, ah, I mean,' she said, quickly improvising. 'All I've got with me is a book and a bag.' She lifted the bag. 'Nothing else. No swimmers.'

The tension broke. Lillian gave Esme a begrudging smile. She took up the tray again, and beckoned Esme inside. 'I've got some you can borrow.' She paused. 'Wait. I didn't agree to this.'

'Too late,' Daniel piped up. 'I'll go get *Talia* ready.'

'Fine,' Lillian sighed, eyeing Esme. 'If you want to go *that* badly, I guess I'll join you.'

'So that's it?' Esme blurted out. 'You really didn't talk to each other for seven years, because of one accident?'

She regretted her words as soon as they came out. But Daniel and Lillian said nothing. All she saw was two guilty faces. It was as if their fight had been going on for so long they had forgotten what had started it.

'When you put it that way,' said Lillian, 'I suppose it wasn't such a big deal. But it felt like it at the time. I guess when lots of big things are happening around you … little things can blow out of proportion.'

'I'll say,' Daniel muttered.

'Hey, I'm trying to apologise here,' said Lillian.

Daniel turned back to her. 'You are?'

'Yeah. You missed it. I'm done.'

Chapter Eight

A short while later, Esme leaned over the side of *Talia*, watching Daniel disappear into the grey-green depths of the lagoon. The water stretched out ahead of her, a sheet of cool relief, waiting for her to slip underneath.

Or drag me down into its depths.

She hesitated, fiddling with the strap of her borrowed swimsuit.

Why did I even suggest this?

It was so unsettling, seeing Daniel disappear beneath the surface, and not coming back up for air. The dangers of drowning had been drilled into her since before she could remember. Her whole life had been spent beside a lighthouse, built to prevent people from perishing in the waves of Splinter Bay. And for years, she had dreamt of her mother sinking beneath the waves.

Daniel resurfaced and kicked away from the boat. Lillian, sitting on the crossbench beside her, watched him with a funny expression on her face.

'Thanks,' she said to Esme.

'For what? I didn't do anything.'

'You got us talking again.' She clambered over the side, mumbling as she went. 'Although I think we might have forgotten how to be friends.' After dropping in, she splashed water up into the boat. 'Come on. This was your idea. Don't leave me alone in here.'

Esme's mind raced back to her experience in the portal: the way the water had closed in on her, the way it had forced her down, the way everything had faded to black.

Get a grip. This is nothing like yesterday. The water's perfectly calm.

She snapped at the strap of her swimsuit again, drew a deep breath out of pure habit, and plunged into the lagoon.

Her first breath under the water was jarring and strange, but air flowed in at once, just the way it had in the rock pool. She fought the urge to kick back up, and soon began to relish the freedom. There were no masks or snorkels to contend with down here, and the water didn't sting her eyes—nor, when she ventured down a few feet, did her ears suffer from the pressure. This weightless world was hers to explore.

Esme stretched out horizontally, her arms and legs splayed out in a star shape, growing more and more aware of a greater, silent rhythm around her. A memory lifted its head, a fragment buried so far inside her that it didn't even seem her own: an echo of ancient seas, and a trace, too, of the more intimate sea in which she had lived and breathed during the months before she was born.

For a while, Esme, Daniel, and Lillian hung a few feet below the surface, observing the movement around them. Small fish flitted above, weaving in and out of water dappled by the sunlight, while larger fish drifted below in languorous procession. A school swept up from the depths, their silver forms flickering around like darts of light. They swayed in time with the currents of the lagoon, a synchronised concert conducted by an invisible hand.

The fish moved off, and Esme watched their departure, captivated by their dance, until Lillian tapped her on the shoulder urgently. A shadow was spreading across the lagoon's surface. They quickly stroked away from it, and then turned to see a rush of gold scales slam into the scattering school.

A dragon.

It swallowed dozens of fish in its great maw before shooting up out of the water. Esme and the others kicked to the surface to see it rising back up into the sky.

Daniel's eyes were shining. 'That was incredible! It came so close.'

'Too close,' Esme breathed, but her eyes were as jubilant as Daniel's.

'Way too close,' said Lillian. 'Let's go, before we end up being dragon food.'

On their way back into the city, *Talia* passed by the spot where the dragon had dived. The fish were long gone, and a solitary ray circled in the water.

'So, what *do* dragons eat?' Esme asked.

'Fish, mostly,' said Daniel. 'They don't eat people.' He paused. 'At least, never on purpose.'

Talia took them up the Palace Canal toward the lake, where they could easily access the waterways leading to Lillian's house. It was getting late: night and day were jostling for possession of the city. The upper storeys of buildings were still lit with gold, but below, the colour faded out to blacks and greys, leaving only oblique lines and shapes in the canals and on the shores.

Just before the canal's end, Daniel directed *Talia* toward one of the squares that filled the gaps between the storeyed mansions. A large statue stood in its centre: an image of a youth who appeared more flesh than marble in the fading light. The vision of sinewy, marbled beauty held a torch aloft, keenly searching out something over the water, muscles straining to escape the plinth that anchored him in place. As *Talia* idled in the twilight, the torch surged into life, tongues of flame twisting high in the air.

'Prometheus,' explained Daniel to Esme. 'By Tarnini, the most famous sculptor in Aeolia. His works so embodied the spirit of the ancient gods, that the gods imbued them with their own power. Those flames appeared out of nowhere. Each night at dusk it lights up—it has for centuries.'

'Ancient gods? And they're still … around?'

Daniel's eyes were dancing. 'Maybe. For all you know, I could be one in disguise.'

Lillian sighed. 'Of course it wasn't the gods. An enchanter must have set it up a long time ago.'

Daniel laughed. 'Maybe, but the legend sounds so much better, don't you think?'

They lapsed into silence as *Talia* drifted on. Shadows flickered in the moving currents behind them. One drew Esme's eye. Strangely, it never wavered with the light. It stayed with them, trailing them up the canal.

It could be nothing, thought Esme, but a shiver skittered up her spine.

She nudged Lillian. 'See that? Behind us?'

Lillian twisted back for a brief look. 'I can't see a thing.'

When *Talia* entered the lake, Lillian turned around again and studied the water more intently. In the deepening twilight, the water was an impenetrable black, and utterly still. The surface broke with a hint of menace, before smoothing out again.

'Daniel,' said Esme. 'Stop a moment.'

Daniel stopped the boat opposite the entrance to the palace and brought it around side-on. He used an oar to splash the surface.

Whatever it was stirred about twenty feet away.

'Did you see that?' Esme asked.

The water rippled ... then rippled again.

Something reared out of the lake.

A grotesque creature—some sort of hybrid creation, with the flared head of a cobra and the diamond-shaped body of a ray—balanced motionless on its long tail. It hovered there like a hooded grey ghost, before sliding back into the water.

'What was that?' Esme gasped.

For once, Daniel and Lillian were as stunned as she was.

The water broke, shearing faster and faster as the creature gathered speed, heading directly toward them.

'Watch out!' Esme yelled, grabbing the oars and throwing one at Daniel.

The beast breached out of the lake and let out a blood-curdling hiss. The curve of its hood framed a face straight from the underworld, its eyes blood-red slits of rage. A forked tongue flickered along two fearsome fangs. The creature fixed its eyes on Esme, and lunged.

Chapter Nine

Daniel swung his oar, but Esme got in first, smashing the creature right in the face. *Thwack!* As it fell, Daniel belted it with the other one. The boat pitched wildly as his oar connected. The creature collapsed backward.

It quickly recovered and propelled itself out of the lake again.

'Duck!' Esme cried, pulling Lillian down into the bowels of the boat.

The ray sailed right over them, its spiked tail lashing across the space where their heads had been only moments before. Enraged, it launched itself at them a third time—

But then stopped in mid-flight. Only inches from Esme.

The air turned cold around her.

Ice was forming around the creature, encasing it in a frozen prison. A blast of pale-blue air, sparkling with countless tiny particles of frost, was emanating from the fingers of a black-uniformed palace official on the opposite shore. Once the creature was fully contained, the official waved her hands in a circular motion, drawing the frozen mass toward her. It made a rough landing on the jetty, spraying chips of ice everywhere.

Lillian had gone white. 'What—what is that thing?'

By now, a crowd of onlookers had gathered on the nearby bridge, and others along the shore had stopped to watch as well. A few children cheered from the bridge, but mostly people just stared, open-mouthed, at the spectacle.

Esme collapsed on the crossbench, her makeshift weapon still in her hand. 'Guess we finally found some use for these oars.'

The palace official called out to them from the jetty, beckoning them toward her. They climbed out of *Talia* and gathered around the comatose creature. Even trapped inside the block of ice, it was a startling sight. Their oars had barely made a mark on it. Its malicious face leered up at them.

'Wait here, please,' said another official, stern eyes sweeping over the three of them. 'All of you.'

He strode back toward the palace, and returned with some water and an armful of blankets. 'The lord mayor wants to see you. I'll show you to his office. Follow me.'

Lillian had regained some of her colour, and she quickly interjected. 'There's no need. I know my way around. My mother works here. I'm Lillian Lovell. My mother's Miranda Lovell, Events Director.'

The official nodded, and went to usher away the crowd.

'The lord mayor?' asked Esme. 'What would he want with us?'

Lillian pointed to a pair of arched windows above the palace's imposing front doors. 'He might have seen what happened from up there. His office looks out over the lake.'

Esme, shaken by the encounter with the creature, and acutely aware of her damp and bedraggled appearance, felt very unprepared for a meeting with what sounded like the highest official in Esperance. But upon entering the palace, her discomfort swiftly gave way to awe.

Dazzling artworks covered every inch of the entrance hall's ceiling: oval frescoes in gilded frames. The largest painting depicted nymphs, sirens, and other denizens of the sea gathered around Poseidon, trident in hand. A series of large blue banners hung from flagpoles mounted along the walls, each adorned with a crest: a crest segmented into four quadrants, displaying a harp, a dragon, a nautilus shell, and a royal sceptre. Each crest was topped with a golden orb.

A long sweep of marbled floor led to a double spiral staircase at the back of the entrance hall. On the next floor up, Lillian led them down a wide corridor, past portraits of distinguished men and women in blue mayoral robes. An official waved them through and they stopped before a set of panelled doors.

Beyond lay the office of the lord mayor. In one corner stood a marble-top desk edged in gold filigree, in another, an ornate fireplace. An oversized globe hung from the high ceiling, revolving slowly in the air. The walls were covered with tapestries, framed documents and royal decrees that looked impossibly old.

Two people stood with their backs to Esme, deep in conversation before the vaulted windows on the far side of the room. The first, a tall, pale woman in a dark suit, exuded a formidable presence. Her black hair swept up in a bun, she was tapping her fingers impatiently on the windowsill. As she turned toward Esme, a flicker of cool surprise passed over her face.

The man beside her had been hunched over, his full attention on the commotion outside. As he registered their presence, his body straightened up until he was almost as tall as the woman beside him. Deep lines creased his dark umber forehead, but there was still a spring to his step and manner, and a coiled energy in his movements. He, too, was dressed in a suit.

'Ah, Lillian,' he said in a smooth voice. 'So it *was* you out there … I thought so. I wanted to make sure you were all safe.'

Lillian stepped forward. 'This is Daniel Swift and Esme Silver. Esme's visiting Aeolia. It's her first time here—she's staying with us. Esme, this is the Right Honourable Lord Mayor Everett Trevelli, High Councillor of—'

'Yes, yes, no need for all that. Just call me Everett.' He smoothed down his thatch of salt-and-pepper hair, which curled up at the front, like a white-flecked comber rolling into shore. 'And this is Celia Skye, Chief Enchantress of Esperance … among other things.'

The eyes of the enchantress, onyx-black and impenetrable, scanned the trio. She nodded at Lillian, but her eyes came to rest on Esme, who squirmed in her still-damp clothes.

'We saw the whole incident from the window,' she said, her curt manner in sharp contrast to the mayor's honeyed tones. 'What exactly happened out there?'

Daniel answered. 'Esme noticed something following the boat. When we stopped to have a closer look, it attacked us ...'

'I see. And you didn't provoke it? For a lark?'

'What? No. Why would I?'

Her eyes bored into Daniel's. He averted his gaze.

'Hm. So you have no idea why it targeted you?'

'No,' said Lillian, with a flicker of annoyance.

'I think it might have followed us in from the lagoon,' offered Esme.

The mayor lifted a warning hand. 'Celia, there's no need to interrogate them like this. They're just children.'

Esme bristled at his remark.

'The most important thing is that you're all right,' he said. 'Let me assure you that this sort of thing is not a common occurrence here in Esperance.' He swung a deep brown hand toward the revolving globe. 'How much do you know about Aeolia?'

'Almost nothing, so far.'

'Well, you deserve a better welcome than this.' The mayor beckoned for her to join him by the slowly circling globe, where countless small islands were scattered across a vast expanse of blue. He reached up and tapped the orb.

'Aeolia is, in many ways, like your world, but much younger. We have no large landmasses comparable to your continents—our islands are spread out over vast seas.'

The orb began to spin around of its own accord, slowly at first, then faster and faster, islands and water blurring together until they were indistinguishable from each other. Eventually it slowed to reveal the large continents of Esme's world.

'Our world and yours come from the same matter, but exist on different planes.' Everett spun the globe again, and Aeolia materialised back into view. He gave a deep sigh, and his next words were threaded with exhaustion. 'And here we are. A pity your visit has coincided with the quakes. Our enchanted borders protect Esperance from invasion on all fronts, but not from attack within—or,' he sighed again, 'from assault by the very ground beneath it.'

The mayor pointed out the various clusters of islands that formed the world's regions, and explained how one day, long ago, they had all risen up from the sea to give Aeolia its present form. When he had finished, Celia turned to Daniel and Lillian.

'If you don't mind waiting outside, I'd like to speak with Esme alone. She won't be long.'

The enchantress guided Esme to one of the armchairs before the fireplace. Once they were seated, Celia's voice softened, and her eyes lost their interrogative gleam. 'You may call me Celia. I've heard that you came across our world by accident. Director Lovell told me yesterday that you were staying with her, and that your mother had gone missing.'

Esme nodded. 'Mum used to visit here all the time, apparently. But she disappeared several years ago. We've searched everywhere back home, but nobody's looked here. It's been so long that—that I'm the only one left looking.'

Everett leaned forward, his brows knitting together. 'I'm very sorry for your loss, but I really don't think it wise for someone so young—'

'What? How old do you think I am?' Esme blurted out.

The mayor's features froze in place.

'Uh,' Esme continued. 'What I meant to say, your honour …'

Before he could say any more, Celia stepped in. 'Really, Everett. Don't underestimate young people. In these sorts of cases, it's often what family or friends uncover that can lead to a breakthrough.'

She leaned in closer to Esme. 'I lost someone close to me, too, when I was younger. I remember how difficult it was. Like a part of me had gone missing.'

Her eyes closed, and when they opened again, her face had snapped back into the expressionless mask of earlier.

Just as Esme left the room, she overheard Everett say her name and immediately tiptoed back to listen at the door. Celia was drumming her fingers on the windowsill again.

The lord mayor's voice was just audible. '... clearly a hopeless case.'

The tapping stopped. 'Why shouldn't I offer to help? She lost her mother.'

After a short silence, the lord mayor spoke again. 'That creature down there. Is it one of Nathan Mare's?'

'Don't tell me *you've* been listening to that nonsense, too.'

'It's not implausible, given—'

'Given what? He's everyone's scapegoat these days. I'm more interested in his connection with Ariane Silver.'

Esme stifled a gasp. She strained forward to hear more, but they had stopped speaking.

Celia gave a short, sharp laugh. 'I know you're there, Esme. You may as well come back in.'

Heat shot up into Esme's face. She pushed the door open, and hovered there.

A semblance of a smile crossed Celia's face. 'It's never a good idea to eavesdrop on an enchantress.'

Esme joined them over at the window, meeting Celia's gaze with a defiant tilt of her chin. Chief enchantress or not—she didn't care. If they had information about her mother, it belonged to her too.

'People back home kept things from me for years. If this Mare person is connected with Mum's disappearance, I'd like to know about it.'

The lord mayor frowned, the grooves on his face deepening.

'All I'm providing, Everett,' said Celia, 'is general knowledge, information that Esme could easily discover for herself.'

He crossed his arms, saying nothing.

Celia moved over to the fireplace and leaned against it. The frontispiece was embellished with the same crest that Esme had seen in the entrance hall. Fluted pilasters ran up either side of it, all the way to the ceiling.

'What you will discover, if you go looking, is that a man named Nathan Mare escaped from prison—here, in Esperance—several years ago. The city's been searching for him ever since.'

What?

Celia's words winded her. She felt as immobilised as the creature trapped in ice downstairs.

'*Prison?* And he knew my mother?'

'When Miranda told me of your situation, I remembered your mother's name from a list of Mare's acquaintances. I'm in charge of his apprehension.'

'Celia deals with security matters for the city,' said the mayor, 'as part of her duties. She oversees the prison from which Mare escaped.'

'I wouldn't be too concerned about Mare's connection with your mother, Esme,' said Celia. 'He had many friends here. He still does. Dr Mare was a well-known figure, highly respected in his field. His conviction was … controversial. In fact, many people still believe he did nothing wrong.'

Everett made his way over toward the door. 'We'd better get down there. I told them to hold the creature for us.'

'Good luck with your search, Esme,' said Celia. 'If you do come across anything important, please let me know. I may be able to help.'

The lord mayor puckered his lips as if he was about to argue with Celia, but stopped himself. 'Now, be sure to take a climb up the Keeper's Tower while you're here. You'll find that it has the best view in the city.'

As *Talia* glided back through silent canals, Esme said little, rocked by this new, unsettling information. At least she had a lead now—thanks to Celia. The lord mayor had been helpful, but blinkered when it came to her situation, whereas the chief enchantress, despite her cold demeanour and forbidding appearance, had shown some empathy for her predicament.

That night, as exhaustion overtook her, Esme remembered something. A name. She took up her mother's notebook and read over the final entry.

Returning to Esperance tomorrow, when the tide is right. Slept badly—dreamt of Nathan.

Chapter Ten

The events of the last few days repeated themselves in the night, jumbled in amongst Esme's dreams. She watched, helpless, as her mother was led into the darkness by a shadowy, sinister figure. Then she was trapped beneath the water's surface, unable to breathe, unable to move a muscle. A gold-scaled dragon sheared toward her, before morphing into the ray-like creature that had charged at her in the lake. Its blood-red eyes were the last things she saw before she woke up.

Her mother's notebook had fallen on to the floor by the bed. Esme took it up again, and puzzled over the last few lines, the way she had the night before.

Couldn't sleep—dreamt of Nathan.

Could the Nathan in this notebook and the Nathan Mare who had escaped from prison be one and the same?

The thought stayed with Esme as she travelled by ferry a few hours later, with Lillian, on their way to the Keeper's Tower. The city sights provided a welcome distraction. Just ahead, sharp-bowed gondolas in vivid blues, greens, and reds made elegant entrances and exits from narrow waterways. Salt-weathered buildings leaned into the glassy water below, as if admiring their own reflections.

Around the bend, Esme started, then stared, open-mouthed. A woman was standing by the next bridge, artfully funnelling water up from the canal with motions of her hands. Esme watched, entranced, as the drops of water came together to form a school of fish, which flipped and wriggled in mid-air before dispersing.

A man beside her was trying to emulate her feats. He brought the water up with no difficulty, but after attaining a certain height, it splashed back into the lagoon, shapeless. The woman consoled him as she continued to fashion more and more elaborate shapes.

Esme ran down the back of the ferry to see more. The woman was now sculpting the water into the shape of a large snapping turtle, moving her hands in and out as if playing an invisible accordion. After the turtle vanished, she flicked her hands in a circular motion, until a wriggling eel swam in the air. It wrapped itself around her hapless companion before dissolving back into the lagoon.

'How's she doing that?' Esme exclaimed. 'She just moved her hands, and—'

'Oh, that's just her Gift,' Lillian said casually.

'What's a—?'

The ferry jolted.

'Oh!' Lillian exclaimed. 'This is our stop.'

They disembarked into a busy square. Mouth-watering smells drifted from a bakery, drawing them to the shop window. A row of flat-topped pastries, pressed with the draconic emblem from the city's crest, lined a tray behind the glass.

Lillian's nose was almost pressed to the window. 'Mmmm. Dragonsbreath buns. The first of the season. They're only around for a few weeks each year—during the month of the festival.'

'My treat.' Esme pushed her way into the crowded shop and ordered half a dozen, counting out a handful of unfamiliar coins into the palm of the shopkeeper. The buns were still warm from the oven, and their aroma accompanied them down the street.

They soon reached the plaza where she had first met Miranda and Lillian. Daniel was waiting by the Keeper's Tower. Esme recognised it as the same tower that she had glimpsed upon her arrival in Esperance. Inside, a stone staircase spiralled up out of sight, lit by thin shafts of light filtering in through tall, narrow windows.

'This—reminds me of the lighthouse—back home,' puffed Esme, after they had climbed the first fifty steps.

'Lighthouse?' asked Daniel.

'The lighthouse where I live.'

'So you have to climb stairs like this every day?' asked Lillian, stopping to catch her breath.

'No ... We live in the cottage next door. My dad's the lighthouse keeper, and—'

'You have keepers there, too?' Daniel asked.

'Uh, well, it just means he looks after the lighthouse. What's a keeper here?'

'The keeper watches over all the magic in Esperance. This tower is named after one of them,' he said, between breaths. 'Thomas Agapios. They come from royalty, originally—there's only one born in each generation—but now they're the last of the royal blood.'

'You have a royal family here?'

'Not really. Esperance was occupied during the wars, and Thomas Agapios was imprisoned here, along with the rest of the royal family. He was the only one who survived. He helped to restore Esperance when the wars were over.'

Esme was the first to make it to the top of the tower, where a flash of gold beyond the parapet drew her over to the side. She leaned over the edge, her heart thundering. Several dragons were hovering close to the tower. The impressive creatures were close to thirty feet long, and dwarfed their human riders. Their clawed bodies rippled with scales, muscle, and sinew straining underneath. Their wings resembled thin sheets of pale, crushed gold leaf. In flight, this was stretched out over a series of slender bones, rather like the structure of a bat's wings.

The dragons' riders were outfitted in scarlet and gold tunics, matching the golden scales of their steeds. One of them raised a hand to wave at Esme, and she returned the greeting, her heart still thudding hard.

Daniel and Lillian showed up behind her, panting from the climb. Daniel's eyes, like Esme's own, shone at the sight of the dragons.

'This tower is as low as they're allowed to fly over the city,' he puffed. 'They used to be able to fly wherever they wanted, but there were too many … accidents.'

Esme's eyes stayed fixed on the creatures as they flew off to join more of their kind across the lagoon. She had a sudden urge to sit down and sketch their sinuous shapes, to record their forms on paper forever. Since Ariane's disappearance, Esme had lost much of her passion for art, but seeing the dragons stirred an urge within her that had lain dormant for years.

This must have been how Mum felt all the time, when she was here.

Lillian broke into her thoughts. 'It's so clear! You can see for miles today. Look. Right out there, past the lagoon, that's the Tiamat Sea.'

Spread out below was the labyrinth of shining waterways, red roofs, towers, and pale domes that made up Esperance. Six wide canals wound out from the central lake, spilling into the wider lagoon. Further out, minute islands bordered the lagoon, on the other side of which lay the Tiamat Sea. Boats appeared as moving white specks in the distance.

One of the dragons was racing across the skyline, spewing fire in spectacular fashion. Another dragon drew too close, and the tip of its tail was caught in the expulsion of flames. The injured creature plummeted toward the lagoon, leaving a trail of smoke in its wake, but both dragon and rider emerged from the water, intact, just a few moments later.

'How do the riders even stay on their backs?' asked Esme, awestruck. 'And what about the fire? That was so close. It could have …'

'Do you still want to be a ranger, Daniel?' asked Lillian, sounding uncertain, as though she were digging far back into her memories.

'Yeah, but my family don't want me to. They're put off by the high … er … fatality rate. But they're the ones who brought me to Esperance in the first place. I'd never even seen a dragon until I left Thalassa! Dad keeps taking me on work trips, trying to get my mind off them. He's dragging me away on one again tomorrow.'

The palace stood to their right, its tallest spire almost level with Esme's eye line, its cool beauty reflected in the lake below. She leaned over to take in a better view. The surface of the lake was crisscrossed with the trails of countless boats.

'It was so empty, yesterday afternoon,' said Esme. 'When that ray …'

'Mum had already heard about the attack by the time she got home last night,' Lillian told Daniel. 'She didn't go on too much. I think she was just glad we were all right.'

'Mine weren't too happy. Dad said there have been sightings of creatures like that in other regions—and other attacks. No one knows where they're from, the creatures, but they'd never been seen in these parts—until yesterday.'

'Well, the mayor seemed to know something about it,' said Esme. 'He thought the creature might be connected with someone called … Nathan Mare. Though he didn't say that to my face. I was listening at the door. I heard my mother's name just as I left, so I hung around outside … Until Celia figured out I was there, and called me back in.'

Lillian looked impressed. 'Did you get in trouble?'

'No, not really. Celia told me that Mum and this criminal—Mare—knew each other. That's why they were talking about him.'

Daniel frowned. 'Why would they know each other?'

'I don't know, but Celia said not to be too concerned. That Mare had plenty of friends in the city, and some didn't agree with his conviction. But when I got home last night, I went through Mum's notebook, the one I brought with me. There's a mention of someone called Nathan in it, in the last entry she made before she disappeared. It might be just a coincidence, but I still want to find out more.'

Daniel pointed out a distant building, rising up over the patch-work of red roofs. 'See that golden dome down there? That's the Temple Library. It'd be as good a place as any to start.'

'I can take you there now, if you'd like,' said Lillian.

Esme shook her head. 'There's no need. You two have done enough for me already. If Mum really is linked with this Mare person, this could get … dangerous.'

Daniel's eyes lit up.

Esme sighed and shook her head again. 'I can do the rest on my own.'

Lillian looked put out. 'But I want to help.'

'I do, too,' said Daniel. 'When I first arrived here, I didn't know anything, or anyone. I barely even knew the language.' He stared out past the parapet. 'That's when I made friends with Lillian. I met her at school. She used to stand up for me when no one else would.'

Lillian's expression was hard to fathom. 'I did?'

'Yeah. You were really sweet back then. Now you're just mean.'

She arched an eyebrow at him, and he laughed.

'Anyway, you'd better let us help, Esme,' he said, in a mock-threatening tone. 'Or we'll throw you off the tower. Like they used to in the old days.'

'*What?*'

'During the occupation of Esperance. The Tyrians did it, as sport. They'd drag prisoners up here and hold them upside-down over the edge. Most of the time, unless the person could offer a big enough bribe, they'd let go. See those marks there, on top of the stone?'

Esme's hand was resting on one of them. She lifted if off like she had just touched a hot stove. Notches in the stone ran right around the perimeter.

'Every notch,' Daniel said, 'is a—'

'Forget it. I don't want to know.'

Her stomach turned as she peered over the balustrade, trying not to picture blood-splattered bodies below. Daniel's stomach, however, didn't seem to be affected.

'Something smells good,' he said.

After taking one for herself, Esme handed the bag of

dragonsbreath buns over to Daniel. The red paste inside the buns was the spiciest thing she had ever tasted. Her eyes brimmed over with tears.

'What's—what's in these things?'

Lillian laughed. 'They've got *dragons* on them. What did you expect, jam? Come on, let's go.'

Chapter Eleven

The Temple Library dominated the square, its entrance flanked with fluted columns of grey-veined creamy marble. The building was crowned with the golden dome that Esme had seen from atop the Keeper's Tower.

'Thanks for showing me the way,' said Esme. 'I can take it from here.'

'Nonsense. I'm staying,' said Lillian. 'But don't you need to go and get ready for your trip tomorrow, Daniel?'

Daniel rolled his eyes. 'You're really not used to having me around, are you?'

A mass flapping of wings interrupted them. A nearby flock of pigeons had taken off in a startled rush.

'Oh no,' cried Lillian, as a rumble came up from the ground below.

It sounded like an enormous subterranean beast, making strange noises in its sleep. The sounds came intermittently at first, before joining together in a deafening, continuous roar.

An earthquake.

Esme's heart vaulted into her throat as the ground beneath them began to shiver and shake. She stared down with mounting horror. The cracks in the pavement—how had she not noticed them before? Hairline cracks, then bigger ruptures, snaked through the square.

Cracks that were now *moving*.

Her instincts told her to run, but there was nowhere to go. She tried to grab hold of something—anything—to steady herself, but everything was moving as much as she was. The ground around her rippled like water. She shrank into herself, willing it to stop. The earth thundered and swayed beneath her.

And then it was over, just as quickly as it had begun.

Esme slid down onto a nearby bench, panting as if she had just run a mile.

'You've gone white,' said Lillian, who looked way too calm. 'Was that your first quake?'

'That was awful.'

Lillian gave her a thin smile. 'You get used to it after a while.'

Unlike most things in Aeolia, this was something Esme didn't want to get used to. The earth was supposed to be solid, fixed, immutable. She thought of the lighthouse back home, anchored into the rocky headland.

'You've really had tremors like this for years?'

Lillian nodded. 'I can hardly remember what it was like before. Usually they're even worse than that.'

Esme shuddered.

Worse?

The cracks left by the quake thankfully stopped just short of the library's steps. Esme and the others ventured inside. As in the palace, rich frescoes decorated the ceiling. The first depicted a man and woman in robes, resting on a sandy beach. Esme recognised them as the founders of Aeolia: Michail and Sofia Agapios. Michail was gazing out to sea, while Sofia cradled a harp, her flaxen hair flowing down toward the strings.

Another panel showed the birth of Aeolia: misty islands rising from the great womb of the sea. Above the islands, red, green, and pink bands of light swathed the sky. Sea dragons played amongst the lights, twisting in and out of enormous curtains of colour.

A long passageway opened up to a sight that took Esme's breath away. A majestic waterfall spilled down from the apex of the library's domed roof, crashing soundlessly onto the ground. The great gusts of spray settled into vapour, obscuring the chequered marble floor. Bookshelves lined every wall, accessible by numerous wooden ladders, which ran along high rails. Thick columns craned upward to support a wide gallery above the main floor.

Esme bent down to try to scoop up some of the mist wafting around her ankles, but nothing cold or wet clung to her fingers.

'Another enchantment?'

Daniel nodded. 'The books wouldn't last very long if it was real.'

'I *love* coming here,' said Lillian, skipping ahead. 'This library holds the largest collection of songspells in all of Aeolia.'

One of the library patrons, a grey-haired man with an armful of books, ambled straight through the waterfall and out the other side. Esme couldn't resist doing the same. She strode up and stepped into the flow. It felt as though the water was falling right through her, the thrum of magic humming in every drop. She emerged, elated.

Then the three made their way past statues of Greek deities, all mired in mist, as if they were floating above the clouds of Mt Olympus.

'The nine muses,' said Lillian, running a hand along one of the sculpted shapes.

Esme tilted her head to read the script that scrolled sideways up a nearby pillar:

The history of Aeolia is writ in water.

A wrought-iron staircase led up to the first gallery, where they retrieved back copies of the city's two most widely read newspapers, the *Aeolian Eye* and the *Esperance Daily*. It took some time for Esme to settle in to her task. The Temple Library, with its marbled floors and magical accoutrements, was so different from the tiny Picton library back home, although it did share the same hushed atmosphere and solemn air.

One article from the *Aeolian Eye*—a weekly column by somebody named Basil Roth—was dated one month after Ariane had vanished.

Trevelli's Tremors
Shaky Start to New Mayor's Tenure

An air of civil unrest—if not outright insurrection—was palpable in Esperance's Town Hall last night, as our new lord mayor, Everett Trevelli, concluded his leadership acceptance speech.

'I would like to give the citizens of Esperance my utmost assurance,' the mayor promised, 'that the disturbances that have been plaguing our fair city over this past month will soon be over. We are working with a team of experts from Pelorus to determine the cause of the earthquakes, and soon all will be well once more.'

These words had barely left the mayor's lips when a tremor struck, the Town Hall itself shaking from side to side as if to spite him. One citizen opined that Trevelli's appointment as lord mayor had brought down a curse upon the city. An elderly man asked what exactly he had done to anger the gods. Your faithful correspondent merely dwelt in silence on the fact that the lord mayor had just hung himself on his newly polished mayoral chains.

Meanwhile, the citizens of Esperance and its surrounding islands wake up each morning wondering if their homes will be reduced to rubble. All will NOT be well, Lord Mayor Trevelli. The election is over, and the hard work of guiding Esperance through these troubled times has begun.

Esme whistled under her breath. *No wonder the lord mayor seemed so worn out,* she thought. Without really noticing what she was doing, she took up a pen and started doodling on her hand.

'Wish I could draw like that,' said Daniel, leaning over to look.

The doodle had turned into one of the spires she had seen on the way here. She had added a sailing ship, balanced on top. 'I haven't really drawn since my mother disappeared.'

When she was younger, drawing had been more than a habit. It had helped her to think, to clear her head. She had defaced plenty of school books, to the horror of her teachers. But in recent years the pages had remained pristine, and her grades, paradoxically, had gone down because of it.

'Here,' said Lillian, pushing a newspaper over. 'Here's something on Mare.'

The headline was splashed across the front page of the *Esperance Daily*.

MARE FOUND GUILTY ON ALL COUNTS

After seven days of deliberation by the jury, the controversial trial of Dr Nathan Mare has at last come to its conclusion. Mare, who was arrested three months ago on charges of manslaughter and medical malpractice, has been found guilty on all counts, and sentenced to fifteen years in prison. Reporters from the Daily *were present on the scene as Mare was transferred to the Citadel.*

A grainy photograph accompanied the article, showing Mare being led through a corridor as uniformed officials held back the press. His head was bent down, so that his facial expression was hidden beneath his silver hair.

Despite the best efforts of the Esperance High Court to keep the details of Mare's trial confidential, the case has attracted an extraordinary amount of public attention. As the investigation progressed, it was revealed that Mare had carried out dangerous experiments on a number of terminally ill patients, who had given the doctor written permission to try out new, untested medical procedures that may have extended their lives. Each one of them died within a month of entering into his care.

A charismatic figure, lauded for his pioneering work in medicine, Dr Mare still retains the support of many. A large number of students and fellow staff members at the University of Esperance continue to express outrage and disbelief at the charges laid against him, as well as at the severity of his sentence. While some believe that Mare did no wrong, others insist that he coerced his patients into agreeing to participate, and that his acts pushed far past the boundaries of ethical behaviour.

Antonia Trask, whose husband, Frank, was one of the patients in Mare's care, had this to say:

'*It was awful, just awful. Those marks on Frank's throat ... And it wasn't just him. I've been told all the others had them, too! If he had known what Mare had planned for him, he would never have agreed to it. Experimenting with Gifts ... everyone knows how dangerous that is. At least now, after today, this will stop.*'

Dr Jonathan Quigley, one of Mare's colleagues at the University of Esperance, expressed a different opinion.

'*Nathan has done nothing wrong. The people in his care consented to these procedures, as a gift to research, with full knowledge of the risks involved. What has happened to him today is a travesty of justice.*'

Dr Mare is the only son of Esperance benefactors, Drs Jules and Eleanor Mare, who were also commended during their lifetimes for their scientific talents and charitable work.

Esme scrutinised the other photographs that accompanied the article. One depicted the silver-haired doctor lounging nonchalantly against a stone arch at the University of Esperance. His parents were shown in a smaller photo, taking part in a ceremony. Their faces glowed with pleasure as they clasped their hands together around a large, golden key.

She sat back in her chair, not sure what to make of it all.

'Any thoughts?' Daniel asked.

'I can see why the conviction was controversial. It's not very clear what he actually did. Or what he's like, apart from being ... shifty.'

Her eyes strayed over the article again, coming to rest on the word 'Gifts'.

'It says here that he was experimenting with Gifts,' she said. 'What exactly *are* they?'

Daniel answered. 'Magical abilities. Most Aeolians have one.'

'But ever since the quakes started, people's Gifts haven't been working the way they're supposed to,' said Lillian. 'Like those water-weavers we saw on the way here. One of them was doing just fine, the other ...'

Esme had assumed that the abilities she had seen demonstrated in the city were limited to only a select few. She regarded Lillian and Daniel curiously.

'What about you two?'

'I don't have one,' said Daniel. 'Not yet, anyway. The Gifts are meant to emerge at our age, but, like Lillian said, there have been problems. A lot haven't come through. It might be different for Lillian ... Come to think of it, there's a Seeing Stone around here somewhere. I'll go and get it.'

He pushed himself up off his chair.

'No, wait,' Lillian called out, but Daniel was already gone, their view of him obscured by the falling water.

Esme buried herself back in the newspapers, where she found another article on Mare. Only a few months after his incarceration, the Citadel had been damaged in an earthquake, resulting in the flooding of three floors and the escape of dozens of prisoners. Mare was amongst them.

Daniel soon returned with something wrapped in an indigo velvet cloth. He set the bundle on the table. Within its folds was a large orb of cloudy quartz, moony in appearance and marked with a number of natural occlusions. He balanced it in the palm of his hand.

'This Seeing Stone is meant to pick up any hints of an emerging Gift. I sometimes check it when I'm in here.'

Nothing happened at first, but then, glowing cinders appeared within the orb. Flames flickered up from them, filling the orb until it began to radiate heat.

'Hot, hot, hot!' Daniel juggled the orb and dropped it back on the velvet. A baffled look came over his face. 'That ... that's never happened before.'

Esme stared at the flames receding in the orb, and glanced over at Lillian. She looked equally stunned, but then she smirked. 'Trust you, Daniel—fire.'

'Your turn,' he said, passing the Seeing Stone to Esme.

'Wait, I don't—nothing's going to happen.'

The stone was still warm from Daniel's touch, but cooled rapidly in Esme's hand. She shook her head and put it back down on the table.

He handed it right back. 'Give it time.'

Esme took up the stone again, and shifted her gaze to Daniel, wondering about the link he'd made with it, the flames that had surged inside. He, however, was concentrating on the stone.

Something *was* happening. Drops of water were bubbling up inside of it, coalescing into rushing streams, which faded away before forming again. 'What's going on?'

Daniel and Lillian's eyes were still fastened on the crystal.

Daniel blinked. 'Wow, Esme. It's seeing a Gift in you.'

Drops of dew had gathered on the outside of the stone, and it almost slipped out of her hand. She put it back on the cloth, shaking her head.

'No, there must be some mistake. I'm not even from here.'

Daniel picked up the orb and wiped it dry. '*You* might not be, but what about your relatives? That's how the Gifts pass down. Through bloodlines.'

Esme let out a sound somewhere in between a snort and a laugh. A passing librarian frowned at her.

'Come on, how reliable is this Seeing Stone?' she whispered.

'About as reliable as everything else is right now,' Lillian whispered back.

'Exactly,' said Esme, once the librarian was out of sight. 'It's just thrown up a false result, that's all—a false positive.'

Daniel gave her a bemused look. 'It's not science class, Esme. It's magic.' He passed the orb to Lillian. 'Your turn.'

'No thanks,' said Lillian.

'Why not?'

Spots of colour appeared on her cheeks. 'I was in here last week and I … I tried it then.'

'So what? Things might have changed.'

Lillian grimaced and took the orb from him. It stayed clear for a few moments, before turning a dull grey. Lillian dumped it back on the table, her voice prickly.

'See? That means there's nothing.'

Daniel sighed. 'Yet. Stop overreacting. It doesn't mean anything. You know how unreliable everything is right now, you said it yourself.' He rolled the Seeing Stone back up in its cloth, and winked at Esme. 'Just think of it as a false negative.'

Chapter Twelve

'It's true, what Daniel said. You could have a Gift—they *are* passed down through the bloodlines. Our worlds aren't as cut off from each other as you might think. Your mother came over here all the time, and your great grandmother, didn't she?'

It was later that same afternoon, and Lillian was standing by the bookcase in her room, rifling through the contents of her shelves. 'You *saw* something,' continued Lillian. 'I've been looking in that stone for years, and ... nothing.'

Esme wasn't sure what to say, or think, about the revelations of the Seeing Stone. The prospect of having a blood relation from Aeolia seemed an impossibility. And even if what she had seen in the stone had been true—which it wasn't—she wasn't planning on crowing about it to Lillian, who, she suspected, had spent most of her life dreaming of the Gift she might one day receive.

So she said nothing as Lillian bent down toward the crowded bottom shelf. It housed a dozen thick volumes, bound in rich claret-coloured velvet. The slippery, silky fabric, worn and mottled, had been woven long ago, and the titles were embroidered in faded gold thread, titles like *Incanto of Marino, Vol I*, and *Incanto of Johannes, Vol IV*.

'Songspells,' said Lillian, brushing a hand along the spines of the volumes, as if the gesture would somehow magically release their essence. She drew out one of the tomes, and plopped down beside Esme on the bed.

'Is this the Gift you want?' Esme asked. 'To be able to cast songspells?'

Lillian couldn't hide the longing in her voice. 'I've always wanted to be a songstress, more than anything. Dad's given me two books of songspells a year, since I was ten.'

She opened the volume on her lap, titled *Incanto of Melisande, Vol II*. Page after page flowed with staves of musical notes. Looping, slanted letters ran beneath each line, in a language Esme didn't recognise.

'The sirens were the first to cast songspells, so it's in their language,' Lillian explained. 'It's phonetic. The symbols all represent sounds, so you can sing it without knowing the meaning of the words. I've been learning what I can. You're not supposed to do this—prepare for your Gift in advance,' she added wistfully. 'You're supposed to just wait and see what you get. But I can't help myself.'

'Are there any songstresses in your family?'

'A few. Mostly on my mother's side. For all I know, I could get nothing, like Mum did—or else my dad's Gift. He's a doctor. Mum keeps telling me to try and forget about it, that it'll happen if it's meant to. She says I'm as bad as the enchanters.'

'What's so bad about them?'

Lillian rolled her eyes. 'Where do I start? The enchanters have always believed they're way above everyone else. They covet their Gifts over all. They only marry each other, to increase the chances of passing them on. They're secretive, too. Songspells are available to anyone. Of course, you have to be Gifted to use them, but there's no waiting around thirty years until your mentor reveals their best magic on their deathbed, if at all. If you put the work in, you can learn as many complex spells as you want to, even create new ones.'

Lillian closed the book and placed it back on the shelf. 'Choosing who you love, based only on what their Gift is—that seems so coldblooded.'

'It does sound pretty clinical.' Esme fidgeted with one of the threads of the bedspread, thinking of home. Her father had certainly been besotted with Penelope, as well as determined to start over, and give Esme a new mother, whether she wanted one or not. Penelope's motives were less clear, but Esme had never seen the same glow of adoration in her eyes that she had seen in his.

'I guess that was the way things used to be, a long time ago,' she mused. 'Love hasn't always been that high on the list of reasons for people to get married. Property, possessions, titles, youth … that's all that used to matter. Not so much now. But then again, what would I know? Although I still don't see what my dad sees in Penelope.'

'Penelope—that's his new wife's name, isn't it?' asked Lillian. 'What's she like?'

Esme's mood flattened. 'To be honest, I've never got on with her. I don't know what it's going to be like when I get back.' She did have some idea—Mavis interfering with everything she did, Penelope icy, her father oblivious to it all. Living in the village, with more of Penelope's relatives to invade whatever privacy she might have left.

She looked down at the bed, suddenly missing Reuben.

Lillian made a face. 'Dad married Mum for love, but it didn't last. He ended up marrying another doctor. Mum tried hard to put on a brave face. She changed the front door knocker from a god to a goddess. Took me shopping a lot—that bit was good. Of course, it was all made worse by Finn leaving as well.'

'Finn left?'

Lillian bit at a nail. 'Yeah. When Dad left, my brother went with him.'

'Oh, Lillian … I'm sorry.'

'I'm used to it now, but back then …' Grief flashed across Lillian's face, revealing a vulnerability that surprised Esme. It was gone in an instant. 'A few days after they left—that's when Daniel burnt my hair. Back then, seeing him reminded me too much of losing my dad and brother. Giving each other a hard time became a habit. I think we both must have taken it too far, in the end, because eventually we stopped talking altogether.'

Esme gave her a sad, knowing smile. She knew how painful it

was to watch others carry on with their lives while there was a great hole in her own.

'Do you see your dad much?' she asked.

'When I can. He's always busy … like I said, he's a doctor. Because of his Gift.' A note of pride sounded in her voice. 'He can see through things. Literally. Dad said that when I was a baby, he could see my tiny heart beating away, little lungs moving in and out.'

Lillian laughed at Esme's look of incredulity.

'Yeah. Dad hated his Gift at first. Now, though, he says he couldn't do without it. Just goes to show that you shouldn't worry too much about whatever Gift you get. It might be the best thing that ever happens to you.'

As Lillian stared longingly at her collection of songspells, Esme resisted the urge to tell her to take her own advice.

'Oh, dear. This one's in a state. Can't work out if it's night or day anymore.'

Miranda stood in the courtyard of No. 8, watering the plants in the old claw-footed bathtub.

'This one's the best remedy for skin conditions: boils, sties, pimples, and the like,' said Miranda, moving the watering can over the middle of the bathtub. The plant's tiny flowers had opened to drink in the sun, but the afternoon rays were long gone. She picked off a couple of dead leaves. 'Every family in Esperance has one, or at least, those with teenagers. But the poor thing's been making things worse lately. It's having a rough time, like most things magically-inclined around here.'

Another plant, with black roots and stems, stood in its own pot to the side.

'A rue plant. For regrets.' She gave it a sprinkle. 'See … the more you water it, the more it cries.'

As the plant soaked in the water, droplets of its own formed on its black leaves. Miranda tipped the can right over to extract the last of the water.

'I'll go fill it up for you,' Esme volunteered.

'Oh, no need. Look!' Miranda tipped the watering can so that Esme could see water creeping up its sides. 'It's enchanted. One of the most useful presents I've ever been given.'

Plump crowns of red-leafed rosettes crowded one of the pots. Miranda touched a finger to the rosette plant, and Esme watched, transfixed, as the tips of its leaves lit up, glowing for a few seconds in the dusk.

A small pot of lavender was tucked in by the herbs, and Esme brushed her fingertips against one of the purple stalks. 'We have this at home. It's Mum's favourite.'

'You must miss her terribly,' said Miranda. 'I can't get used to the news that she's gone. It's the same with my mother—she passed away a few years ago. I still think about going to visit her, and then remember she's not here anymore. Such a long goodbye, that forgetting and remembering that seems to go on forever. Like a little death each time. I can't imagine what it must be like for you.'

She tucked the watering can away behind the bath. 'Ariane was never here for long, but when she was, she made the most of her time. Her art was always uppermost in her mind.'

Miranda paused and tipped her head slightly to the side, something Esme had noticed she often did when she was regarding Lillian with affection. 'As were you and your father. I think it was hard on her, not being able to tell people where she really was. We know of the existence of your world, but it's not quite the same for you, is it?'

'No. Not at all. Mum did tell Dad about Esperance, but he didn't take it well. He thought she was ill, that she had made up Esperance—Aeolia—in her mind.'

Miranda's face turned down, but before she could reply, her expression changed. Small wisps of light were drifting toward them from the canal, their reflections streaming in the water behind them like the tails of comets.

'Look.' Miranda leaned over the low wall, holding out a hand toward them. Esme reached out hers as well, and a couple of the lights drifted her way.

'They don't come round so much anymore, but I used to see these all the time, when I was younger.' Her voice took on a dreamy timbre. 'It's said that when the islands were first created, the ocean was full of them.'

One of them floated tantalisingly close to Esme, and she guided it into her palm. Through the haze, she glimpsed a nebula of light, like a piece of a galaxy torn from the far reaches of the sky. Its essence drew her in, making her feel part of something wider, a vast ocean bathed in a celestial sea of light, a body of water untrammelled and unrestrained.

She glanced over at Miranda, whose face had relaxed into blissful serenity. When the last wisps of light floated off into the night and Lillian called to Miranda from the kitchen window, the spell was broken. The fine, worried lines that usually crossed Miranda's face returned. She was almost at the door when she stopped and turned back.

'Oh, Esme, I meant to tell you—I've contacted a Professor Sage from the university here. Ariane worked with him. She illustrated one of his books. He's away at the moment, but I sent a letter, telling him the news.'

Miranda's words took a moment to sink in. 'A book?'

'Yes, I never saw the finished product, but it was about the myths and legends of Aeolia. A compendium. I'm sure the professor will give you a copy.'

Miranda went inside.

A compendium—such a book sounded weighty, substantial. How had Ariane found time for a project like that? On her way back inside, Esme stopped by the rosette plant and touched a finger to it. Its phosphorescent glow winked again, a red beacon in the night. Like a warning light. The more she found out, the more she wondered what else she didn't know about her mother.

Chapter Thirteen

Esme sat on her bed, rummaging through a sack of her mother's clothes that Miranda had found for her. With Lillian away on an overnight visit to her father, and Miranda at work, the house was quieter than usual. The only sounds at No. 8 were those floating in from outside: fragments of conversations from passing boats, the slap of water against the sides of the canal, the faint peal of a distant bell.

She tipped the sack's contents on to the bed. Ariane's clothes tumbled out: jeans, dresses, skirts, and jumpers, along with the faintest whiff of lavender. She picked up a soft wool sweater and hugged it to herself.

As she lifted one of the skirts, a crumpled piece of paper fluttered out of its pocket. A receipt: yellow and faded with age.

La Peregrina
14 Sofia Square

A. Silver.
50 merles, paid in full.
Collect in one week.

A date was faintly inked in the top right hand corner. Ariane had placed and paid for the order, whatever it was, only two days before she was last seen in Esperance.

Goaded into action, Esme quickly searched around the house for a map. Of course, whatever had been ordered would be long gone—the shop might have even closed down. But any information about her mother's last few days in the city was worth pursuing. She soon found a map under a pile of papers in the bottom of the hall-table drawer.

There it was: Sofia Square, in the far south-west of the city.

A ferry along one of the main canals took her only part of the way. She disembarked just as a gondola entered the narrow waterway off to her left. It stopped to let off a passenger, and she hurried to take the passenger's place, pressing a silver coin into the straw-hatted gondolier's palm.

This was her first trip in one of the elegant flat-bottomed boats that graced the waterways of Esperance. The interior was snug, but with enough seating for seven. As the boat glided along, its glossy surface caught the light and reflection of the world around it. Buildings rose up on either side, the gondola drifting so close to some of the walls that it almost caressed the brickwork.

Travelling by gondola was like slipping into a dream: a dream where nothing mattered except the passage of water beneath, and the banks drifting by. The gondola's pointed prow speared upward, arabesque, saluting the bow-shaped bridges under which it passed. It was the same way Esme felt when she was immersed in a good book: cocooned in character and place, reality temporarily suspended, her troubles forgotten.

The gondolier's cry startled her out of her reverie.

'Last stop,' cried the gondolier. 'Canal's blocked ahead.'

Esme peered ahead, trying to gauge the state of the canal, but a bridge impeded her view. She could only see the roofs, a number of which were ruined beyond repair, and had been left open, abandoned to the vagaries of the weather. She scrambled out of the boat.

'Can you point me in the direction of Sofia Square?'

The gondolier waved her off, pointing vaguely into the distance. The square led off into a web of lanes that kept doubling back on each other.

This part of the city was more worn down than worn out, the patina of centuries showing underneath every surface. Peeling paint and exposed brickwork only served to accentuate the city's ancient and noble underpinnings.

One of the doors was so riddled with age that it had partially disintegrated, but the owners had merely nailed a few equally decrepit boards across it. When Esme passed by the exact same door a few minutes later, she realised she was completely lost.

The map proved little use. Even though it faithfully recorded the squares and main canals of Esperance, it offered scant detail of the squiggle of lanes that veined the city. Passers-by were happy to give directions, but their instructions were about as useful as the gondolier's had been, and she was soon lost again in a twist of narrow alleyways and dead ends.

After a while, she passed into an area mired in an oppressive gloom. The houses here were set close together, and cast long shadows; the stone paths underfoot were slippery and damp. The former welcoming aura of the neighbourhood had vanished. Statues of fang-jawed fish, tortured faces, and stern three-headed goddesses silently marked Esme's passage from their shadowy alcoves.

Nobody was around to ask for assistance, so Esme trudged on, trying to shake off the gloom that had begun to envelop her. Streets that appeared to lead out of the maze proved to be dead ends; more than once she found herself in a courtyard walled in on every side except one.

On her way out of one of these blind alleys, she spied someone whom she could ask for help. She hurried toward him, down a lane so narrow there was barely enough room for two people to pass. A moist, musty smell lingered in the air, and it was soon overlaid with another odour: something fetid, like a decaying animal. The stench grew stronger as the figure came closer. By the time he was only a few feet away, Esme had decided to pass right by without stopping.

The man squinted at her as he shuffled by. While a hood shadowed most of his face, what she glimpsed of it was scarred, scaly, and spotted with fungus. He smelled as if he was rotting away, and looked that way too.

Esme's stomach turned. She tried not to gag. The shuffling stopped a few feet on and then started again, growing louder. With a bolt of fear, she realised that he was coming back toward her. She quickly turned into the next lane. She could hear the murmur of people ahead, and exhaled with relief as the next street opened up into a busy square. It wasn't Sofia Square, but it was full of shops and people. Her thumping heart slowed a little.

The unusual display of a shop named 'Akitsu' drew her attention. Miniature paper creatures—birds, tiny butterflies, whirring bees, and bug-eyed beetles—flitted around in the windows in a frenzy. All at once they flew toward her, crowding together, pressing up behind the glass, before rushing away again.

In their stead, she glimpsed a reflection: the hooded man, coming up behind her. Before she could turn around, he grabbed at her. His eyes had taken on a glittering madness.

'Where is it, Ari—?'

His fingers dug into her arm. The stench of decay overpowered her; it was the smell of encroaching death, a rotten, sickly sweet smell, invading every pore. She wrenched her arm away from him, just as an aproned shopkeeper, armed with a broom, rushed out of the store.

'Get your hands off her!'

The man slunk away, and the shopkeeper bellowed after him. 'And if I see you around here again, I'll be calling the authorities. I've told you before—get yourself to a doctor!'

The squat, black-haired shopkeeper took off his spectacles and wiped them on his apron, before balancing them back on his nose. He glared after the disappearing figure, but the outrage on his face shifted to concern at the sight of Esme. 'Are you all right? Would you like a glass of water or something? I'm—'

'Akitsu?'

He smiled. 'Yes.'

Esme followed him inside.

'No need to worry, he's a harmless vagrant,' Akitsu said, as he filled a glass with water. 'I don't know what's gotten into him though, he doesn't usually bother people.'

'What's happened to him?'

'I don't know. A Gift gone wrong, perhaps.'

Esme nursed the glass, the man's stench still in her nostrils. Once again, she had been mistaken for Ariane. But how could that man have known who her mother was? Panic stole her nerve and stalled her breath.

She took refuge in the distraction of Akitsu's colourful paper menagerie. Above her, schools of striped fish swum through the air together. Beside them, the mouths of a string of baby birds opened and closed, the mother bird swooping in turn toward each one. Most of the creatures hung from mobiles attached to the ceiling, but bees, bugs, and small birds flew about the store, unencumbered. A red and black spotted ladybird settled on her sleeve for a moment before whizzing off again.

'Do you make all these yourself?' she asked.

'I do. My grandfather had the same Gift.'

Esme returned the glass. 'I'm on my way to Sofia Square. Is it far?'

'Sofia Square? It's very close. I'd show you the way myself, if I could leave the shop. But here, let me draw you a map ... or wait, better still ...'

He selected a square of yellow paper from the pile in front of him, cutting and folding it so quickly that Esme couldn't discern the shape of it. Then he escorted her to the door, where he held out his hand. A paper butterfly rose up from his palm, dipping and swaying as if showing off its newfound wings.

'This little one will show you the way.'

Esme's eyes stayed on the fluttering wings of the butterfly as she felt around in her pocket for some merles. 'Here, I ...'

'No need. It knows the way home,' he said, slipping back into the shop.

The butterfly alighted on her shoulder, and after a few wing beats, flew off erratically toward the edge of the square. It ducked and weaved just like a real butterfly, flitting here and there as it led her through the streets. The shopkeeper was right; Sofia Square was close by, only a few streets away. In the centre of it stood a statue of Queen Sofia, and Esme spied the butterfly there, settled on Sofia's breast. It was resting, moving its wings up and down in a stately fashion, like a living brooch on the queen's stone cloak.

Sofia Square was lined with artisan workshops and small tea-shops. One window displayed the washed blues, greens and pinks of tumbled sea glass, set into bracelets and necklaces; in another, glass vases and bowls had been hand-blown into exquisite shapes. The next shop along was La Peregrina. In its window stood a wooden treasure chest, overflowing with strands of dazzling pearls and glinting gold and silver.

She entered La Peregrina to find an older man at the counter, his long, severe face brightening at the prospect of trade. 'Can I help you?'

Esme offered him the old receipt.

'I found this with my mother's things. She's gone now. I was wondering if what she ordered would still be here. Or if not, a record of what it might have been?'

His smile turned to a scowl. 'This was my brother's shop, until he passed away. There's stock here from years back. If this was unclaimed he could have sold it again, though I very much doubt he did. He was good at making jewellery, but not so much at turning a profit.'

'Really? You might still have it? Ah, I'd be happy to pay for it again—for your trouble.'

The shopkeeper immediately cheered up at the sight of Esme producing her purse. He disappeared into the back of the store, and eventually returned with a small, black box in his hands, which he set down on the counter.

'Let's see. I came across these the other day, stuck right in the back of one of the cupboards.' He rifled through a dozen pouches. 'Ah. You're in luck. Here we are.'

He unpinned the note and passed her a red velvet pouch.

'I—I can't believe it's still here,' Esme stammered. 'Thank you.'

'You have my brother to thank,' he said, while depositing her merles in the till. 'For leaving the place in such a mess.'

Outside the shop, Esme crossed the cobbled square and took a seat on a bench by the statue of Sofia. She fumbled with the string before drawing out a small package, wrapped neatly in tissue paper.

Her heart twisted when she saw what was inside. She held it up to the light. A silver chain glinted in the sun, and the pendant at its end twirled lazily in the air: a small pearl set above the letter 'E'.

A tear traced down Esme's cheek. Her mother had once possessed a necklace just like this, but with an 'A' instead of an 'E'. It had been Esme's favourite, and she had often asked for one of her own. Since the disappearance, she'd forgotten all about it.

And just like that, Esme was eight years old again, hugging her mother goodbye, hearing her say she would be home soon, the two of them tangled up in the smell of each other's clothes and skin and hair, the silver 'A' in there, too, Esme touching it like a talisman.

She fingered the creamy pearl above the 'E', then undid the clasp and put the necklace on, her eyes still wet. She hardly noticed as the paper butterfly alighted on her shoulder, as if in a show of sympathy, before lifting off and fluttering back to its master.

Chapter Fourteen

'Oh, wow. That's pretty. Is it new?'

Lillian had just returned from her father's, and was emptying her overnight bag on the kitchen table when she glanced up and noticed Esme's necklace.

'Uh ... sort of.'

Lillian threw her an enquiring look.

'I found a receipt for it, in with my mum's things. So I went to the address, a place in Sofia Square, and the shop still had it.'

She unhooked the chain, and spilled it into Lillian's outstretched hand.

'Mum used to have one just like it ... I was always asking her to get me one.' She swallowed and shifted her gaze to the patterned tiles on the kitchen floor. 'I guess she was thinking of me, even then.'

Lillian squeezed her arm in sympathy. 'Of course she was.'

'Something else happened too, on the way there. Someone—'

Thump, thump, thump.

Esme started. A small flap door, set at the base of the wall below the kitchen window, had begun to tremble violently. She bent down to open the latch.

'Wait! Don't!' cried Lillian, a moment too late.

As soon as the words came out of Lillian's mouth, the flap door burst open. A blur of blue rocketed past Esme. Lillian grabbed the flying object just before it could smash into the wall.

It was a bottle, shaped like a fish: wet, slippery, and blue, with glass scales that fanned out to a wide tail. Lillian wiped it with a tea towel, held it up to the light, and peered through the translucent glass.

'We've been having a few problems with these jiggers lately. Message bottles,' she added at the confused look on Esme's face. Then she handed it to her. 'It's for you.'

'Really?'

The note inside was written under the letterhead of the University of Esperance:

Dear Esme,

May I extend my deepest condolences and profound sympathies as to the loss of your mother. Ariane was a much-esteemed colleague of mine, and a wonderful friend, who will be sorely missed. Please visit me, at your convenience, at the Department of Cultural Studies at the University. I will be here in my office each afternoon for the next week. Again, I offer you my heart-felt sympathies.

Regards,

Professor Theodore Sage

Later that day, Esme and Lillian boarded one of the black, gold-trimmed ferries that plied the city's waterways. After departing the ferry at the university stop, they lingered at the jetty to watch another water-weaver, busy juggling orbs of water brought up from the canal. Some kept their shape on their upward flight, but others flumed into spouts, reforming into glistening balls on the downward arc. Faster and faster the man juggled, balancing more and more orbs until Esme could barely see him for the water rushing everywhere.

For the first time, she began to seriously consider that she might have a Gift like his, waiting to emerge. She looked down at her own hands and imagined them sculpting water into glittering shapes. Would she feel the same way she had under the waterfall in the Temple Library—magic thrumming through her? Coiled excitement leaped up inside, like the liquid in the water-weaver's hands.

The gates to the university stood nearby, flanked by two black granite gods, proffering books of knowledge to all who passed by. The names 'Oceanus' and 'Tethys' were etched into the plinths beneath them. As Esme stopped to admire them, she heard a sound like the distant rumble of surf.

Another earthquake, she thought, bracing herself.

Soon the ground beneath them was howling and groaning as it had the other day, the racket reverberating through their bodies. Water sloshed up the sides of the canal. Esme grabbed Lillian and they clung to each other, swaying in unison, as the earth tore apart every notion of an ordered existence.

Time stretched and lengthened, as if the universe was folding in on itself—and then, the tremors began to subside. Esme's heart began to slow from a break-neck gallop—

CRACK.

She jumped. It was like a gunshot at the start of a race. Esme's heart bolted off again.

A large fissure appeared in the ground, splitting the base of the statue of Oceanus. With a terrifying, cataclysmic creak, the statue began to lean over.

'Lillian!' Esme cried. 'Get down!'

She threw herself at Lillian, pulling her out of the way just as the statue came crashing down. Its head shattered, dust clouding the air around them.

Esme, coughing, pushed herself up off the ground, eyeing the fallen god. What remained of Oceanus' face was now planted in the dirt, as if it were indignantly searching for someone down below to blame for its undignified demise.

She held out a hand to Lillian, who scrambled up, dazed, looking like she had just stepped out of a dust bath.

'Are you okay?'

Lillian's glazed eyes cleared as they focused properly on Esme's form. 'Thanks to you,' she exhaled, dusting herself off. 'Let's find somewhere to clean ourselves up.'

Just ahead, strung out along the lagoon's edge, stood the

University of Esperance: a set of imposing stone buildings, topped at intervals by gothic turrets. The buildings' façades bore sculpted terrors from the ocean's underbelly: fish with bulbous eyes, colossal squid with hooked tentacles, gargantuan sea serpents that slithered around the pilasters. A hunched-over stone creature, with dark holes for eyes, yawned down at them from atop a pillar.

The summer vacation had stripped the university of students, and the Cultural Studies department was just as deserted as everywhere else. After cleaning up as best they could, they followed the whiff of departed academia down a dimly lit corridor, stopping by the last door on the left. Esme knocked, and a voice bid them enter.

The door fell open to reveal an office in total disarray. Papers, books, and artefacts lay scattered everywhere, amongst a mountain of boxes.

'Come in, come in. You made it through the terrors! You must be Esme and Lillian.'

Professor Sage stood up from behind his desk, as shaky on his feet as the ground outside had just been. His face was as wrinkled as a walnut shell, but so full of life that it looked as though the creases could iron out any moment. Ridges ran down his face like dried-up rivers in a drought. He waved a silver, claw-tipped walking stick toward the seats on the other side of his desk.

'Have a seat. My apologies for the disorder—I'm meant to be retiring this week.' His voice hollowed, his rheumy eyes grew wet. 'So ... it's really true? Ariane's gone?'

The professor lowered himself into his chair and wiped his eyes with a handkerchief. 'And all this time, I thought she had been home with you. I sent letters, but got no reply. You say there's no clue—no clue at all as to what happened?'

'None. She was only meant to be away for a few days, but she never came home.'

Sorrow wounded his voice. 'How is this possible? It seems like only yesterday she was sitting there, right where you are now, discussing our book's progress. She seemed just fine to me, perhaps a little worn out, but that was understandable. She was so happy. We were almost done.'

He reached back and pulled out a volume from the shelf behind him. 'This is what we worked on for so long. Sadly, she never got to see it in its finished form.'

He pressed it into Esme's hands, a weighty leather-bound tome titled *Aeolian Myths and Legends: A Compendium.* The names of the author and illustrator—Professor Theodore Sage and Ariane Silver—were embossed beneath a painting on the front cover.

The compendium was filled with stories and illustrations of lost islands, cursed beaches, ancient dragons, and mysterious caves. She stopped at one page, where her mother had painted the same colourful sky Esme had seen in the fresco at the Temple Library. According to the compendium, this was the 'Aurora of Aeolia'.

'It's incredible,' said Esme. 'There are so many paintings ... Mum did all of these?'

'Oh, yes. But over a long period of time—years and years.'

Years and years?

Esme stared down at the compendium, a ringing in her ears. It wasn't an aftereffect of the quake; it was something completely unrelated. She closed her eyes and tried to calm the blood roaring in her head.

She'd felt this before—sometimes a trace of it, sometimes more. When she was younger, and she'd watched, alone, while other mothers picked up their children after school. When she had listened to other students complain about their own mothers, wishing they had someone else's—anyone else's. She'd felt a hint of it, too, back when Miranda had first told her about the compendium.

It rose up in full force, wedging in her throat like a blocked scream.

Envy. A violent, raw rush of envy.

Her mother had been missing from her life for seven years—but how much of the time before that had she spent in thrall to Esperance instead of to her daughter?

She passed the book to Lillian and excused herself. It was silly, being jealous of a book. And it wasn't as if her mother had *known* she would disappear, that her time with her daughter was painfully limited. But logic had no foothold in this twisted green thicket. All Esme could think was that time spent on this compendium had been time spent away from her. She passed it to Lillian, and started pacing the room.

The professor joined her, assuming she had gotten up to examine the wonders displayed all around. A bright light shone in his aged eyes as he toured her around a lifetime's worth of artefacts. The professor's office was packed with pieces that wouldn't have looked out of place in a museum: stuffed and mounted specimens, ancient manuscripts, bones, statues, even skulls.

She tried to listen, but couldn't concentrate on anything but the picture that had formed in her mind: a picture of her mother contentedly painting away, rapt in the legends and mysteries of Aeolia.

'Don't touch that,' Sage called out to Lillian, who was investigating a plant on the other side of the room. 'That flower looks innocent enough, but it can balloon out to twice its size in an instant, and it rather likes … how shall we say … finger food.'

'Why is it even in here then?' Lillian exclaimed, snatching her hand away.

'Because it's rather excellent at warding off uninvited guests. And keeping them from coming back. As you can imagine, some of these artefacts are priceless.'

The flower burped.

At the end of the room, Esme came to an abrupt halt. Above her, the dead, black eyes of a giant moth-like creature, hanging from the ceiling, bored into her own. It was a monstrosity: a mass of brown fur and tangled limbs, with hooked wings and a set of furred antennae.

'What *is* that thing?' Esme asked, pointing up at it.

The professor beamed, eager to enlighten her. 'You mean the Moiran moth? Something I picked up on one of my research trips.

They smother their prey, human or otherwise, in their wings, before eating them very slowly, bit by bit. I managed to save one of my expedition members from this one—well, most of him—and ended up bringing it home with me.'

'It reminds me of my step-aunt,' Esme muttered to Lillian.

She prevented the professor from launching into another monologue about the moth by pointing out a model on the shelves behind his desk. Three enormous, grisly claws spiked the air, renting at an imaginary foe.

'Those claws. I think I've seen them before. In my mother's notebook.'

'They're not really claws,' the professor said, as they took their seats again. He pushed the model toward her. 'They're closer to horns.'

'Horns?' Lillian asked.

'Yes, the horns of a stygian, or so it is claimed. No one really knows what they looked like. They're said to have lived out their miserable existence centuries ago, in caves and tunnels beneath the sea. Stygians abhorred sunlight, and devoured anything that came near—or failing that, each other. Fascinating creatures. The way their venom worked was unlike anything else. Just one scratch from a stygian's horn causes one's skin to mutate and decay, ultimately resembling the stygian's own. A painful transformation that could take years—an agonisingly slow decline.'

'Forget I asked,' said Lillian.

The professor restored the model to its home. When he turned back around, his brows furrowed.

'Perhaps all this is my fault, encouraging your mother to delve into these things. I've spent my whole life in this field, but sometimes she seemed to know even more about the myths than I did.' The professor put his elbows on the desk, and formed his fingers into a steeple, leaning his chin into it. 'Ariane was always so thorough. But unfortunately, the sort of knowledge that she possessed—that I possess—can often bring unwanted attention.

Treasure hunters wander in here all the time, trying to grill me for information, but I always give them short shrift.'

'Treasure hunters? But aren't these just myths? Stories?'

'Ah yes,' he said, taking back the compendium, 'but stories as old as these ones can take on a power of their own.' He ran his wizened fingers along the cover. 'Some people spend their whole lives combing through Aeolia's legends, seeking treasures that may have never even existed in the first place. Some lose touch with their moral compass ... and, in the end, lose everything. If Ariane ever crossed paths with someone like that, I ...' He rapped his knuckles on the desk. 'Life is such a fragile thing. Like butterfly wings.'

Just as Esme was reflecting on the profundity of these words, he waved a hand at a glass case full of pinned butterflies, hanging behind his chair. Esme glanced over at Lillian, whose face had assumed the expression reserved for aged folk whose minds have gone slightly astray.

Lillian pushed back her chair in preparation for their departure, but Esme motioned for her to wait.

'Professor,' asked Esme, 'did you ever work with a Dr Nathan Mare?'

'Mare?' The professor's face clouded over. 'No. We never worked together directly. But he is—was—a colleague of mine. A promising scientist, who took a wrong turn. Ariane was a close friend of his, she used to talk about him all the time. I asked her once what she saw in him.'

Esme leaned forward. 'What did she say?'

'Not much. Only that she was "indebted" to him. I never liked him myself, but plenty did. I suppose I've seen too many people in my time pretending to be something they're not.' He flexed his fingers. 'To be honest, part of my dislike—and that of others—could have stemmed from a case of envy. Everything came so easily to him.'

He paused.

'I suppose there is one thing I should thank him for. He was the one who introduced Ariane's art to me and encouraged us to work together. It was my first sight of her art that really spurred me on to create the compendium.' He inclined his head. 'If you turn to the end, you'll find a photo of your mother and me in happier times.'

On the end flap was a photo of a sprightlier professor, together with Ariane, taken in front of the bookshelves across from his desk. The professor wore a satisfied smile, and her mother her usual enigmatic one.

'Look!' said Lillian. 'She's wearing the necklace.'

A pearl hung above the silver 'A' that rested over Ariane's chest. Esme gingerly put her hand to her own necklace, concealed beneath her top. The professor levered himself out of his chair and passed the compendium over to her.

'Please, take it with you. I've plenty of copies to spare. I'm just sorry your mother isn't here to show it to you yourself.' He limped to the door, taking a roundabout path through the boxes, leaning on his walking stick for support.

'Good luck with the move,' said Esme.

He wagged a finger. 'Take care. Both of you.'

While they were waiting for the next ferry, Lillian flicked through the compendium and smiled. 'I'd be so proud if my mum did something like this.'

Esme nodded, shifting awkwardly on her seat.

She had always assumed that her mother's long absences from home were necessary, in order for her to keep doing what she loved. She had always thought that her mother *had* to spend time away, so that she could make money from her art. Surely, given the choice, Ariane would have preferred to stay at home with her family. The compendium in Lillian's hands told her otherwise.

Her real grievance, she realised, was that she hadn't always been the centre of her mother's world.

Her long-cherished image of her mother was fading like an old photograph, memories painfully rearranging themselves. But as the crest of her anger passed, she started to see things in a clearer light. If tragedy hadn't struck, she probably would have met Lillian years ago. It was Lucinda who had brought Ariane to Aeolia in the first place, and Ariane must have been planning to do the same, once Esme turned old enough to keep the family secret.

Her eyes strayed across the water, following the path of the ferries. The city's beauty was utterly intoxicating. No wonder her mother had been drawn here time and time again. How could anyone ever compete with this place?

Lillian handed back the compendium. The illustration on the front cover depicted a glistening bead of water, suspended in the air. Within it spun islands, people, and fantastical creatures.

'That's from the legend of Aeolia's creation,' said Lillian, running her hand over the cover. 'Everything in our world—Esperance, the islands, the magic—is said to have flowed from one enchanted drop of water.'

Chapter Fifteen

Later that afternoon, Esme took the compendium into the Lovells' courtyard and settled down at the mosaic table. The first tale in the heavy hardback book corresponded with the image on its cover: the creation of Aeolia.

Aeolia's story begins in the Other World, almost two thousand years ago, during a long period of war and strife. The armies of Rome were sweeping across the city-states of Ancient Greece, subsuming a great and powerful civilisation that had thrived for centuries. As the Greek city of Corinth fell to Roman rule, a pair of lovers fled their home: Michail and Sofia Agapios.

The exiles came to rest on the sands of a deserted beach, where their troubles were soothed by the sounds of the lapping sea and the song of the breeze as it played across the strings of a wind harp. These sounds were soon joined by unearthly voices. One rose above the others and told them of the existence of another world, pristine and unspoiled by human folly and avarice.

This voice led them into the water, to another world, to the place that would become known as Aeolia. At this time, Aeolia was nothing but one vast ocean, rolling unimpeded around the globe.

Michail and Sofia were transported high above the seas, and from their eyrie, they witnessed a series of extraordinary events. A drop of water, infused with light, appeared in the sky before them. It hung there, impossibly suspended in the air, before bursting into the water below. The ocean was filled with light and song, and the islands of Aeolia rose from the seas.

Esme stopped reading and leaned back in her seat, imagining the drop of water plummeting into the sea and spreading its magic throughout Aeolia. When Lillian had mentioned the story of Aeolia's creation, Esme had found it hard to believe. Now that she read it in her mother's compendium, the tale didn't seem so strange after all.

It had only been a few days since that wisp of oceanic light had alighted on her hand. Had it really been a remnant of those ancient times? With startling clarity, she remembered the sensation that it had evoked, the sensation of a connection with something much bigger than herself.

She read on.

The future king and queen were led to their new home, a water-riven island in a sheltered lagoon by the Tiamat Sea. Here, the god left them with parting gifts: great mounds of pale, rough-hewn abyssal stone, flung up from the ocean depths, and a shimmering pearl, formed from the very last essence of the water drop. With the pale godstone, Michail and Sofia built the Palace of Ephyra, which would later become the centre of the city of Esperance.

The water drop also summoned an aurora, which hung over Aeolia for fifty years, and birthed the sea dragons that still roam through the skies today. The pearl and the aurora are lost to legend, but the dragons, and the Godstone Palace, remain, as do the Gifts: the legacy of the ancient gods.

Esme closed the book and set it on the table. Somewhere in Esperance there had to be a stack of research underpinning the contents of this compendium. Her mother had always painstakingly documented everything. The bookshelves back home were evidence of that, packed with Ariane's art diaries, filled with notes and preliminary sketches for her paintings. Perhaps, this material would provide the leads she needed.

She pushed herself up from the chair. Miranda had already told her that Ariane rarely painted at No. 8—but the professor might know something.

Esme hunted through the kitchen cupboards for a jigger. On a high shelf, she found a whole school of them, perched upright on their splayed tails. She tore a sheet off the pad beside them, and penned a note to the professor.

After rolling up the letter, she slid it into the message bottle and hurried out to the stone steps that led down from the courtyard to the canal. She leaned down and lowered the jigger toward the water, not sure what to do next. It flipped out of her hand of its own accord, dove in to the canal, and sped off along the waterway.

The next time the flap door *thumped*, a few days later, Esme was prepared. She grabbed the bottle before it could ricochet around the room, and unfurled the note inside.

It was from Daniel; he had arrived back from his trip, and was coming over in the afternoon.

Upon hearing a knock on the front door, Esme opened it, not to Daniel, but to a stranger: a deliveryman, laden with three large rectangular parcels.

'Delivery for an Esme Silver.'

Lillian helped her carry them into the living room, where they deposited them on the glass-topped piece of driftwood that served as a table. Squishy striped sofas sat on either side of it, and only a few feet away, glass doors led out to the canal.

A note accompanied the parcels.

Dear Ms Silver,

Theodore Sage informed me yesterday of your tragic loss. I was deeply saddened to hear of the passing of your mother. Ariane was an inspiration to us all: a talented and hard-working artist, and a gracious client.

My gallery is in temporary hiatus, but after checking my stock, I have found three of Ariane's paintings, ones that arrived too late to be included in her last exhibition. Please accept them with my heartfelt condolences, and do not hesitate to contact me if you require any advice or assistance.

All the best,

Raphael Cinto

With Lillian's help, Esme unwrapped the canvases and propped them up on the opposite sofa.

The first painting depicted the deserted dunes of a long beach. Sandy hills of ochre and mauve stretched obliquely into the distance, while the sea itself was squeezed into a small triangle of pastel-green in the bottom right-hand corner. In the next painting, the sea was prominent, but the focal point was a gap-toothed gash between slanting, dark rocks: a grotto, half-submerged in the water.

The last oil depicted a lustrous pearl, resting on a pedestal in a dark chamber. This painting both fascinated and repelled her, but she couldn't pinpoint why.

Lillian gestured toward the picture of the dunes.

'I know about this one. The Singing Sands. One holiday, we were staying nearby, so I pestered Mum to take me there. The sands sing all day and night. You can only view them from a far-off boat, though—no one wanders the sands anymore.'

'Why not?'

'It's said that they're cursed. The singing mesmerises people, and the sand swallows them up.'

Their viewing of the paintings was interrupted by another knock at the door. It was Daniel, back from his trip. His eyes were glazed over, his skin flaking with sunburn. He peeled a long strip of it from the back of his neck and presented it to them on his palm.

Lillian looked repulsed. 'Charming.'

He headed straight for the sofa, where he stretched out and closed his eyes. 'If Dad wants me to follow him into his profession, he's not doing a very good job of convincing me. He had us working around the clock.'

'Where were you?' Esme asked.

'Pelorus. Dad's team is helping restore a section of Pallas, a sunken city. It's hard work, but the place is worth preserving. There's lots of history to it. And it pays well. The Pelorusians are eager to preserve as much as they can; people are always down there scavenging and the ruins are getting ... well, more ruined.'

He heaved himself up and took in the canvases on the opposite sofa. 'What's all this?'

'Some of Mum's paintings turned up this morning. Ones that didn't make it into her last exhibition.'

He leaned forward to view them, his eyes coming to rest on the painting of the grotto. A glimmer of recognition showed on his face. The cave was partially obscured by the waves, but a faint turquoise light was just visible within.

Esme showed him the compendium. 'They're all illustrations from this. I got it the other day at the university, from a professor there. It's full of Mum's paintings.'

'Really?' said Daniel, taking it from her hands. He turned the pages slowly and stopped at the artwork of the cave. 'This is it,' he said grimly. '"The Oracle's Grotto". My grandfather Leo was obsessed with that myth. After Gran died, he'd go off on long trips with his friends. He vowed that one day he'd go looking for that cave and find the oracle that lived there. One day he claimed that he had found it, and that the oracle had spoken to him.'

'Really? What did the oracle say?'

Daniel looked even more downcast. 'None of us know. All we know is that going into that cave did something to him. After that, he was never the same again. Whatever happened in there addled his brain. He died a few years later. My parents don't really like to talk about it.' He gave a wry grin. 'Except to say I take after him.'

✤

After Daniel left, Esme stayed in the living room a little while longer. The pearl, glowing atop its pedestal, was watching her like an unblinking eye. The painting still invoked an odd response in her. She took up the compendium and thumbed through it until she reached the relevant tale.

The Pearl of Esperance

Also known as the 'Pearl of Promise', this magnificent jewel was formed from the last essence of the enchanted water drop from which the isles and magic of Aeolia sprung. The Esperance Pearl is said to possess such inordinate beauty and power that all who set eyes on it are smitten. Why exactly is the pearl so coveted? Many theories abound, but the most common versions of the tale claim that the pearl will grant its possessor whatever he or she desires.

The true extent of its power, however, can never be known. The pearl was lost in the first century of Aeolia's existence, during the reign of King Michail and Queen Sofia, and has never been seen since. It only resided in Ephyra for a short while, before being stolen by the city's first keeper: Anna Agapios, the daughter of Michail and Sofia, and, at the time, Aeolia's rightful heiress.

Over the centuries, many expeditions have been mounted in search of this precious heirloom, and so many lives have been lost in its pursuit that some say the pearl is cursed. Others believe that the pearl can only change hands safely when it is gifted from one guardian to the next, for if it is taken by force, terrible calamities will befall its possessor.

Esme set the book back down and took the canvas outside to the canal, where she could examine it in a better light. The pearl, softly glowing in the centre, naturally drew the eye. The rest of the painting was in shadow, but as Esme examined it more closely, the details became clear. A murky pool surrounded the pearl's pedestal, the waters radiating a vague menace. The base of the pedestal was scored with countless claw-like markings. Her head jerked back.

It's just like ...

She ran upstairs and grabbed her mother's notebook.

Back in the living room, Esme opened it to the sketch of the ferocious three-horned creature that Professor Sage had spoken of. There was no mistaking it: the pedestal was covered with stygians.

After another examination of the painting, she noticed something else: the mottled texture on the surface of the pool wasn't mould or leaf matter. It was the backs of more stygians, their leprous jackets all blending together.

The water was seething with them.

Her skin crawled. Flashes of the hooded man—the man who had stalked her to Sofia Square, the man who had mistaken her for her mother—came back to her. He had been scratched and bleeding in parts, as if he'd been clawing at himself. She had never seen anyone in such a state, like something was eating him up from the inside.

What was it the professor had said? *Just one scratch from a stygian causes one's skin to mutate and decay, ultimately resembling the stygian's own.* The foul odour of the man returned, along with his pockmarked face and misshapen hands, covered with weeping sores. *A painful transformation that could take years ... An agonisingly slow decline.*

He hadn't looked human. He'd looked ... stygian.

Esme shook her head. This was absurd. She went outside to the courtyard and tried to clear her head. Stygians were extinct. There could be any number of explanations for the man's state. The shopkeeper himself had raised the possibility of a Gift gone wrong.

She picked a few dead leaves off a plant in the tub. One of the leaves crumbled in her hand, and she let the fragments fall to the ground. The hooded man rose up again in her mind, and she relived the scene: his deterioration, the rough grasp of his arm on hers, and the desperation in his rasping plea.

Where is it, Ari—?

Chapter Sixteen

Esme and Lillian entered the kitchen early on Saturday morning, drawn by the aroma of brown butter and spilt flour. Miranda was transferring breyberry hotcakes from a pan to a blue and white platter. This was a rare treat; Miranda was usually at work at this hour.

The three of them sat in silence for a while, working their way through the mountain of hotcakes. When they were done, Esme leaned forward and showed Miranda the pearl necklace.

'I found a receipt for it in that sack of clothes you gave me, so I went on a search. The shop still had it.'

Miranda put her hand to her heart. 'Your mother wore a necklace like that all the time! I remember now ... She told me she'd lost it, just before I last saw her. I looked out for it, all around the house, but never found it.'

She stood up to clear the plates, and her words came out muffled, like she'd just developed a cold. 'You've collected quite a few of her things now.'

The last bit of hotcake stuck in Esme's throat, and she swallowed, hard. This was how it must seem to Miranda and the others, like she was just gathering what was left of her mother's things, as a way of saying goodbye.

After breakfast, a frantic knocking sounded against the side of the house. A jigger had come from Raphael Cinto, the art dealer, replying to Esme on behalf of Professor Sage. He had sent her the address of her mother's former studio: No. 136 Conte Street.

A few hours later, Esme and Lillian stood on the pathway beside Conte Canal. Daniel was with them; he had dropped by earlier, and offered to take them over in *Talia*. Conte Canal was part of the same neighbourhood that Esme had passed through on her way to Sofia Square. The waterways were blocked here too, full of debris from dwellings that had toppled over.

Lillian wrinkled her nose at the dank odour. 'This doesn't look promising.'

A crow sounded overhead. A rat scuttled into an abandoned house, which was teetering on the water's edge. Esme heard the sound of laughter, and caught a glimpse of a face behind a dirt-streaked window. Two hollow eyes scrutinised her, before melting away into thin air.

She jumped back. 'Did you see that?'

'See what?' asked Daniel.

'That … oh, nothing.'

Around the next bend, the houses had fared a little better. The far left side of No. 136 had collapsed onto the bank, but the rest of the house was intact. Daniel walked over and picked up a tattered sign from amongst the debris: 'Studios For Rent'.

Just as Esme knocked on the front door, a ginger tabby cat sidled up behind them.

'Hi, there,' said Esme.

With its mashed-up nose and haughty countenance, the cat looked anything but welcoming. In fact, it looked positively hostile, as if it would unsheathe its claws at any opportunity. But when Esme tentatively bent down to check its collar, it rubbed up against her leg. Discerning green eyes met hers, a wrenching reminder of Reuben's, waiting for her back home.

'Hello, Hunter,' she said, reading its name from its collar.

Hunter responded with a languid arch of his back. He purred deeply, before butting his head into Esme's hand. Meanwhile, the house stayed silent.

Lillian knocked a few more times. 'No answer,' she said, putting her ear to the door. 'I don't think anyone's home.'

Hunter padded off and disappeared around the corner of the house, his tail still visible, waving behind him. The cat ducked its head back and threw them a baleful glance.

'Looks like he's inviting us in,' said Esme, following him round with the others.

Hunter slinked down the side of the house, into a garden well past its prime. A table and chairs were buried under dense growth. Tangled grapevines had spread beyond an arbour, before running into brambles six feet high. At the end of the neglected garden, the gabled roof of a building was just visible.

'Maybe his owner's down there,' said Esme.

Hunter led them through the undergrowth via a barely visible winding path. Trees, bowed out of shape, bent toward them, and spreading vines caught at their feet. The cat stole ahead, impatient at their slow progress.

There were few signs of recent visitors inside the deserted studio at the bottom of the garden. An army of ants marched up the leg of one of the tables, and a spider slept in its web, spun across a high window in the roof. Sunlight shafted in over a worn wicker sofa. The strong odour of oil paint was present. When Lillian unlatched a window, it squeaked in protest. Hunter stalked out the door, as though insulted by the infusion of fresh air.

Dog-eared sketches hung from the walls, and tables, lined with old art supplies, lay in perpetual wait for their owners' return. Esme crossed over to one of the canvases. It was an oil of the abandoned end of the canal, painted in a loose, impressionistic style. The canvas was signed 'Maria'. The oil on it glistened. It was still wet.

Daniel glanced around. 'I wonder where this Maria is.'

They spread out around the studio, looking for Ariane's work.

'Here! Over here,' called out Lillian.

The far corner of the studio was covered in cobwebbed sketches and studies for paintings—Ariane's paintings.

Only the spiders' handiwork, and the thick dust everywhere,

revealed to Esme that her mother hadn't been here in a very long time. A stack of canvases leaned against a table before the wall. On the table itself lay unfinished work: sketches of Esperance landmarks, including the Keeper's Tower, and the palace grounds.

The studio was eerily similar to the state of Ariane's painting nook back at Spindrift; this was an artist who had gone for a break, but fully intended to come back and continue her work. Even some of the tubes of paint on the table had their lids off. Esme took a deep breath, rubbing at the silver letter around her neck. Her mother's past presence wound around her until she could hardly bear it.

What happened to you, Mum?

Esme froze as she saw, out of the corner of her eye, one of Ariane's brushes lift off the end of the table by itself. A tube of yellow paint followed; it hung suspended in mid-air, and drops began to squeeze out onto the palette beneath it.

The room darkened a little as the sun passed behind a cloud. In the more subdued light, Esme could see a faint silver shape clasping the painting tools. A female figure, clothed in a filmy dress covered partly by a bib, a bonnet on her head.

Esme took a few paces back, her heart beating so fast that it drummed in her ears. Daniel and Lillian had spoken of ghosts in Esperance, but Esme hadn't ever expected to see one. The thought that it might be Ariane seized her, but then the figure turned in mid-stroke, paintbrush raised. This woman had a long, thin face, and large, sad eyes. Esme blurted out the first words she could think of.

'I'm—I'm Esme. These are my mother's things. You're welcome to use them, er … Maria?'

The ghost inclined her head and gave a slight curtsy, before resuming her work at the canvas.

Esme retreated to the wicker sofa, hypnotised by the movements of the ghost. Whenever the sun dappled the spot before the canvas, Maria would temporarily become invisible, and the painting would create itself. Then shadows would fall over her and she would flicker into existence once more. Daniel and Lillian joined

Esme on the sofa. They seemed more concerned for her than bothered by the sight of Maria.

'You've gone so pale,' said Lillian.

'I … I've never seen a ghost before.'

'Really? You don't have them back home?' asked Daniel.

'Well, yes, no—what I mean is, there are *stories*, but no one ever
really sees them … I don't think.'

The three of them gazed at Maria's form, flickering in and out
of the light.

'One of my best friends was a ghost,' said Daniel. 'A little boy, the
same age as me. I don't know how he died, we never talked about it.
As the years went by …' He paused, barely concealing a grin. 'I saw
less and less of him.'

Esme and Lillian groaned. Feeling a little less intimidated by
the proximity of Maria, Esme began to search the studio with the
others. However, there was no sign of anything in Ariane's corner,
nor in the drawers and cupboards littered around the rest of the
studio.

After a fruitless search, Esme sat down heavily on the sofa
beside Lillian. Dust flew everywhere, and Lillian bent over in a
coughing fit. Esme patted her on the back.

'I don't understand. I was so sure we'd find them. Mum always
had her art diaries close by.'

Lillian, still coughing, pointed straight ahead.

Esme leaned forward and spied a small cupboard set far back
under Ariane's desk. She sprinted across the room and pulled out
a pile of black notebooks.

'They're here!'

Back at the sofa, she distributed them evenly. Each book was
bursting with notes and sketches for her mother's projects.

'Wow,' said Lillian. 'She really did document everything.'

The first notebook Esme checked was dedicated to drawings of
Esperance's fountains. 'I don't remember seeing any of these in the
compendium.'

Daniel leaned in to see. 'Maybe not, but there are plenty of stories attached to the fountains of Esperance. Is the Merle Fountain in there?'

Esme leafed through the book.

'Stop there. That's it,' said Daniel.

Her mother had sketched a large fountain, presided over by Poseidon. He stood at the helm of an immense chariot, riding the wild waves beneath him. The teeth of a giant stone shell formed the waterspout, and around the base, marbled sea dragons disported in the water.

Daniel grinned. 'Mum and Dad say that fountain was how they first met.'

Before he could continue, Maria glided over and swooped down between the two of them. The goose bumps that rose on Esme weren't just from the shock—Maria was freezing cold. Daniel and Esme moved apart, and the chill lessened.

'And?' asked Lillian.

'Well, Dad was over here, visiting from Thalassa. He threw a coin in there one day, made a wish to find the love of his life, and the next day he met Mum. When he told her, she said she'd made the same wish, at the same fountain, on the same day.'

'Who made it first?' asked Lillian.

'I don't know. I've never thought to ask them.' Daniel laughed. 'Unfortunately, nothing *I've* ever wished for in there has come true.'

'I think I'd like to see this fountain for myself,' Esme mused.

Maria floated back to her canvas and the three of them bent back down over the notebooks. Esme soon came across Ariane's preparatory work for the painting of the pearl. A number of pages were filled with sketches of the gem, and the pedestal on which it stood. The stygians were in there, too. Her mother had drawn them from every angle.

'Ugh,' said Daniel, peering over Esme's shoulder. 'What are they?'

'Stygians,' said Esme.

'Oh, I've heard about them, in stories.'

From a top view, Esme could see that the stygian's claw-like horns stuck out from its shoulders, and were the same length as its body. Beneath those horns, the creature had no head, only a bumpy, decaying torso, with four sinewy limbs, curved talons, and a long tail.

A final drawing showed the creature rearing up, revealing a gaping, sucker-like mouth on its fleshy underside, lined with countless rows of sharp teeth.

The sketch on the following page was markedly different from her mother's usual style. Hundreds of thin lines veined the page like a web, scribbled as though Ariane had been trying to exorcise a bad dream. At the top of the page lay the islands of Aeolia. A misshapen hand reached up toward them, the Pearl of Esperance visible in its palm. Dark tendrils shot out from each fingertip, strangling the lands, turning the seas into maelstroms.

Later that night, Esme sat at the desk in her room, reading over the letter she had just written to Aaron. Lillian had told her she could send it the next morning, by messenger bird. Her dad would be back from his honeymoon in just a few days. She had planned to be home by then, but she couldn't leave now. Not until she knew more.

Dear Dad,

You'll probably be back from your honeymoon by now, and worrying about me, so I'm writing to let you know that I'm perfectly safe. I can't say much more now, except to let you know I'm spending the summer with some people who knew Mum. Don't go looking. You won't find me. But if you'd like to write, send a reply back in the same envelope, and give your letter to the messenger bird that delivered this one.

Don't blame yourself for my leaving—I'll be back sooner than you think.

I miss you.

Love Esme

PS: Please give Reuben extra hugs from me.

PPS: Please tell Mavis I'm not missing her at all.

Esme wanted to say more, but she was conscious of how her father had reacted in the past to talk of other worlds. There was also a chance of Penelope reading it over his shoulder, or worse, getting to it first.

After sealing the letter in the thick waterproof envelope that Lillian had given her, Esme placed it on the chest of drawers, ready to send in the morning. Beside it lay the indigo shell from her mother's handbag. She picked it up and listened to the murmur of the ocean inside.

To her surprise, the sounds faded after a while, and in their stead came a song: a melody filled with such longing it brought tears to her eyes. She listened a while longer, before setting it back down, figuring it must be some sort of songspell, like the one in the bell downstairs.

Esme was almost asleep when she heard a shrill cry from outside. A bird had landed on the rail of the balcony. It perched there, motionless, ghostly in the moonlight. It was the sea eagle from home, the same messenger bird that had been so attached to her mother, and led Esme to Aeolia.

She ventured outside, letter in hand, not sure what to do or say.

'You brought me here on purpose, didn't you?'

The bird twitched, its eye on the letter.

'Do you know where she is?'

If only it could talk—tell her something, anything. But the bird just ruffled its feathers and motioned toward the envelope with its beak.

'All right. Suit yourself. Uh, take this to Picton. To my dad—to Aaron.'

Esme held the envelope out, and the sea eagle folded a talon around it, before soaring off into the night.

Chapter Seventeen

Esme and Daniel wound their way through the palace's manicured gardens. It was the following day, and they were on their way to the Merle Fountain, where Lillian had arranged to meet them after seeing her mother at work.

The gravelled path took them past several draconic shapes, fixed in flight. The trees had been clipped in preparation for the upcoming festival, becoming leafy green imitators of the real dragons looping in the skies above.

Esme stopped by one of the topiaries, and brushed a hand against the scribble of leaves that formed a dragon's outstretched wing. Daniel was in the middle of yet another long soliloquy about dragons, but Esme's mind was elsewhere.

'The Rows have asked for me again this year,' said Daniel. 'Rowana always bring a contingent of dragons to the festival. I got asked to help out in their den, after one of the volunteers was hospitalised with severe burns.'

Esme nodded.

'Hey, you know how you can tell when people aren't really listening? They nod in all the wrong spots.'

Esme nodded again.

'Like that.'

'Oh.' Esme winced. 'Sorry. I'm looking forward to the festival. It's just … I can't stop thinking about those drawings from Mum's notebook. The ones of the stygians.'

'What about them?'

'The other day, when I was out on my own, on my way to Sofia

Square, there was a man following me. And I'm pretty sure he mistook me for my mother. He was sick—really sick. His skin … he looked like a corpse. Like he was rotting away. Smelled that way, too.'

Daniel grimaced. 'What happened?'

'Nothing. A shopkeeper shooed him away. Said he was always skulking around that part of the city. But when I got home that day, I saw stygians in one of Mum's paintings—the one of the Pearl of Esperance.'

'I don't remember any,' said Daniel.

'In the pool. You have to look twice, but they're in there, loads of them. Professor Sage told us—Lillian and I—that once a stygian infects you, your skin starts to decay. It takes a long time, years, but eventually it starts to look like the stygian's own.' Her voice faltered. 'The man—his skin looked like theirs.'

Daniel rubbed a hand over the waves tattooed on his face, the way he sometimes did when he was trying to puzzle something out.

'Stygians are extinct, aren't they? There's not much proof that they ever existed at all.' He shrugged. 'I wouldn't get too wound up about it. He could have looked that way for plenty of reasons. Especially with things in the city the way they are.'

'I know.' Esme reddened. 'It's stupid.'

'No it's not. You've only just arrived here. You're still learning how things work.' He started on the path again. 'Why didn't you say anything earlier? If something like that was worrying me, I'd tell you.'

'You would?'

He gave her a searching glance. 'Why not? Isn't that what friends are for? So you don't have to deal with this stuff all on your own?'

Esme fell silent. Daniel had caught her out. She *was* used to dealing with things on her own. It had been easier, over the years, to do things by herself rather than ask for help. Eventually, this had turned into a sort of stubbornness she wasn't sure how to shift.

'Bad habit, I guess,' she finally mumbled.

The path led them into a wide grove of clipped conifers, which encircled the Merle Fountain. Poseidon sat atop the fountain, trident in hand, broad chest thrust out before him. The god and the horse-drawn chariot he commanded were streaked and grey, as tired and worn as the sculpted sea below. Beneath the marble waves, real water sprayed out over countless coins that rested on the fountain floor. Stone sea dragons were partly visible around the base, their winding forms dipping in and out of the water.

Esme watched as a small girl ran over to the fountain and threw in a coin. The child stood there on tiptoe, following the coin's descent, before returning to her mother and whispering in her ear.

'There's a fountain like this back home,' said Esme with a wistful sigh. 'Except much smaller. I used to love going there when I was younger. That story, about your parents making a wish—did it really happen that way?'

He took out a coin and flipped it in the air. 'They say it did.'

'So that's why your dad moved here, to Esperance? Because he met your mum?'

'Not right away. They were married in Thalassa, but Mum couldn't get used to living there. She missed Esperance too much.'

He felt around in his pocket and produced a coin, imprinted with the face of Sofia Agapios. Then he offered it to Esme.

'No thanks,' she said softly. 'You can only wish for the same thing so many times.'

Daniel's expression was hard to fathom. He flipped his coin into the fountain, and Esme leaned over the thick marble edge to watch it fall. It disappeared into the depths, joining the innumerable coins on the marble floor.

The spray danced on Esme's skin, and the notes of the fountain lulled her into a relaxed state. On impulse, she took off her shoes, perched on the edge of the fountain, swung around, and dipped her feet in. She closed her eyes, listening to the murmur of the water.

Her respite was short lived. A tight band of pain clamped

around her head, and a roaring filled her ears. The gentle murmur of the fountain had turned into the thundering of a mighty waterfall. She tried to cry out, but she was frozen, as immobile as the marble statues that decorated the fountain.

Esme's consciousness shifted, until there was only her, the water, and the clinking sound of hundreds of coins being thrown into the fountain.

In her mind's eye, a blur of water rushed past. She could hear voices: the voices of hundreds of people, thousands of people, all making wishes.

First she heard Daniel's, and then the little girl's. The voices came faster and faster, tumbling over each other, hopes and prayers pouring into the fountain from the lips of the people of Esperance: wishes for the earthquakes to end, for a sick child to get well, a longed-for baby to arrive, a pair of lovers to reunite.

The wishes ran on and on. The language changed, but somehow Esme could still understand the requests. A mother struggling with a difficult pregnancy; others who begged for no more children—ten was too many mouths to feed; and hundreds, thousands of wishes for the end of a terrible war. They came faster and faster, jumbling together into an indistinguishable wall of sound, before fading away.

All at once, she could see again.

She was still in the same place, on the edge of the fountain, her legs dangling in the water. But Daniel was gone, along with the little girl and her mother.

The fountain was shiny and new—or at least it seemed that way. The marble had lost all marks of age, and no coins littered the fountain floor. The tall firs no longer lined the perimeter. She twisted around to see the palace, glittering like cut glass in the distance.

Am I dreaming?

The sky above was no longer blue. Pinks, icy greens, and mauves arced across it: waves of vivid light, receding and reforming, as if some celestial artist was at work, experimenting on a never-ending canvas. Flecks of gold danced across the horizon—sea dragons, chasing each other in and out of billowing curtains of colour.

Above her shone the Aurora of Aeolia.

Gravel crunched nearby.

Two people were approaching the Merle Fountain: a tall man garbed in black robes, and a slighter woman, in blue. They stopped only an arm's length away from Esme, who was still sitting on the lip of the fountain.

With a start, Esme recognised the patrician face of Michail Agapios, and the gentler visage of Sofia Agapios. Faces she had seen many times before: on the coins of Esperance, on the busts in the plaza, and in Professor Sage's compendium. The founders of Aeolia stood before her.

Queen Sofia disengaged her arm from the king's. Her face was white and drawn, her long hair hidden in a hood.

'I sense a presence. Someone is here.'

The king paced around the fountain, searching out strangers. Esme froze as the queen's gaze fixed upon her. Sofia's eyes were a startling blue, and meeting them was like staring into a bottomless pool that was impossibly wide and deep. But then Sofia looked away, and Esme realised she was as invisible to the king and queen as she had been to her own mother, during that strange vision back on Picton.

The king returned from his circuit. 'No one is here, Sofia.' He spoke with care and concern, more like an anxious husband than a monarch.

The queen glanced behind her, before drawing a bundle from her robes. She unwrapped it and cradled the object within. The colours of the aurora rolled across the gleaming surface of a large, perfectly formed pearl.

The Pearl of Esperance.

It was just as Ariane had painted it: a lustrous orb that subsumed everything around it. Its flawless beauty sung out, igniting a painful longing inside her. It called to the very depths of her soul, promising to grant all her heart's deepest desires.

Overcome with a burning compulsion to possess it, Esme reached out toward the radiant prize.

The queen fixed her gaze on Esme again, her blue eyes so penetrating that Esme jerked her hand back. Sofia frowned, as if she could sense the intruder's intentions. Her eyes became shadowed and dim, and she hid the pearl away in its cloth.

Now that it was out of sight, the pearl's sway lessened. The wider world mattered again. Esme's eyes stayed, however, on the shrouded bundle in Sofia's hand, as did the eyes of the king and queen, silent in their thoughts.

The queen spoke first, her voice tight with emotion. 'The last gift of the gods—surely they sent it to us as a test.' Her face creased with grief. 'Anna, our poor Anna.'

The king beheld the queen tenderly.

'Come, Sofia. We have done our duty. Aeolia's travails have ceased, now that the pearl has been returned to Ephyra. The earth will no longer split and sigh beneath us.'

The queen's voice trembled. 'But what of Anna? Who will save her?'

He shook his head. 'Anna is beyond our help, beyond anyone's help. Come now. I have prepared a place for it. The pearl will be safe here, guarded by stygians. No one must know of its return. It can never leave Ephyra again.'

The king climbed into the fountain, but the queen hesitated.

'Will they harm us?'

'No, but if others attempt to enter the chamber, they will not fare so well.'

As soon as the king and queen disappeared into the depths of the fountain, Esme's headache started up again. The scene faded, and her eyes opened of their own accord. The first thing she heard was Lillian's voice.

'Daniel! She's all right—I think …'

The fountain was ringed with high firs, and the sky was blue again. The colours of the aurora had retreated to the past. The fountain was cracked and chipped in places, the marble mottled with age once more.

Esme had never been so glad to see something so ruined.

By the time they arrived back at No. 8, Esme's headache was almost gone. She sank down onto the couch and tried to explain her vision. The details were fading fast. Only the image of the pearl retained its clarity.

'I heard everyone's wishes—hundreds, thousands of them. When they stopped, the fountain looked new. There were great waves of colour in the sky above me. It was the Aurora of Aeolia … I think. I went back to the beginnings of the city … of the world.'

She took up the compendium, which had become a permanent fixture on the driftwood table, and turned to the entry on the Aurora of Aeolia.

'That's what it looked like. And then the king and queen showed up.'

'What?' Daniel exclaimed. 'Michail and Sofia?'

Daniel's shock mirrored her own. She levered herself off the sofa. She needed air. The doors to the canal were wide open, and the sun was at its zenith, sharpening the shadows cast by the buildings along the canal. Esme slumped down on one of the steps that led to the water and rubbed at her temple, willing away the last traces of the headache. Doubt overwhelmed her.

'What if I made this all up? What if my mind's just playing tricks on me?'

Lillian joined her on the step, while Daniel leaned against the edge of the open door.

'Has anything like this happened to you before?' Lillian asked.

'Once ... back home. Just before I came here.'

'I know how we can tell if it was real,' said Daniel. 'If you heard everyone's wishes, you must have heard mine, too. So, what did I wish for?'

It was true. In the trance, Daniel's was the first voice that she had heard, and even with all the thousands of voices following it, she hadn't forgotten his words.

'You ... You wished I'd find my mother.'

'Exactly. So you didn't make it all up. This must be your Gift.'

'My Gift?'

'Of course,' said Lillian. 'What happened was clearly magical. People don't just dip their feet in fountains and travel back through time. You saw the aurora! It *must* have been your Gift.'

Esme and Daniel returned to the sofa. Lillian began to pace the room.

'I wonder what sort of Gift it is?' she mused. 'There are people who are able to see the future, water-scryers and the like, but I've never heard of being able to see things in the past. And scryers don't really see the future, not like this. They just get glimpses. They're notoriously unreliable.'

'There's more,' said Esme. 'The queen was holding something in her hand. The Pearl of Esperance.'

Daniel sat down beside her. 'The pearl your mother painted?'

'I still can't get it out of my head. Seeing it up so close. It was so ... perfect.'

She could remember the pearl in minute detail: the colours of the aurora scrolling over it, its radiant, enchanting beauty. Strangely, it was growing stronger, not weaker, in her mind.

'The queen was talking to the king about their daughter, Anna— the first keeper, the one who stole the pearl. They'd gotten the pearl back, but they hadn't been able to rescue her. The queen was inconsolable. The king was trying to calm her. He said that they'd done their duty, bringing the pearl back to the city. He said that the pearl had to stay in Esperance—Ephyra, he called it—so that the earth would "no longer split and sigh beneath them".'

'What?' Lillian was chewing her fingernails. 'They were having earthquakes back then, too?'

Esme nodded. 'The king said that they couldn't tell anybody about the pearl's return, and that he'd prepared a hiding place for it. In the Merle Fountain. They went under the water with it. That's when I came back.'

Daniel had taken up the compendium, and was reading though the entry on the pearl.

'In here, it says that the pearl was stolen by the first keeper, and never found again. If what you saw really did happen, then part of the story is missing. The earthquakes, the pearl … maybe this is the link we've all been looking for.'

Just the possibility of the pearl being so close sent shivers of anticipation through Esme, followed hard on its heels by guilt. She was meant to be looking for her mother, not for the pearl. But, maybe searching for one would lead her to the other.

'I want to go back,' she said, 'and see if it's still there.'

'Wait,' said Lillian. 'This might be really important, Esme. Shouldn't we just tell the authorities?'

'Not yet.'

'Why not?'

'I think my mum might be involved in all of this, somehow. I think she might have known where the pearl was hidden.'

Esme retrieved the painting of the pearl from the back of the room. She took it over to the steps beside the canal, where the light was best. The others joined her there.

'Look. Not at the pearl—the water, beneath it.'

Daniel and Lillian peered into the gloom surrounding the pedestal, where the stygians lurked, swarming in the murky water.

'The king said that the hiding place was guarded by stygians.'

'Is that what they are? They're revolting,' said Lillian.

'I was going to tell you earlier—but when I was on my way to Sofia Square, there was a man who mistook me for my mum. His skin ...' she paused, shuddering. 'It was like he had been infected by stygians, just like the professor said.'

'So?'

'She knew. Somehow, my mother knew something nobody else *could* know—she knew about the stygians in the chamber. Why else would she have painted them around the pedestal?'

Lillian flicked her eyes from the painting to Esme, and back again. 'So they could still be *in there?*' She turned her gaze full on Esme. 'And you want to go and see? Have you gone completely *mad?*'

'I have to get to the bottom of this,' said Esme firmly. 'I'll go there on my own. When no one else is around. Tomorrow, before dawn.'

Chapter Eighteen

Esme left No. 8 well before dawn. Darkness stalked her as she stole through the streets, past snaking canals and over pitch-black water. Her way was lit only by the occasional yellow glow of a street lamp, or a forgotten light burning inside a dwelling.

The Merle Fountain was set at the border of the palace's formal gardens, swaddled in the darkness by the mass of parkland behind it. From a distance, it appeared as though a vast black beast had swallowed Poseidon whole.

The decision to return here had made sense the day before, but not during the sleepless night that had followed. Esme had regressed into the night terrors of her childhood, falling asleep only to snap bolt upright in bed, sure that there were strangers in the room, shadows that could mutate into monsters at any moment. Disembodied skulls, femurs, and other human bones clicked together in dark corners, preparing to spring on her. The dread of those small hours was yet to dissipate.

The sound of the fountain's spray was amplified in the night. Inside the circle of trees, Poseidon loomed out of the blackness.

The gravel crunched behind her, and she jumped.

It was Daniel. Lillian wasn't far behind him.

'You don't have to do this, you know,' said Esme, when Lillian had caught up with them.

'Do you really think we'd let you go in there on your own?' said Lillian.

'On your own *and* unprepared?' asked Daniel, extracting a small pouch from his bag. He dipped his hand in, and when he removed it, his fingers glowed green in the night, trails of phosphorescent light snaking out from each fingertip.

Esme coated her fingers with the dust, too, feeling a slight tingle. 'What is this stuff?'

'Ashlight. From wood burnt by dragons' breath. I was given it for helping out at the festival last year. Lasts ages.'

'Dawn's not far away,' said Lillian, climbing over the lip of the fountain.

Esme gave up arguing and clambered in with the others. The water slid over her, sealing her in. The three of them separated and worked their way around the central plinth, searching for any irregular grooves or markings. A mass of algae had colonised the marble centrepiece, including the dragons that adorned the base. Great fronds of it waved in the water, brushing against her face as if seeking a new host, making her skin crawl.

She was about to move on to the next carved section when Daniel tapped her on the shoulder. She followed him to the other side of the plinth. The raised relief of a stygian claw was fixed on the throat of one of the stone dragons.

Esme's heart hammered at the sight.

They set to work, trying to uncover some sort of entrance. Part of the dragon's maw was buried in coins, so Esme cleared them away, making enough space to see inside. She squeezed underneath, ignoring the coins digging into her sides, and shone ashlight up into the cavernous interior of the dragon's mouth. Nothing there.

The water around them was rapidly lightening with the advent of day. Esme withdrew her hand from the dragon's maw and signalled to the others. They shook their heads and surfaced, beckoning for Esme to join them.

She stayed where she was for a moment, staring up into the darkness, algae drifting across her field of vision. Only then did she see it: a pinpoint of faint green light, far up in the dragon's throat. The green glow of the ashlight had masked it.

Something *was* here.

Her pulse raced. She jammed her shoulder and arm up as far as she could into the cavity, straining toward the green light. The tips of her fingers brushed against a small round stone, embedded in the ancient marble.

A light blazed out from the dragon's mouth, and swallowed her whole.

A great weight pressed in on her, crushing her sides until she could barely breathe. Then it let go, and she fell, plummeting into darkness.

Esme crashed, spreadeagled, onto a wet, uneven floor.

Something had broken her fall. She pulled herself to her feet and threw ashlight around her, stifling a scream.

She had landed on the remains of a feast. Bones were strewn everywhere: ribcages, vertebrae, curved horns, and long, lethal claws, lying half-submerged in shallow puddles of water.

The air was thick and clammy, and the chamber silent, apart from the steady drip of water from behind her. She stood up and drifted ghostly streams of green from her fingertips, illuminating a place that was devoid of light. Water drizzled down a row of yawning stone dragons fixed to a wall, which curved up out of sight.

Desolation pervaded the air. She inhaled and exhaled in violent little waves. She couldn't remember how long Daniel had said the ashlight would last. The dank air pressed in on her, whispering on her skin:

You are trespassing.

Fear curdled her breath.

The ashlight lit up the perimeter of a large pool, and Esme followed the trail of bones around it. They crunched beneath her feet, but thankfully, none of them resembled the bones of humans. They were all too small, or of a strange shape. Soon, she was back to where she had first entered the chamber. She'd gone full circle.

So far, Esme had avoided illuminating the pool itself, but now, taking cautious steps, she edged closer and threw ashlight out over the water. There it was, in the centre of the pool: the faint outline of a pedestal, just like in Ariane's painting.

The sight of the pedestal sent a stab of longing through her. Her lust for the pearl came back with a vengeance, warping her judgement and clouding her vision.

Patches of scum covered the pool, but Esme convinced herself that they looked benign—sheets of lichen, like the algae that covered the plinth in the Merle Fountain. Her logic, her instinct, her intellect tried to stop her, but she was possessed.

She slid into water that had never felt the warmth of the sun.

As she made her way through the water, the algae parted harmlessly before her. *See,* she told herself. *It's perfectly safe. The stygians must all be gone by now—they must have eaten each other out of existence.*

When she brushed against another patch of lichen, it twitched.

Stygians.

Countless stygians were floating in clumps throughout the pool, sleeping close together, a tangle of monstrous skin and claw. One of them stirred, stretching out a limb toward her. Esme froze.

The limb retracted.

Go back. Get out of here—now.

Every part of her recoiled, screamed at her to flee. But Esme pressed on, consumed with desire. She paddled around the stygians, keeping her hands as still as possible to avoid generating light. Her prize was only a few strokes away.

She clambered on to the stone island. The top of the pedestal was bare, but in the middle it funnelled down into a cavity, big enough for a human hand, but not a stygian claw.

The pearl must be hidden within.

Esme reached inside, her hand trembling. Something was in there—the smooth, cool, surface of a pearl—but it was too small. She drew it out.

It *was* a pearl, but not the Pearl of Esperance.

It was fixed to a broken metallic chain, and the letter 'A' hung a few links above it, in tarnished silver.

A low growl sounded from close by.

The passing of prey had registered somewhere deep in the creatures' slumber.

Reality returned in a sickening rush. The spell that had propelled Esme through the water was gone, replaced by paralysing fear. Her knees buckled out from under her. She had risked her life for nothing. Now she was marooned in the middle of the pool, surrounded by waking stygians.

She crammed the necklace in her pocket and frantically searched for a clear path back through the water. The clumps were coming apart and spreading out over the pool. A green glow, concealed under the lip of the pedestal, caught her eye.

Another stone, like the one in the dragon's maw, was fixed underneath. She brushed her hand against it—*come on, come on*—impatient for the light to stream over her and take her back to safety, hardly believing her luck.

Instead, a rumble came from beneath the pool: the sound of stone grinding against stone, making enough noise to wake the rest of the slumbering creatures.

A set of sharp, curving horns scraped at the platform. The stench of death preceded her. A stygian reared up out of the water: a mass of scabbed, decomposing skin, three feet across. Its sucker mouth yawned open, wider and wider, spraying Esme with globules of saliva.

More stygians breached the platform. Esme leaped on top of the pedestal.

The beasts continued to gather, a writhing mass of flesh, claw, and horn, climbing over each other to be the first to devour her. One fell, and the others sliced it wide open, gorging on its flesh and innards.

While they were feasting, Esme threw ashlight across the pool.

The rumbling had ceased. Columns of stone had risen out of the water, providing a path to the other side.

Esme took a deep, shuddering breath and flew off the pedestal. A stygian swiped at her, barely missing her leg as she landed clumsily on the first column. Three more leaps to safety. It looked impossible.

She jumped.

One, she counted, landing heavily on the next column. The stygians' cries filled the air. She sucked in another juddering breath and jumped again.

Two. She slipped across the mossy surface, almost falling off the edge.

Three.

Esme crashed to the wet ground with a thud. She was up again at once, crunching over the bones to the stone dragons. Five heads were fixed to the walls, but which was the way out?

Splashes behind her and roars of fury signalled the approach of the stygians.

They were almost upon her, their breath fouling the air. Finally, she spied a glow inside the very last dragon's maw. Esme thrust her arm in. Light poured out over her, just as the very tip of a stygian's claw slashed across her thigh.

Warm blood seeped down her leg, and then she was gone.

The guttural roars of the beasts, enraged at the disappearance of their prey, followed Esme out of the chamber.

Chapter Nineteen

When Esme rematerialised in the bottom of the Merle Fountain, Daniel's concerned face was hovering inches away from her own. She surfaced to hear Lillian's frantic voice.

'Esme! Are you all right? What happened?'

The last rosy streaks of dawn were fading over the horizon. Blood streamed from Esme's leg into the water, clouding the surface of the fountain. She answered in an unsteady voice.

'I found the chamber … and the stygians.'

Daniel and Lillian helped her out of the fountain and over to a wooden bench. Black dots crowded Esme's vision as she gazed down at her leg, uncomprehending. The flesh around it had already taken on a greenish tinge.

'Oh, Esme,' said Lillian, her face white.

Daniel took a spare shirt from his bag, tore strips from it, bound the wound, and tied it off. 'That should stop the bleeding.'

'What now?' Esme couldn't keep the raw edge from her voice.

Lillian touched a hand to her forehead. 'She's burning up.'

'We should go see the keeper—right away,' said Daniel.

'Can he help?' Esme asked uncertainly. 'Is he a doctor as well?'

'No, but I don't know what an ordinary doctor would make of this.' Daniel's eyes strayed to her leg. 'People visit him when they don't know where else to go. My grandfather used to go see him, sometimes, at his clinic. He deals with all sorts of things. His treatments are … unconventional. But then, so is this.'

'I've never met him, but I've heard he's very experienced,' added Lillian, sounding less sure than Daniel.

Esme limped with them to the ferry stop, where they boarded a boat bound for the Crown Canal.

'We couldn't see where you'd gone,' said Daniel, as they took their seats. 'We couldn't see anything. How did you find the way?'

'I was about to leave. But I looked in the dragon's mouth one last time, and saw a green glow. The ashlight had masked it. It took me straight to a chamber, just like the one in Mum's painting. The floor was covered with bones—but no human ones, just stygian.'

She couldn't bring herself to tell them what had really happened in there: how she had been consumed by the allure of the pearl, and risked her life swimming to the pedestal; how she had found her mother's necklace there, in its place. Her thoughts swung wildly between self-recrimination and panic.

'Did you find anything in there? Did you see the pearl?' asked Lillian.

She shook her head. 'It wasn't there.'

Along the Crown Canal, shops and businesses were opening up for the day. A figure in rags had fallen asleep on some steps. The man from her visit to Sofia Square flashed into her mind. He had been infected by stygians. She was sure of it.

Did he go looking for the pearl, too?

A wave of nausea rolled over her. She placed her hand on the wooden rail to steady herself. When she glanced down at it, she jerked backward. The skin had already started to decay, and foul-smelling pus was oozing down her wrists.

'Are you all right? Is it hurting badly?' asked Lillian anxiously.

'My hand—look at my hand!'

'What's wrong with it?' asked Daniel.

She could hear confusion in Daniel's voice, and opened her eyes again. Her hand was completely unharmed. The skin was soft, pink, and healthy.

'I thought … the venom …'

'Must be playing with your mind. We'll be there soon,' said Daniel, putting a comforting hand over hers.

A short while later, they arrived at the outer reaches of the city, where the Crown Canal merged with the wider waters of the lagoon. A maze of narrow, cobbled streets opened up onto Keepers' Row, a wide thoroughfare fringed by row upon row of red-leafed trees. Partway down, Daniel stopped before a large set of old bronze doors, decorated with hammered reliefs of shells. The lintel above was decorated in cursive script: '*Memento, verentur, secundum*'.

Esme's pulse was racing. She tried to calm down as they went inside, reasoning that slowing her heart rate might help to prevent the spread of poison. They passed by a series of painted scenes, depicting an assortment of Gifts. Figures moved amongst whirling water or emerged from the midst of fire, while others cast enchantments in front of great crowds, or sung in robed choirs. At the hall's end, steps led down to a waiting room, where a uniformed attendant took a quick glance under Esme's bandage and immediately escorted her to a treatment room.

Esme limped into a long, narrow chamber, past shelves bowed with leather-bound tomes and crowded with vials. Dim forms crawled around behind the smoky glass of a large cabinet. She had entered an apothecary of sorts, redolent with the smell of waxy camphor, dried out herbs and hand-brewed concoctions. Thick blue curtains were hooked back around a large window, and Esme sank into one of the low chairs beside them.

Beside her sat a glass cabinet, which held a single object: a knotted, gnarled rod, which was twisted into a spiral. The rod hung in mid-air, seemingly suspended by nothing.

A droll voice sounded from above. 'I haven't seen you around here before ...'

Esme froze, then lifted her head to see a spectral shape lolling in a chandelier made of whitened coral branches. A waistcoated figure slid between the antlers, hovering a couple of feet over Esme. This apparition was much easier to see than pale Maria from the studio, but still, the air turned frosty around her.

'Mortimer, at your service.' He bowed, stretching his body out like an ethereal rubber band, until it was twice its normal length, before snapping back into his original shape. 'First visit?'

Esme nodded.

'I see. State your purpose.'

'Er, I've come to see the keeper about my leg.'

He floated down and poked an icy digit at her. 'Hm. The keeper's a busy man, you know. He often sends me in for a first opinion, saves him time. Let's see what's under this bandage.'

'All right, I suppose ...'

Esme undid the bandage and regretted it at once. The discolouration had spread even further. Mortimer grinned, but Esme was too busy winding the bandage up again to notice. By the time she finished, he had assumed a grave expression once more.

'Hm, that looks nasty. I must be frank—from my experience, with an infection like that, there's a good chance you'll lose the leg. Augustine won't tell you the truth, but if he sets one of his insects on you, you'll know you're in desperate straits.'

He floated over to the cabinet, where shadows moved behind the hazy glass.

'They're in here. The horrid little things.' Then he zoomed back up to his skeletal branches and settled there. 'I much prefer the coral with all the life bleached out of it,' he mused. 'Don't you?'

A branch was sprouting out of Mortimer's right cheek, but he didn't bother to move. He just splayed out his ghostly hands, and more coral spikes pierced through them.

Esme was still fixated on the ghost when the door opened, and the Keeper of Esperance strode into the room. He was olive-skinned and looked around the same age as her father. He wore a black robe, and his white-blond hair was tied back in a ponytail; in his right hand, he grasped a long, springy rod.

Esme remembered his royal lineage only when she saw his eyes: brilliant pools of blue, like those of Queen Sofia. His brow looked permanently furrowed, but there were also humour lines around his eyes and mouth. The rod in his hand strained upward, and a stern expression crossed his face, once he saw who was keeping his patient company.

'What are you doing in here, Mortimer? I've told you countless times to leave my patients alone. Go and find something useful to do.'

Mortimer disentangled himself from the antlers. 'Just cheering her up. This one's very poorly, I'm afraid.'

'Off! Or I'll set Willow on to you.'

Mortimer dived through the wall, his hand elongated in a long parting wave.

The keeper let go of the rod, and it floated over to rest on the table. He strode up to Esme and greeted her with a smile. 'You must excuse Mortimer. He's not of this world any longer, but he can't seem to move on from it.'

He took the other seat, and splayed out his delicate hands on the clawed arms of the chair. 'You're not from this world, either, it seems.'

It was not phrased as a question; it was as if he knew without having to ask.

'I'm Augustine.'

His eyes ranged over her in a practiced assessment, before he pushed his chair away and whipped out two stools from under a table. He propped her leg up on one and sat astride the other, then unwound the bandage. Esme cringed at the sight. The keeper scrutinised her leg with great interest, and considerable concern.

'When did this happen? I've never seen anything like it.'

'Earlier this morning.'

He turned the stricken limb gently from side to side. 'What could have done this to you?' he murmured, half to himself, before giving Esme an enquiring glance.

When Esme stayed silent, the keeper regarded her quizzically.

'I can assure you that I have heard many remarkable things over the years. Nothing much astonishes me anymore. And I would never betray a patient's confidence.'

His kind eyes melted her reserve. Weighed down under all that had happened to her, Esme told him the truth.

'It was a stygian.'

The wrinkles on his forehead almost disappeared into his hairline. He sprung out of his chair and headed for the bookshelf, talking all the while. 'You were attacked by a *stygian*? But ... they've been extinct for thousands of years.'

A book slid out from the topmost shelf and fell into his hands; after he had finished with it, another flew toward him in the same fashion, and then another, until he had consulted half a dozen of them. 'I want to hear more, but not now. Time is of the essence.'

He scribbled some notes and moved over to the rows of bottles. Esme's nose wrinkled at the fumes from a glass of black, odorous liquid that he handed to her.

'You have my sympathies. Not the most pleasant of tastes. Try to drink the whole thing at once. If you stop, I doubt you'll be able to start over.'

Esme gulped the drink down as quickly as she could, almost gagging on the last few drops. In the meantime, something had landed on her leg: a black and yellow striped beetle, about the size of the bowl of a teaspoon. She shrunk back in horror—it took all her self-control to stop herself from flinging the beetle off her leg. The keeper, on the other hand, was regarding the insect with a disquieting fondness.

'I breed them myself,' he said, with an air of pride. 'Let's see what this one can do.'

Mortimer's doom-laden words rang in her ears as the keeper prodded at the beetle. All it did was roll over and jerk its legs feebly in the air.

Augustine tutted, scooped it up in a bowl, and moved over to the sink. He returned with another, more ferocious-looking beetle, twice the size of the first. Neon orange circles ringed its black shell. It flipped itself over in the bowl, legs waving wildly, pincers gnashing in a frenzy of fury. Black dots swam in front of Esme's eyes.

She closed them tight, but that made her feel even woozier. The moment the bug landed on her leg, it began to attack the affected area with a vengeance. Esme had to bite down on her lip, hard, to stop from crying out every time it dug in her.

'That's more like it,' said Augustine, prodding the beetle into greater fury.

The orange bullseye on its back grew bigger and bigger as the beetle worked its way around the wound, extracting the stygian's toxin. Soon it had become so engorged it could no longer move.

The keeper took it over to the sink, but returned with it a short while later, shrunk back to its original size. 'Not quite finished, I'm afraid.'

The bug was just as vicious on the second application, and the third, but eventually, its violent ministrations had some effect. The spreading infection was shrinking, and by the time the beetle had finished, all signs of it were gone.

'That's better,' said Augustine, returning the beetle to the cabinet.

Esme's voice trembled. 'So I'm not going to lose my leg?'

'Lose your leg? Whatever would give you that idea?'

'Mortimer said—before you came in, he told me that you only use your beetles as a last resort, and—'

'I see.' Augustine gave a grunt of annoyance as he threaded a needle. 'That Mortimer's a menace. I'm afraid his greatest joy is toying with anybody who comes to see me. He's an ex-patient of mine, who, for some reason, blames me for his untimely demise. He seems to have made it his death's duty to punish me for my supposed misdemeanours.'

The keeper finished stitching up the gash, and then busied himself preparing a mixture in a stone bowl. Esme couldn't quite see what he was putting into it, but she thought she heard something crunch.

'I've done what I can,' said the keeper. 'But the venom is unlikely to completely leave your system without putting up a fight. Be prepared for things to get worse before they get better.'

Esme shivered, remembering the hallucination on the ferry.

'This will help. Take a large spoonful each day, until it's all gone. And drink plenty of water.'

He poured the contents of the bowl into a dark blue bottle, and handed it to her, before sitting back down.

'Stygians,' he breathed. 'This is a momentous discovery. The City Conservator must be notified at once. Where exactly were you attacked?'

'In … a secret chamber.'

'A *secret chamber*?'

Esme stared down at her lap, twisting her hands together. 'That's all I can tell you for now. You did say that you would never betray a patient's confidence.'

'Well, yes, but I hardly think this is the sort of information that—'

Esme cut in. 'It's to do with my mother. She's gone missing, and I think she knew about the chamber. I want to find out more before I tell anyone.'

'But … how did you even find this chamber in the first place?'

Before Esme could respond, the keeper's rod swooped down in front of her, and hovered inches from her face. Augustine leaned forward, his eyes shining like the sun on the water of a wide lake.

'Ah … I see,' said the keeper. 'Willow wishes to examine your Gift.'

Chapter Twenty

'Gifts are my area of expertise,' said Augustine, 'and they are Willow's prime interest, too.'

He gestured to the rod, which soared back into his hand. 'Willow is a diviner—she has been with me since birth. I was just one of many cousins with royal blood; nobody suspected that I would be the next keeper. But when Willow materialised beside me on the day I was born, my path was set.'

Augustine filled a bowl with water and set it down on the low table beside Esme. 'Willow is very interested to see your Gift, as am I. May I?'

'Uh … sure.'

'Rest your hand in the water. Relax, close your eyes.'

She did as he instructed, and almost at once, one of her interminable headaches started up. A rushing sound filled her ears, but just as quickly, it was gone. Her eyes opened and the keeper leaned toward her attentively.

'Tell me what you know about this Gift of yours.'

'Nothing, really, except that it's to do with water—according to the Seeing Stone in the Temple Library.'

'That is correct. Your Gift can only manifest when you are in contact with water. Has this been the case so far?'

Esme thought back. The first time, she had been washing the blue vase; the second time, she had been dangling her feet in the Merle Fountain. 'Yes, but I don't understand. If it is a Gift, what kind is it?'

'Water has a memory of its own. It stores within itself the history of all it sees. The waters of both our worlds share this property, but, as you are no doubt aware, magic has largely faded from your world. Still, the water's memory remains. In your world, nobody has been able to access these memories, at least, as far as I know. Nobody, that is, except you.'

'Me?'

'It seems so. Your Gift is a rare one, but not unheard of. Through your Gift, you form a kinship with the water's memory—you are able to see all that it has seen. You have borne witness to visions from the past, have you not?'

Esme nodded, somewhat dazed by the keeper's revelations.

'These visions are pieces of history, shown to you through the water. Your Gift functions as a conduit to the past.'

The inscription on one of the pillars in the Temple Library floated back to her:

The history of Aeolia is writ in water.

Augustine beckoned for her to join him at the window. The waters of the lagoon rippled by outside, the prow of an occasional gondola or ferry rearranging the patterns upon its surface.

'Here, just as in your world,' continued the keeper, 'every drop of water has been present since the very beginning. The same drops circulate over and over again in an endless cycle, falling from the skies to form oceans, rivers, streams. When Aeolia was formed, the gods enhanced the magical properties of our water, as their gift to us. We have always been able to breathe beneath its surface and explore its depths, as easily as we can travel across the land.'

His voice had in it a hint of wonder and longing.

'It is a rare and enviable ability to be able to ride the waves of history, to visit the far shores of centuries past. Others can only reminisce, or read about such events.'

As they resumed their seats, Esme noticed that the gnarled rod in the glass cabinet had moved. It had wedged itself up against the pane, facing them, as if it had been listening in on their conversation.

'What *is* that?' asked Esme.

The keeper followed her gaze. 'Hm? Oh, that diviner belonged to Anna Agapios, the first keeper. When keepers die, their divining rod is buried with them, or else it quickly disintegrates. But Anna's rod is still here, separated from her. I can only surmise that she must still be linked to this plane, in some form or other.'

'I've read about her. Before my mother went missing, she illustrated a compendium on Aeolian myths and legends. And one of the entries mentions Anna. The bit about the Pearl of Esperance.'

'Ah, I see. Yes, history tells us that Anna stole the pearl, but why she did, and what happened to her afterwards, is a mystery to us all. It has been the subject of much speculation over the years. I have a theory of my own, of course.'

Esme leaned forward, intrigued.

'Every keeper possesses a little of each Gift,' said Augustine. 'A small taste, which, in itself, can whet the appetite for more. The pearl promises keepers what they can never have: the chance to fully experience all of them—a temptation that proved far too much for Anna Agapios to bear. Well, that's my hypothesis, anyway.'

Willow, who had been roving around the room, flew back to the keeper and tapped him on the shoulder.

'Yes … let us get back to the matter at hand. You must resist using your Gift, at least for now. The magic of our world has become increasingly unstable, and if such a Gift went awry, it could have devastating consequences.'

He swung Willow over her again. 'Let me see one more time.'

Esme dipped her hand into the water and closed her eyes. When she opened them, a storm was passing over the keeper's face.

'What is it?'

The thunderclouds on his brow shifted, but his expression remained solemn.

'Willow and I have spied a thread of darkness in your Gift. Someone has tampered with it. It's something I've seen before, in the Gifts of others. Its presence in you just ... doesn't make any sense. You've only just arrived here. And yet, there it is.'

Augustine said nothing for a long time, the rod spinning in his palm.

'I must caution you again, to avoid using it, at all costs. I've seen the results of Nathan Mare's handiwork.'

Esme drew a quick breath, sure that she had misheard him.

'Did you say Nathan Mare?'

For several long moments, she sat in a daze. The whole room seemed to be spinning. This whole day had been one trauma after another: the discovery of the chamber, the shock of finding her mother's necklace, her close call with the stygians, the keeper's bizarre treatment methods ... and now this.

Augustine regarded her with concern. 'Do you need to lie down?' he asked.

'No,' she blurted out, forcing herself to focus, pushing through the fuzz in her head. 'I need to know more. How could Nathan Mare have tampered with my Gift? I've only been in Esperance a few weeks.'

'I can't even begin to fathom,' the keeper sighed. 'But it sounds like you've heard of him.'

She nodded. 'Apparently he was a friend of my mother's. Mum—Ariane—used to come here all the time, years and years ago. Then she vanished, just before he escaped from prison. No one's seen her since—neither here, nor back home. I've been trying to find out more about him, in case he has something to do with it.'

He leaned back in his chair, looking weary. Willow, who had retreated to the table on which the glass cabinet stood, flew over and rested on his lap.

'Then I will tell you what I can. Mare's parents, Jules and Eleanor, brought him in here once, when he was about your age. Both were scientists, well known in their field. Highly regarded at the time. But I saw another side of them that day.

'Jules and Eleanor wanted—no, *demanded* to know why their son had shown no signs of possessing a Gift. At first I refused to examine him. I'm not in the business of soothsaying, I told them. But they refused to leave.'

Augustine twisted the emerald ring on his finger.

'Willow examined the boy, searching in vain for a hint of something that might emerge in his future. Nothing showed itself. Mare was clearly a brilliant student, destined for great things, but his parents couldn't see that. All they could see was what he lacked. I'll never forget the way they discussed him in front of me. Like he was some sort of failed experiment.'

'All because he didn't have a Gift?'

Augustine nodded. 'Unfortunately, some families in Esperance place such great store on their Gifts that they order all of their affairs around them. Enchanters tend to be the worst offenders, given that enchantment is one of the most powerful Gifts one can possess. Jules and Eleanor Mare, both highly skilled enchanters, assumed that their son would carry on their legacy.'

The keeper twirled Willow in his hand.

'But chance intervened in their plans. Gifts are passed down in the same way as family traits—there's no guarantee they will surface in every generation. Which is exactly what happened when Nathan was born; the Gift skipped a generation. Why there would be any shame in that is beyond my comprehension. I felt sorry for the boy, and when he later expressed interest in my activities, I agreed that he could spend some time here, assisting me at the clinic.'

A pained look crossed his face.

'I suppose I hoped that with my influence, I might be able to undo some of the damage inflicted on him by his parents. While he was here, I tried to instil in him the keepers' code. *Memento, verentur, secundum* ... "Remember, revere, respect." Keepers funnel their energies into nurturing and protecting the magic that flows though this world, thus protecting the world itself. One of

the primary ways in which this is accomplished is through assisting with Gifts, ensuring that they work as they are meant to.'

He heaved a sigh.

'But in the end ... Nathan Mare took everything I taught him
and twisted it to his own ends.'

A rap on the door interrupted him. 'Coming!' he called, rising
from his chair.

'Duty calls,' he said, turning back to her. 'I must go, unless I want
to have another Mortimer on my hands. But I have told you almost
all I know. Mare's court case only confirmed my views of the path
he had taken. Among the remedies that he had prescribed to his
victims were powerful concoctions of his own design, designed
to manipulate one's Gift. It was the volatile combinations of these
elixirs, most of which were derived from illegal substances, that
killed those in his care.

'What made it even worse was that he had claimed to model
his treatments on mine. I had to stand up in court and set them
straight on that point. Nothing,' he said firmly, 'could have been
further from the truth.'

Chapter Twenty-One

'Good news?' asked Lillian, when Esme appeared back in the waiting room. 'You were in there for so long, I thought ...'

'The worst? I did, too.' Esme gave her a shaky smile, and held up the tonic. 'My leg's better, but I still have to take this, to clear out the last of the venom.'

Outside, it was still only mid-morning, but it felt like days, not hours, had passed since their search of the fountain. Delicious smells wafted from an outdoor café only a few doors away. They headed straight there, and ordered breakfast.

'So did he use his beetles on you?' asked Daniel.

Lillian thumped him. 'What? You knew about the beetles? You could have *warned* her.'

'I did—sort of. I said that his treatments were unconventional. I thought if I said any more, she wouldn't have gone to see him.'

Esme was in the middle of recounting what had happened when she felt a faint tickling sensation. It soon turned into a maddening itch, as if thousands of ants were swarming around under her skin. She scratched viciously at her arms, desperate for relief.

'What's the matter?' asked Lillian.

Esme forced herself to stop. Angry red welts now crisscrossed her skin. 'The keeper said something like this might happen.' She poured herself a glass of water and gulped it down.

Daniel stopped chewing momentarily. 'Did Augustine talk to you about your vision while you were in there?'

'He did. After he set the beetles on me. He said it was my Gift. That I can link in to the memories of the water ... and see the past.'

Lillian's smile could have lit up the whole city. 'I *told* you it was a Gift.'

Daniel looked impressed. 'So now you know where your visions come from,' he said. 'The Seeing Stone was right. It *is* to do with water.'

They both gazed expectantly at Esme, who was fully occupied by her breakfast. Lillian made a noise somewhere between a sniff and a laugh.

'Look at you. Here I am, waking up every morning hoping that this will be the day my Gift comes through. I'd be overjoyed ...'

Lillian was right. This should be a cause for celebration. She should be joining in with her friends' jubilation. What she mostly felt, though, was numb shock.

'I wish I was, but ... it's complicated. Augustine said not to use my Gift at all. But how do I avoid using it? It happens on its own. I mean, obviously it's triggered by contact with water ...' Esme was about to take another sip. Instead, she set the glass back down. 'Oh.'

Daniel smiled. 'I don't think you'll last long doing that. And I'm sure he says that to everybody, with the way the magic's been lately—'

'It's not just that.' Esme shook her head. 'He saw something in my Gift. Someone's ... interfered with it.'

A thread of darkness had been his exact words, but Esme left that part out. She didn't like how it made her feel—violated, somehow.

'What? Who?'

'Nathan Mare.'

'*What?*'

'Mare?' said Daniel, crunching a mouthful of toast. 'That can't be right.'

'Augustine didn't understand it either. He did tell me more about Mare, though. He said that when Nathan was about our age, his parents, both enchanters, brought him into the clinic, demanding to know what his Gift was. When the keeper said he couldn't see one, they practically disowned him. What you said about the enchanters, Lillian, might have some truth to it.'

'The keeper would have hated Mare's parents bullying him like that,' said Daniel. 'Grandpa Leo asked him once to help make his Gift more powerful, and I can still remember Augustine's face. He carried on and on about "upsetting the balance of the world". That wasn't the same time I released all the beetles. At least, I don't think ...'

'You *what*?' cried Lillian.

'I felt sorry for them.'

Esme ordered a cup of coffee, craving the taste of something familiar, and desperately tried to keep her mind off the urge to scratch. If she could turn herself inside out and shake off her tormentors, she would.

'What was your grandfather's Gift?' she asked Daniel.

'Echolocation.'

'Wow,' said Esme.

Lillian frowned. 'Is that something to do with soundwaves?'

'Yeah. He could sense his surroundings even in total darkness, like whales do. He worked a lot underwater, with the rangers. And he was always fooling around at home, showing off.'

The coffee arrived, thick and black. Esme added copious amounts of milk and sugar, until it tasted vaguely like the version she was used to. Lillian had gone unusually silent.

'Something on your mind?' Daniel asked.

'I've been thinking about the pearl,' said Lillian. She focused on Esme. 'If your Gift is to look back at the past, then everything the king said in your vision must be true. When Anna took the pearl, the city started having earthquakes.'

Daniel was rapidly coming to the same conclusion. 'They put the pearl back,' he said, 'and the earthquakes stopped.'

Lillian nodded. 'So, if it wasn't in the chamber, then maybe it was taken again. Seven years ago, at the start of *these* quakes. But who would do such a thing?'

'The stygian guy!' Daniel exclaimed triumphantly.

Lillian frowned. 'But if he had a pearl that could grant his every wish, why would he still be in Esperance, living on the streets? Surely, if the pearl is as powerful as the compendium says, it could cure the effects of stygian venom. There must be more to it than that.'

Daniel looked disappointed, but Esme froze inside. The memory came rushing back to her—the man's tortured eyes, his pleading rasp:

Where is it, Ari—?

Suddenly, her coffee didn't taste so sweet. Ariane's necklace felt like it was burning a hole in her pocket. The worry that had been hovering in the back of her mind finally crystallised into something solid.

'What do you think, Esme?' asked Lillian.

Before Esme could answer, cries came from further down the street. Fingers pointed toward the sky.

Daniel glanced upward, his face beaming. 'Look! The Rows are here—the dragons from Rowana!'

Rainclouds were moving in from the east, along with a dozen growing specks of vermillion. The dots were soon recognisable as a flight of orange dragons, their wings beating like sails beneath the bolting clouds. Every eye locked on the majestic beasts as they passed overhead. Daniel shouted out greetings, and one of the rangers, a boy with a mane of fiery red hair, waved back at him.

'That's Rhys.' Daniel scrambled to his feet. 'I'd better go. I'm meant to be at the Esperance den as soon as the Rows arrive. Hey—why don't you both meet me there, the day of the festival? Come around noon.'

During the ferry ride home, the storm clouds that had been gathering all morning finally broke. The rain fell in sheets, slick against the side of the ferry, but Esme hardly noticed. Fear could take many forms, but, right now, it felt cold and small, like an icy fist, clenched within her.

Could my mother have stolen the pearl?

Esme didn't even know what she, herself, would have done if she *had* found the pearl in the chamber. She could easily imagine just slipping away with it, the way Anna Agapios had, the way her mother might have.

Sleep that night was elusive. The events of the day kept running through Esme's mind, like debris down a swollen river after a flood. At some point, she picked up her mother's shell from the bedside table. Eventually, she drifted off to the sounds of the otherworldly voices within.

In her dreams, Esme teetered on the edge of a vast precipice. Beneath her lay a dark pool, full of ravenous stygians. Something else glinted beneath the surface of the water. Its glow filled the pool with light. A violent push from behind propelled her off the cliff. She screamed as she plummeted down toward the beasts' yawning mouths, each one straining up toward her.

She plunged into the water between them, but there was no welcome there, no reprieve, no glittering pearl—only darkness and oblivion.

Esme woke in a fit of panic, convinced that the infection had worsened overnight. She gingerly lifted her blankets to inspect her leg. A quick glance was enough to reassure her that the keeper's cure had worked. The wound was still healing. She heaved a sigh of relief.

The house had slept in, too. A spider had found its way into the room and spun a web overnight. Quiet filled the corners. Outside, rain still fell, soft and steady, pattering on the roof above.

In the bedside drawer lay her mother's necklace, entangled with her own. Esme took them out and teased the two apart. The chain she had found in the chamber was black and pitted, the once-shiny letter 'A' corroded from its years in the dank chamber. The dirt-encrusted pearl hung, forlornly, a few links below it.

She wanted to put away this scarred memento of her visit to the chamber, pretend that she'd never found it. Instead, she examined it more closely. One of the links was sheared right though. At least, Esme thought to herself, this proved that her mother had escaped the chamber alive. Miranda had told her that Ariane had lost this necklace just before they last saw each other.

The itching started up again. Her skin was still raw from the day before, but the urge to scratch was unbearable. Esme ran a warm bath and soaked in it for a while. When she closed her eyes, images of the stygians appeared behind them. They flew back open in distress.

Her hand was oozing pus, the way it had on the ferry. Her gaze travelled down the rest of her body. Her arms, legs, stomach, and chest—all had turned a leprous, weeping green.

She staggered out of the bath and stared in the mirror. Her face was unrecognisable, reduced to craters of putrid flesh, begging her to claw at them. Only her eyes were recognisably her own, frightened and filling with tears.

'It's not real,' she told herself, over and over again. 'It's not real.'

The visions came and went as she towelled herself dry, one moment a creature's hand drying her, the next her own.

Nobody else was home. Lillian would be gone for most of the day, helping her mum with the last-minute rush before the festival. Downstairs in the kitchen, Esme gulped down a spoonful of the keeper's medicine. She followed it with glass after glass of water, gripping the kitchen bench to keep herself steady.

Desperate for something, anything, to distract her, Esme decided to search through Ariane's notebooks and the compendium, yet again. She flipped through page after page and studied drawing after drawing, seeing everything in a painful new light. Now that she suspected her mother of having stolen the pearl, it was like she was looking through the life of a stranger. It gave her a kind of vertigo, like her world had tipped and she couldn't set it right.

Often, she would pick up the indigo shell and lose herself in its song. It had a curative effect, especially when the itching started up again, or the venom tried to play with her mind.

By the end of the day, Esme had gone over everything so many times that her head was a whirl of sea monsters, water demons, vortices of doom, and cursed islands. Her mother's notebooks had yielded no real clues, but Esme kept being drawn back to the compendium. If her mother had travelled outside Esperance, it would make sense for her to have visited the places associated with the compendium's myths and legends. According to Professor Sage, Ariane's research had been very thorough.

She searched around the house for an atlas and some blank paper, and started to draw a makeshift map. On it, she marked all of the places linked with the book's myths and legends. When she had finished, she eyed the map with misgivings.

The supposition that her mother had visited any of these places was thin, and it would take months, even years, to travel to all of them. Unless she could narrow down the list.

A few minutes later, she stepped out into the courtyard and dropped a jigger into the canal. It contained a letter for Professor Sage, asking him if he could recall any places outside of Esperance that her mother may have visited.

Chapter Twenty-Two

Esme woke to the sound of Lillian's voice, floating up from below. The threads of everyday life tugged at her, but Esme lay still for a while, tangled up in her fading dreams, letting the music wash over her. Then reality barged back in. She put the pillow over her head and groaned.

The last few notes of Lillian's song ended, followed by the sound of feet coming up the stairs, and a tap on the door.

'Morning,' said Lillian, peeping around the side. 'How are you feeling? Do you still want to go to the dragon festival today? I've got plenty of clothes you can borrow, if you're worried about what to wear—with your leg the way it is.'

Esme threw back the covers and checked her leg. The infection was slowly, but surely, abating. The itching, too, seemed to have died down for now.

She rolled out of bed. 'Of course I'm coming. I wouldn't miss it for anything.'

A short while later, she stood before the long mirror on the door of Lillian's wardrobe, garbed in a floaty chestnut-coloured dress. It was hemmed with red and gold, and in a style she had never worn before, but it was long enough to hide the injury, and loose enough to avoid aggravating it.

She retreated to the edge of Lillian's bed, where she played around with the hem of the dress, lifting it a little and watching it float back down onto her legs.

'What are we going to do about your hair?'

Esme shrugged. 'I know … it's always a mess.'

'It looks like the garden around your mum's studio,' Lillian laughed. 'I can fix it for you, if you like.'

Lillian was always doing something with her hair—sweeping it up and trying new styles—but Esme tended to ignore her own. 'It's okay,' she said. 'I'll just run a comb through it and—'

'But it's always easier when someone else does it, and it's the perfect sort of hair for plaiting.'

Lillian had already advanced on her with the comb, and was deftly separating the strands before Esme could protest any further.

As Lillian worked, Esme's thoughts strayed to the pitted necklace, hidden back in her room. This was her chance to tell Lillian about all that had happened in the chamber: the pearl's allure, the way it had possessed her to swim through the pool, the discovery of her mother's necklace where the pearl should have been.

If Ariane really had taken the pearl, then she was singlehandedly responsible for the earthquakes that had plagued Esperance for the past seven years. She wanted to confide in Lillian, to break down and apologise for her mother's mistakes, but she couldn't bring herself to say it. Her hands fidgeted nervously in her lap.

'Almost done,' said Lillian, misreading Esme's agitation.

Esme went along with it. 'I'm not as patient as you,' she said. 'I was thinking of getting it cut off before I came here.'

'Well, I'm glad you didn't. Look!'

Esme was astounded when she saw Lillian's efforts in the mirror. Her hair was piled up on top of her head, her wayward knots transformed from snares into intricate braids. Something that looked like it would take half a day to accomplish had only taken Lillian a few minutes.

'Thanks,' she said guiltily.

She knew she would have to tell someone what she had discovered. Someone older and more experienced might be able to advise her. To whom could she turn? Celia came to mind—but Esme had misgivings about her now, after all that Lillian and the keeper had said about enchanters.

Outside, the rain of the previous day was gone, and the city smelled fresh, as though it had been rinsed clean overnight in preparation for the day's events. It had donned festive garb as well. Boats were bedecked in blue and gold, and silky banners hung from balconies and windows along the waterways.

In the rush for the ferry, Esme was sure she felt something close behind her—but when she checked, there was nothing there. She dismissed it as another strange effect of the stygian venom.

'What are you waiting for? Come on!' said Lillian, pulling her aboard.

In the din, neither of them noticed as a strange shadow, cast by nothing, slithered behind them onto the ferry. It quickly slipped down the outside of the boat, and became a dark patch lost in the movement of the surging water.

The ferry, full of enthusiastic festivalgoers, soon drew close to the northeast end of the city. It rounded a final bend and pulled up at the mouth of the lagoon. Esme had taken only a few paces on land before she stopped, transfixed at the sight before her.

Far-off clouds mushroomed on the horizon, like distant hills in a vista of blue, forming a serene backdrop to the frenzy of activity above the lagoon. Dragons with scales the colour of jade glittered in the distance, like jewels dropped from the heavens. Beyond them flew a contingent of the vermillion-coloured dragons from Rowana. The Scions—the Esperance dragons—fanned out over the lagoon, where numerous floating platforms were anchored.

Esme and Lillian hurried along to the dragons' den: an enormous, open-roofed building, adjacent to the lagoon. Daniel was waiting for them outside the entrance, although they didn't recognise him at first. He looked as if he had just staggered out of an inferno: his clothes were black and tattered, his face streaked with soot.

'What happened to you?' asked Lillian.

'Part of the job.' He squinted at Esme, the sun shining in his eyes. 'I like your hair like that. How's your leg?'

'Much better.'

As Daniel ushered them into the den, Esme could have sworn she felt a strange presence behind them. She shivered and spun around to see, but, once again, saw nothing.

Inside the den, there was a faint whiff of sulphur in the air, and an acrid odour emanating from blackened patches all over the floor. A pair of Esperance Scions lounged only a few feet away, regal in demeanour, with scales that shone like hammered gold. Excitement spiked through Esme at being in such close proximity to these living furnaces, but still, she kept her distance. Daniel, however, seemed quite at home amongst them. Esme didn't know whether to award him marks for foolishness or for bravery.

He soon led them through an open set of doors, where rangers and dragons milled around on the bank outside. It was a prime spot to view the feats being performed in the lagoon.

The atmosphere was electric. The lagoon was a frenzy of activity, stoked by the whooping and cheering of the crowd. Stands lined the banks; other people watched the spectacle from boats, kept well back from the proceedings by numerous officials.

'It normally costs hundreds of merles to be up this close,' Daniel said smugly. 'But you're getting in free, since you're with me.'

'I'll bear that in mind when I'm being burnt to a crisp,' quipped Lillian.

Esme, however, was riveted by the activity taking place on the lagoon. One group of rangers was simulating rescues, using volunteers from the crowd; further along, a horde of black dragons, distinguished by the thick spikes that ran all the way down their spines to the ends of their tails, flew head-on into a barrage of ice, wind, and rain. Many of the riders toppled from their saddles into the water, to the amusement of the onlookers. The creatures themselves emerged unscathed, shaking off the water and ice, before swooping down to pick up the fallen.

'They're from Tyria, those dragons,' said Daniel. 'That's the sort of weather they have to deal with all the time.'

He kept up a running commentary as the rangers came up with new obstacles and barriers, using their Gifts: whirlpools, water-spouts, and walls of fire.

'Watch out!'

A Scion was flying directly toward them, on its way into the den. Lillian pulled Esme out of the way, just in time. They hung on to each other as the dragon passed overhead, so close that Esme could have reached up and touched the tip of its wing.

Daniel beamed. 'Isn't this great? We're right in the middle of the action.'

Lillian groaned; Esme grinned in wholehearted agreement.

'So, what exactly does a ranger's job involve, apart from—this?' she asked Daniel when there was a break in the festivities.

'Plenty. Rangers patrol Aeolia, lead rescue teams, offer emergency aid, and help with stuff like mapping the seafloor. Look! Those dragons are from Pelorus.'

He pointed toward some dragons further out in the lagoon. Their teal-coloured bodies were fringed with white, and watching them fly was like watching waves crest in the sky. One climbed high above the others and hung there, motionless, before dropping down in a spectacular vertical dive. It contracted its wings completely, its head straining forward until it resembled a tightly wound chrysalis. The rider flattened out, and Esme's breath hitched as she watched their fearless descent. The pair torpedoed into the water, and she quickly trained her binoculars on it to see how they had fared. The Pelorusian dragon resurfaced almost at once, propelling itself out of the water in one fluid motion. For a moment, its body appeared smooth, until it unfolded its wings and its scales rippled back into view. Its rider, safely astride its back, punched the air to tumultuous roars from the crowd.

While the spectators were noisily demanding an encore, a uniformed man strode over to speak to Daniel. He was of stocky build and his face was flecked with red and grey bristle. His gruff voice cut through the applause.

'Ah, Daniel said that a few of his friends would be coming to watch. He's the best helper we've ever had. I'd like to steal him for our own den, one of these days.'

Daniel shoved his hands in his pocket and shuffled with embarrassment. 'Er, thanks.'

'Just needs to work on his manners. Aren't you going to introduce us?'

'Oh, yeah, sorry. This is Tristan, the Rowana dragonmaster. Tristan, this is Esme and Lillian.'

Before Daniel could say anything else, a dragon and its rider landed effortlessly beside them. The rider slid off the dragon's back; it was the boy who had waved at Daniel from the sky two days ago. He was redheaded, like Tristan, with deep green eyes, and his long shag of hair was tied back in a ponytail. A large scar covered most of the left side of his face.

The boy clapped a hand on Daniel's shoulder, and his eyes ranged over the two visitors. 'You must be Esme and Lillian,' he said. 'Daniel mentioned you might turn up.'

'My son Rhys,' said Tristan. 'And his dragon, Tango.'

The resemblance between father and son was more than just physical. It was the way they held themselves: relaxed, but also alert.

'She's not quite mine yet,' said Rhys.

'True. Rhys is still in training,' said Tristan. 'He finished school last year, and works with the dragons full-time now, but he won't be a ranger until next year.'

'The minimum age, usually, is eighteen,' explained Daniel.

'I suppose you know by now that your friend is quite the expert on dragons,' said Rhys.

Lillian laughed. 'That's all he'd talk about if we didn't shut him up.'

'Well, I've told him he's welcome to come stay with us anytime, in Rowana. You, too, as long as you don't mind sleeping in the den.'

While the others talked on, Esme was distracted by the presence of Rhys's dragon, Tango. Primal energy radiated from her even as she rested, wings folded over orange scales that glowed richly, like the afternoon sun shining through the autumnal hues of a forest. Without thinking, Esme walked straight up to her and put her hand on her flank.

'Wait, I wouldn't—' Rhys called out.

Upon Esme's touch, Tango's scales retracted, the same way the Pelorusian dragon's had when it had emerged from the water. They flattened against the dragon's body to form a tight, impenetrable shield—like living armour.

Esme drew back. 'Sorry, I didn't think ...'

'It's okay,' said Rhys, coming over. 'You're fine. Tango's young and unpredictable, that's all. And usually not too keen on strangers.' He smiled. 'But she seems to be all right with you. Their scales do that to help them move through the water ... but it also means that she likes you.'

Tango raised her fiery orange head toward Esme. Her black, slit-like pupils, islands of molten lava, drew Esme into their depths. The festival swirled around her, forgotten.

'What's it like, riding one?' she asked.

'Better than anything you could ever imagine,' said Rhys. 'But being on a dragon's back doesn't mean a lot—to them. Half the time, it feels like they know what needs to be done before we do. We're often the ones playing catch-up. Makes it interesting.'

'But dangerous,' said Tristan, approaching them.

Rhys nodded. 'The dragons are used to their power. Sometimes they forget—and we forget, too—that we aren't made of the same stuff.' He put his hand to the scarred side of his face. 'But it gets in your blood. I couldn't imagine doing anything else.'

Tristan and Rhys departed, but Esme lingered by Tango a little longer. She tentatively rested her hand against Tango's flank again, feeling the dragon's warmth thrum beneath her fingers.

As she watched the pageant of colour in the distance, Esme was reminded of the Aurora of Aeolia: the dragons' effortless flight through the huge corridors of colour. She was reminded, too, of the pearl, resplendent in Queen Sofia's hand, another force just as potent as Tango's. The dragon's power seemed to magnify the pearl's presence within her, its cool beauty calling out to her.

Esme's bravado slipped away, and she felt her own insignificance in between these two monumental forces. She stepped away from Tango and walked back to join the others, feeling deeply disturbed. She, and her mother, had become entangled in matters far beyond their capacity—with forces far beyond their understanding—and it seemed there was no right way forward.

Chapter Twenty-Three

The sun was disappearing behind the rooftops when Esme and Lillian took their leave of Daniel, wandering through the arts quarter on their way to the palace plaza. It was quieter here than usual, like a ghost town compared with the frenzied atmosphere in which they had immersed themselves all day.

The many buskers who were normally a fixture of these streets had made themselves scarce. Only the moody notes of a wind instrument drifted toward them on the breeze. It had a mournful tone to it, and Esme half-expected a ghostly musician to float around the corner—one of the long-departed residents of the quarter, reclaiming the streets from the living for just a few hours.

Esme paused before a wreath of twigs hung on one house's front door, threaded with shells, tiny tridents, bells, starfish, and seed pearls. 'I've seen a few of these before, on other doors around the city.'

'They're put out for protection,' said Lillian. 'It's an old tradition.'

On the banks of the wide waterway that bordered the arts quarter, they stopped to watch a girl performing feats on the canal's surface. She moved like the wind, executing leaps and pirouettes that were already difficult to perform on solid ground. From the shore, other performers were sending trails of fire across the water, which she teased toward her, before twirling away from them. The fire was coming from their outstretched hands, the same way Esme had seen other people send out ice and water. Occasionally the girl's Gift would fail, and she would sink down in the water, only to bravely rise again.

A few steps on, Esme sensed the same eerie presence she had felt earlier that day. Out of the corner of her eye, she spied a shadow running along the wall a few feet behind them—stopping when they stopped, and creeping along behind them when they started up again. It stretched and shifted as it moved, dissolving into pockets of black, where corners bent into darkness, and night already nestled.

Her pulse quickened. 'Look. On the wall behind us,' she whispered to Lillian. 'A shadow, but it's not attached to anything. I think it's been following us all day. What *is* it?'

'I don't know, but it's giving me the creeps.' Lillian shook a fist at the dark blot. 'Go away!'

The shadow merely retreated up under the eaves.

'Let's get out of here,' said Lillian.

'There's not much point. I think it can follow us wherever it wants.'

The preternatural thing hung there in the gloom. Fear glued itself to the bottom of Esme's ribs, making it difficult to breathe, but she stayed there, staring up at it.

It's only a shadow, she said to herself, trying to imbue herself with courage.

Esme stepped toward it, and spoke in a level voice. 'What do you want? Why are you following us?'

The shadow did not reply; instead, it began to grow in size. It played along the walls, sliding over the bricks, expanding until it was much bigger than both Esme and Lillian. Then the shadow spoke, in a voice that was hollow and devoid of life.

'You ... You seek what is not rightfully yours. The pearl belongs to her now.'

'Her?' The hard mass of dread beneath Esme's ribs rose up into her throat. 'Who is she?'

The shadow fell silent. It shrunk again and slid back up under the eaves.

Lillian's face had gone white. 'What was all that supposed to mean?'

Esme shook her head. 'I don't have a clue.'

But the words hounded her as they made their way to the plaza, echoing the fears that had already taken hold within her.

The pearl belongs to her now.

By nightfall, Esme and Lillian had arrived at the plaza, where lanterns swung from a multitude of market stalls. Tantalising aromas filled the air, wafting from stalls that offered meats and seafood grilling above burning coals; children's cries rang from the direction of the palace gardens, where the dragon topiaries had been enchanted, and now prowled the grounds.

Other children strayed around the plaza, queuing to buy trinkets and temporary tattoos. Esme watched as one boy rubbed at a fresh tattoo on his arm; it leaped up into the air, a ghostly miniature dragon in flight, before fading away.

Daniel joined up with them shortly afterwards, minus the soot, and together they ended the evening leaning against the balustrade of the palace bridge. Will-o'-the-wisps, conjured up for the festival, drifted over the canals. Music echoed across the water as a trio of ethereal musicians—two violinists and a cellist—entered the lake.

The boat they travelled in was virtually transparent, dark water visible through the hull. The musicians raised a bow in acknowledgement of the audience on the bridge, and continued under—or rather, through—the solid stone structure. The diaphanous figures floated on, leaving only the strains of their plaintive air on the wind.

'That's what's left of the Tobias family,' remarked Lillian. 'The story goes that a few centuries ago, they were serenading the city, just the way they are now, when a bridge collapsed on them. They returned to the canals a few months later, still making music, as if nothing had even happened.'

Esme watched the trio depart, rather horrified by the story, while Daniel and Lillian barely blinked.

'That'll be me one day,' said Daniel. 'Shot out of the sky by a Gift gone awry. And then I'll fly around, astride my ghostly dragon, haunting the city.'

'And what? Scare the birds?' jeered Lillian.

As if on cue, the birds in the palace gardens suddenly went silent. The trees shook as the birds flew off, frightened by something unseen. Moments later, a tremor rumbled beneath the bridge, ruffling the surface of the water. It died away as quickly as it came. Minor tremors had been disturbing the city on and off all week, but this was the first of the day.

'Lucky again this year,' said Lillian. 'Like last year. I'm sure Mum's been on tenterhooks all day.'

'Lucky,' echoed Esme, but her words felt fraudulent.

'Aeolia's travails have ceased, now that the pearl has been returned to Ephyra. The earth will no longer split and sigh beneath us.'

If the health of the world really was dependent on the Pearl of Esperance, then it would take more than just luck to remedy it.

Mum … What have you done?

Chapter Twenty-Four

Esme and Lillian stood by the lagoon at the northernmost point of the city, in the midst of the ruins of an old fortress. Heavy clouds dimmed the face of the water. Wind whipped at Esme's face and hair, and shrieked through arched stone doorways that led nowhere. Beneath her, grass and weeds ran wild between ravaged blocks of stone.

A letter had come from Celia the previous day, asking Esme to meet her at the Citadel. Lillian had brought her here, but Esme wasn't sure why.

Maybe it's across the lagoon, she thought.

When she searched the water to the west, she couldn't believe her eyes.

Debris littered the seafloor: hazy shapes that didn't belong underwater, the shapes of submerged houses with crumbling chimneys. And people—she could see several figures weaving in and out amongst the buildings.

'It's like a whole other city—underwater,' Esme breathed, transfixed.

'Part of a city,' said Lillian. 'Our city. A few years ago, a whole district of Esperance sunk into the lagoon after one of the worst quakes.'

'And people still live there?'

'Not many … just a few. The council tried to relocate them, but there wasn't enough space in Esperance for everybody whose home had been destroyed. When the council tried to send them to other islands, some refused to leave their homes.'

Appalled, Esme stared down into the crumbling metropolis. 'Of course. Because you can all breathe underwater.'

Lillian nodded. 'But even with all the enchantments to make life bearable down there, it can't compare to life above the surface. I just hope the rest of the city manages to stay afloat.' She sighed. 'Better go, or you'll be late.'

'About that—where exactly *is* the Citadel?

Lillian pointed to the ground beneath them. 'Down there.'

'Here? There's nothing here but ruins.'

'It's underground. The Citadel used to be a key post for warding off Tyrian attacks during the wars. But when the top half was destroyed at the end of the war, the rest of it became a prison.'

A small building, adjacent to the ruins, proved to be the entrance. A silent, scowling sentry stood motionless by the door; he let them pass only after Esme told him of her appointment with Celia. Lillian stayed above ground while a uniformed guard escorted Esme down a dungeon-like stairwell into the Citadel proper.

Lamps flickered at intervals along rough-hewn rock walls, and Esme was plagued by visions of prisoners being marched down here to begin their incarceration. She had to remind herself, more than once, that she was only visiting. When she reached the bottom of the stairs and turned into a corridor, something clicked.

I've seen this place before.

It didn't come to her at first, but then she remembered: she had seen it in the pictures accompanying the article about Nathan Mare's trial.

The sense of oppression was so great that by the time they arrived at Celia's office, Esme was convinced she was about to receive some terrible news. The guard stopped before a door at the end of the passageway and gave it a sharp rap.

'Come in.'

Celia occupied a desk at the far end of the narrow room, before a thick glass window, cut into the rock. The unbound world of the lagoon floated by outside. To the far left, Esme could glimpse part of the drowned district. Light diffused into the water from above, and indistinct shapes moved further out in the gloom.

The chief enchantress had dressed in her usual severe attire. Her only accessory was a jewelled brooch, glinting on her lapel.

'Have a seat. Thank you for coming.'

The councillor grimaced as howls of distress came up from below. She drummed her fingers on the desk, as if trying to tap the noise away. 'I'm afraid this isn't the most pleasant of places to meet, but I'm required to spend a few days a week here as part of my duties.'

Esme braced herself. 'Is this something about my mum? Bad news?'

The enchantress had perfected the art of revealing nothing about herself. It was impossible to tell whether her cold demeanour was part of the armour she wore to survive her job, or whether it was something else. She didn't answer directly.

'You may not know this, but any matters related to the security of Esperance find their way to me, eventually. A vagrant by the name of Quigley was brought into hospital yesterday. He'd been afflicted with some terrible disease; he barely looked human. And he was raving—delirious. Close to death. But before he passed away, he moaned about the same things, over and over again. Nathan Mare, a lost pearl, experiments, the earthquakes—even the ray that attacked you in the lake. And he said something about being … "betrayed".'

Esme took in every word, thinking quickly. There was no doubt in her mind that this man by the name of Quigley was the same person who had mistaken her for Ariane. Furthermore, the name rang a bell, somewhere in the back of her mind. She could feel Celia coolly assessing her, the way she probably did with prisoners every day.

'But what has this got to do with my mother?'

Celia tapped her nails on the table again. 'He mentioned her by name. Multiple times.'

Celia's words shook Esme to the core. Quigley had mentioned both the pearl and Ariane in his dying breaths. Outwardly, Esme worked to maintain an illusion of calm. Inside, things had taken a chaotic turn. She thought back to the dark, dank stygian chamber, to the force that had propelled her through the murky water.

If Esme, herself, had found the pearl there—if the spell over her hadn't been broken—she was sure that she would have taken it without a second thought.

But did that mean her mother would have done the same?

When she spoke again, Esme couldn't hide the slight tremor in her voice. 'I—I don't understand. How could they have even known each other?'

Celia leaned forward, her eyes pinholes of black. 'I know that you have been conducting your own search into your mother's affairs. Have you come across any information that may shed light on what this Quigley was saying?'

Esme's hand went to her necklace.

Only information that would incriminate her.

During the whole conversation, the howls from below had continued unabated. Now she heard a crack, like wood against bone, and whoever had been complaining abruptly stopped.

Celia raised her eyebrows. 'No?'

She pushed back her chair and stepped over to the window, beckoning for Esme to join her there. A school of small fish swam past, then flicked away, diving deeper. Seconds later, a much larger fish swept by, one with brilliant stripes and menacing fangs.

Celia turned away from the window and absently rubbed at the brooch pinned to her black jacket. Esme's eye was drawn to the small golden trident, formed from a three-headed sea serpent. Embedded in each head was a tiny sparkling jewel.

Celia noticed Esme's interest, and deftly unpinned the brooch. 'This is the emblem of the enchanters. Here, take a closer look.'

As soon as Esme held it in her hand, her mind was freed. It was as if she was out there beyond the glass window, riding the open ocean's endless rolling waves and swells. Along with the sense of freedom came a strong urge to confess all the information she had on the chamber. Only a moment ago, she'd been clear on her reasons for not telling Celia all the details; now a fog obscured her thinking. The full tale was about to spin out of her when other, unpleasant memories rose up in her mind: dreams of her mother drowning, the broken link in Ariane's necklace, the yawning stygians beneath her, the danger she was in. She opened her mouth, and Celia leaned forward. Then she snapped it shut.

Esme blinked. She returned the brooch and Celia pinned it back on her lapel.

'What—what was that? I could see the ocean, and ...'

'Just a little something we use on recalcitrant prisoners.' A slight smile played around Celia's lips. 'Of course, it doesn't work on everyone. With your presence of mind, I think you would have made a good enchanter.'

Esme glared at her. 'You can't use something like that on me. I'm not one of your prisoners. I came here of my own free will.'

Celia sighed. 'I am merely trying to ascertain the truth, but perhaps I did overstep the mark. Please accept my apologies. I also asked you in because I have something for you to see.'

She returned to her seat, opened a drawer in her desk, and produced a folder. 'As Mare's case remains open, the city still has all of his medical files. I thought you might like to see your mother's.'

Esme blanched. 'She was a patient of his? I thought she was just a friend.'

'She was both, it seems. You have my permission to go through it, but only while you are here. I must warn you: the prosecutors of his case have been over the evidence many times. But, if it can give you peace of mind, you should have the chance to see it for yourself. I'll get the guard to take you to a room upstairs.'

The chief enchantress escorted her to the door, and handed over the file, but not before giving Esme a smile tinged with regret. 'Good luck, Esme. And remember, I'm on your side, no matter what anyone might say.'

❧

Esme and Lillian were ushered into a small room off the waiting area, furnished with only a battered metal table and half a dozen chairs. A lamp hung from the ceiling, casting a ring of light over the dented table top.

'This place gives me the creeps,' said Lillian. 'Like they're going to lock us up if we stay too long. What did Celia say?'

Esme's jaw tightened. 'She questioned me like *I* was a prisoner. And then she used something enchanted, a brooch, to try and squeeze information out of me.'

Lillian snorted. 'That's just like her. Mum says Celia's only good at her job because she can find out everything about everyone. And use it against them, if it suits her.' She noticed the folder in Esme's hands. 'What's that?'

The manila folder, yellowed with age, bore the name 'Ariane Silver', inked in black.

'A medical file on Mum. Celia gave it to me. Apparently Mum was one of Dr Mare's patients.'

Esme leafed through the thin pages. It was difficult to decipher the entries on each page, all in medical shorthand, but Mare's signature was there, after each log. Each entry was dated.

That's odd, thought Esme. *He started treating Mum the year I was born.*

A letter was clipped into the file, in her mother's handwriting.

Dr Mare,

I'm sorry to have taken so long to write back, but with this letter comes wonderful news. Last week I was blessed with the arrival of a beautiful baby girl. I took your elixir every day as instructed, and Esme now sleeps peacefully beside me, thanks to you. Everything has progressed the way we hoped, although I've begun to develop terrible headaches. Until my next visit to Esperance, take care. In the meantime, please accept my heartfelt thanks. I remain eternally in your debt.

Ariane Silver

There were more entries in the file for further visits in the years after her birth. All of them were in Mare's handwriting. Once she had finished reading, she passed the file over to Lillian and rocked back on her chair, too shaken to speak. Now she knew why Ariane was 'indebted' to Mare.

This was no longer just about her mother. It intimately involved *her*. A strange flutter started up in the pit of her stomach. She had no idea that her mother had experienced any problems with her pregnancy.

Lillian stopped at the page with the letter.

'I don't know what to make of it. It sounds like he saved your life … but what else did he do?'

'I think this is what the keeper meant, when he said that someone had tampered with my Gift. I said it couldn't have been Mare, as I'd only just arrived in Esperance, but I *had* been here before. I just didn't know it.'

'But if he was helping your mother through her pregnancy, why would that have anything to do with your Gift—and hers?'

'I don't know. But I remember reading about his trial. When he was meant to be helping all those people who were dying, he did something to their Gifts, too. Maybe he just couldn't help himself,' she said bitterly.

The sound of approaching footsteps spurred Esme into action. She hurriedly unclipped the letter, and secreted it in her pocket.

Esme's sleep was troubled again that night. Stygians still haunted her dreams, but so did images of faceless men and women, standing cold and merciless over Ariane's body. A baby whimpered in the distance, its cries turning into screams of pain. Her eyes flew open, and the images evaporated into the night.

She woke with a start, and her feelings of helplessness shifted to fury: fury at the fate of her mother, and at the faceless figures who had taken advantage of her; fury at people like Dr Mare, who wrapped themselves in shadows, leaving riddles in their wake.

Chapter Twenty-Five

The first light of day was peeping through the shutters, but Esme's body still clung to sleep, protesting the early hour. As she leaned over to sip some water from the glass beside her bed, she noticed that the water's surface was dancing to a fine vibration, one that she couldn't feel herself. A moment later, the lampshade hanging above her bed began to sway.

Esme snapped bolt upright.

Soon the whole house was pitching from side to side, like a ship caught in a storm. The swaying went on and on, and so did the deafening roar. Dust came out of the walls and clouded the air. Drawers flew open, and the mirror hanging over the chest of drawers shivered and shook, threatening to smash into a thousand pieces.

I have to get out of here.

Any moment now, the floor was going to drop away, collapse in on itself like a house of cards.

Esme reeled out of bed and lurched across the floor.

Once, when she had been very little, she had lost her parents at a crowded fair. The same terror seized her now. The thunder coming up from below seemed to have no end. She grabbed the things that were about to topple off the dresser, and took refuge under the desk for what felt like an age.

When the earthquake finally faded, she opened her bedroom door to find Miranda and Lillian standing outside, their faces solemn and pale. Miranda's dressing gown was slipping off her shoulders, her hair askew. Lillian was in a similar state.

'We were coming to see if you were all right,' said Miranda, in a strained voice. 'Lillian said you've never been in an earthquake that bad before.'

Esme dropped down onto the top step and wrapped her arms around her legs.

'That was horrible,' she said shakily. 'I can't believe this has been going on for so long.'

Lillian hunched down beside her.

'There'll be some real damage this time,' said Miranda. 'We're probably okay, but ...'

Miranda was right. No. 8 had suffered only minimal damage. Downstairs, the kitchen was littered with broken crockery, while outside, more roof tiles had been thrown off into the courtyard. One of them had struck the table, further chipping the siren's tesserae. Esme tried to gather up the fragments and piece them back together. It proved a hopeless task.

Miranda left shortly afterwards to help with the citywide clean up, while Esme and Lillian spent the rest of the morning assisting the family who lived behind No. 8. Lillian's neighbour, heavily pregnant, greeted them with a weary smile.

'Thanks for coming. Morning sickness was bad enough, but waking up to this?'

Much of the scaffolding that surrounded the house had collapsed, taking some of the new brickwork with it. The young children of the family played amongst the debris while Esme and Lillian picked up around them.

Back at No. 8, they discovered two jiggers knocking against the flap in the kitchen. One was from Lillian's father, asking if they were okay; the other from Miranda. The colour drained from Lillian's face as she read her mother's note.

'What is it?' asked Esme.

'Mum says the Keeper's Tower has collapsed.'

Esme's face fell. 'The Keeper's Tower?'

The ground underneath her wasn't moving anymore, but it felt like it was. The most recognisable landmark in the city, gone in an instant.

'But we were there just the other day!' she cried. 'Was anyone hurt?'

'Not seriously. Just some minor injuries. Mum said to go out and help if we want, but to be careful.'

Daniel turned up in *Talia* a short while later, and the three of them spent the rest of the day traversing the city by boat, offering to help out where they could. Yellow rescue boats plied the canals, carrying the injured to safety. More roofs had fallen in; more windows had been blown out, more canals closed off. Nobody on the shores said much as they stacked fallen bricks or swept up broken glass, grime and resignation etched upon their features.

As the boat rounded each bend, a fresh wave of guilt passed over Esme. The sight of the families they passed, mired in grief beside their ruined homes, pressed down on her until she couldn't bear to see any more.

From time to time, *Talia* passed by the plaza, where the spire of the Keeper's Tower, the tallest building in Esperance, had once crowned the city.

'I keep looking out for it,' said Lillian. 'How can it be gone, just like that? It's like there's a hole in the sky.'

Esme glanced over at their forlorn faces, still gazing up into the empty sky. Her insides churned like magma.

There was too much at stake to hide the truth any longer.

Later that afternoon, the three of them slumped down, dirt-streaked and exhausted, around the kitchen table of No. 8. Esme pushed herself up from the table and excused herself. A few minutes later, she returned with her mother's necklace, and laid it on the table.

'I've got something to tell you.'

It could easily have been a relic of the day: something ruined but still precious, rescued from the rubble. Lillian took it up and rubbed at the pitted letter 'A.'

When she finally spoke, the rigours of the day showed in her face; her voice was tired and strained. 'Isn't this your mother's necklace?'

Esme's fears crowded in on her. She took a deep breath before answering. 'I think so. I found it in the chamber in the Merle Fountain.'

'*What*? Didn't Mum say that Ariane lost this just before she disappeared? So she must have gotten out of there okay. This is good news, isn't it?'

'I think so.' Esme twisted her hands together. 'Except—I can't help thinking that Mum might have taken the pearl. If she did, then … the earthquakes must be all her fault.'

'Why leap to that conclusion?' asked Daniel. 'I doubt she was the first person to have discovered the chamber. We weren't.' He exchanged looks with Lillian. 'Why didn't you show us earlier?'

Heat flooded Esme's face. 'I'm sorry. I should have. It was lodged in the pedestal, where the pearl was meant to be. I swam out to the pedestal, past the stygians … They were sleeping in the pool. I should have got out once I saw them, but I didn't. I kept going.'

Lillian stared at her in shock, while Daniel looked a little impressed.

'Don't get the wrong idea. I didn't swim out there because of Mum—I *wish* that had been the reason.'

'So why did you?'

'Because of the pearl. All I could think about in there was seeing it again … the way I saw it in my vision. It *does* something to you, corrupts you, compels you, makes you want it for yourself. I *had* to see if it was on the pedestal.'

The plea for understanding in her voice wasn't just for them. It was for herself, too. She hated the pearl for its hold on her, but her anger could never last. Whenever she thought of the jewel, it flooded her mind with its beauty, and she was helpless again under its thrall.

'I can't help but think … What if Mum took it when she went

into the chamber? The king and queen returned it to the city, but now it's gone again. Maybe all of this—the earthquakes, the problems with the Gifts—is all her fault.'

No one spoke for a long moment. Water swished outside. A boat passed, a tapering shadow in the encroaching darkness. Esme waited for her friends' recrimination, her ears burning in advance.

'Oh, Esme,' said Lillian. 'What were you thinking, keeping all this to yourself?'

Esme blinked. Lillian looked sympathetic, not angry. Daniel cast her a long, quizzical glance, then took up the compendium and leafed through the pages, until he found what he was looking for.

'According to this, people have *died* looking for this pearl. It leaves a trail of destruction everywhere it goes. It seems pretty clear—from what it says in here, and what you've said—that you've fallen under the pearl's sway. It's not like you could have helped it.'

'Daniel's right, for once,' said Lillian. 'Don't blame yourself. We just have to get on and deal with this—together.'

They adjourned to the living room, where Esme stayed on edge, waiting for her friends to realise how much she had let them down. They had every right to be angry, to close ranks. Instead they plied her with questions. Daniel wanted to know everything about her visit to Celia, and what the enchantress had said about Quigley. As Esme spoke, her defences fell away, bit by bit.

'Quigley. That was his name: the man who chased after me, on my way to Sofia Square. He'd been brought into hospital, close to death, and delirious. Before he passed away, he raved on about Mare … about the pearl. He even mentioned the creature from the lagoon. And he kept repeating my mother's name, over and over again.'

'Quigley …' said Daniel, staring off into the distance and rubbing at his tattoo. 'Wasn't he mentioned in that article on Mare, the one we read in the Temple Library? One of Mare's colleagues?'

So that's where I've heard his name before.

Esme passed him the letter from Ariane's medical file.

'At the end of her interview, Celia gave this to me. My mother wasn't just a friend of Mare's. She was a patient of his, too.'

There's no getting away from him, she thought. Mare's fingerprints were everywhere, when it came to her mother—and herself.

As Daniel read the letter, his features settled into a deep scowl. Meanwhile, Lillian picked up the indigo shell, which Esme had left on the driftwood table.

'Put it to your ear,' said Esme.

'Hm?'

'It takes a while to come through, but there's a song inside. Like the bell in the hallway.'

'Really?'

Lillian held it to her ear and listened with keen interest. Finally, she lowered it, and gave Esme a look of wonder.

'There *is* a songspell in there—only, it hasn't been put in there by a songstress.'

'What do you mean?'

'It's a *siren's* song. Sirens are so reclusive … they only associate with highly accomplished songstresses. How could your mother have gotten hold of something like this?'

'I don't know,' said Esme, picking up the compendium, 'but I'm sure there was a part about sirens, somewhere in here.'

She found the relevant entry, and began to read aloud.

The Isle of Mists

The Isle of Mists is reputed to have been the ancestral home of the sirens. Sirens lived in the waters of Aeolia long before humans ventured here, and when the islands of Aeolia rose from the sea, they were given their own paradise, shrouded in a healing, life-giving mist. The isle has long since vanished, but its fate is forever enshrined in the sirens' legends: a solemn reminder of the heavy price they once paid for setting themselves above the gods.

When humans first came to Aeolia, and the gods spread magic through the oceans, the sirens were entrusted with the guardianship of Aeolia's song magic. All songspells draw upon the same source when they are cast, and legend has it that this magic stems from a vast pool in the centre of the isle. However, after many years of composing songspells, the sirens began to forget their origins, and became consumed by the power within their grasp.

This angered the gods. A shadow soon passed over the isle: a curse that made the mist poisonous, crystallised the pools and waterfalls, and turned the sirens' home barren. The sirens, seeing the errors of their ways, scattered to every part of the globe, each taking with them some water from the isle's pool.

Before leaving, they threaded songspells of healing into the shells on the isle's beaches, hoping that one day they might return and find their home restored. Alas, this was never to be. Chastened by their actions and forever grieving their beloved home, the sirens resumed their appointed tasks as guardians of the songspells, and worked diligently to train songstresses and bards in their ways.

Esme examined the painting accompanying the text: an Eden-like isle, replete with flowing streams, springs, and waterfalls. A shell-strewn beach curved around the island's edge. Her mother had painted the island at sunset, and the shells in the foreground glittered like a galaxy of stars.

A galaxy of stars ...

Her eyes fell on Ariane's shell. 'Look!' She grabbed the shell and placed it beside the painting. 'It matches.'

Lillian bent over the page and studied the painting. 'You're right! It looks just like it belongs on that beach. Maybe your mother went to see the sirens, when she was researching their home.'

'Well ...' Esme went to retrieve the rough map she had drawn a few days earlier. 'I made this the other day, after going through all of Mum's things. I assumed she would have visited some of the places she painted, but there was no way of knowing which ones. So I sent a letter to the professor asking him, but he couldn't remember much. And there was nothing in her notes. But I didn't mark the Isle of Mists, of course. How could I?'

Lillian picked up a pen. 'Give it here.' She began to scribble on the map, pondering out loud. 'The sirens live in isolated caves, scattered around the globe. I've always wanted to visit them, but it's not so easy. Like I said, they keep to themselves; they're very private. No one can enter their caves except select songstresses and bards. But, we have the shell ... that might help.'

Lillian finished drawing, and laid the map on the table. Five tiny sirens dotted the ocean.

'The oldest cave of them all is here,' she said, pointing at one to the north of Esperance. 'We could get a clipper part of the way there. They go most days.'

'What? You really think we should try and visit them?' asked Esme.

'Why not? I'm telling you, Esme, I don't see any other way your mother could have gotten this shell. The sirens wouldn't give something like this to a stranger.'

Daniel eyed the map with great interest. He drew a line with his finger, from the sirens' caves to a nearby squiggle. 'This is Asha, the capital of Rowana. Tristan and Rhys said we could visit whenever we like, remember?'

Esme gazed down at the map, remembering how terrible she had felt the day she had drawn it. That day, the venom-induced visions had been at their worst; that day, she had never felt more alone in the world. The future was still as fearful as ever, but at least now she wasn't facing it by herself.

She turned this revelation round and round in her head. It didn't feel real enough to stick, but she felt lighter than she had all day. She folded up the map and nodded at the others.

'Then let's take them up on their offer,' she said.

Chapter Twenty-Six

The *Windspur*'s golden prow, carved into the shape of a dragon, scythed effortlessly through the waters of the lagoon. Sails ruffled overhead, great white flags billowing below an expanse of blue sky.

Two days had passed since Esme, Daniel, and Lillian's decision to travel to Asha. Miranda, who knew Tristan and his family from their regular trips to the annual dragon festivals, had been more than happy to let Esme and Lillian escape for a few days. Daniel's parents had proved harder to persuade, only giving their begrudging consent after Daniel promised to accompany his father on two more work trips before the end of summer.

Now they were on their way, coasting by the last of the tiny islands fringing the Esperance lagoon. The city shrunk steadily behind them, until it was only a faint line in the distance. As the towers and spires of Esperance dipped beyond the horizon, Esme tried to ignore the sinking feeling inside her. She may have successfully retraced her mother's steps in the city, but now she was venturing out into the unknown, with nothing to guide her but a shell and a map.

And my friends, she reminded herself.

Daniel and Lillian were leaning over the ship's rails, watching Esperance disappear into the distance. She'd never had friends like these. After all her worrying, they didn't think any less of her, despite what her mother might have done. And she needed them—she realised that now. They could think clearly where she couldn't; they had her back, even when she felt like she had one hand tied behind it.

She had been so sure they would reject her; but then, Esme had never really had many friends, so how could she be sure? After her mother had disappeared, she had learned to rely on herself. She had holed up in the lighthouse, waiting for Ariane to come home, so she could prove everyone wrong.

It was hard not to become infected with the sheer joy of their windborne journey. Salty air rushed past, the sails straining to catch every last bit of wind. The piercing cries of gulls faded as the birds wheeled back toward land, only to be replaced by the voice of the shipmaster, crying out orders for the working of the sails. No crewmen did his bidding; the craft responded by itself, the sails furling and unfurling as though invisible sailors were working the ropes.

The sleek clipper soon entered the wilder waters of the Tiamat Sea. Esme braced herself against the side of the boat as the *Windspur* rode the swell.

Daniel tapped her on the shoulder. 'Look.'

Just ahead lay a large patch of calm water, bang in the middle of the rough sea. The swell heaved at the edge of the anomaly, but fell back at an invisible barrier. It didn't look real; it was as if someone had cut out a piece of the ocean and forgot to put it back.

Maybe it's a mirage, Esme thought. *Like the waterfall in the Temple Library.*

The *Windspur* sailed straight on to the glassy expanse. At once, the ship stopped rolling about, and the deck steadied under their feet. The sails flapped due to the loss of wind, and the ship's ropes ran up and down to adjust them.

'What's going on?' Esme asked the others.

'We're taking a shortcut through a portal,' Lillian explained. 'Otherwise, it would take us weeks to get to Rowana.'

'Next stop's Palmina, in Pelorus,' said Daniel.

The temperature rose several degrees as the boat sailed through the calm water. Esme peeled off a layer of clothing. After a short while, the deck began to toss beneath them again, and a sprawling island blinked into view. The *Windspur* docked at Palmina Island, the main settlement in Pelorus, to discharge passengers and take on more.

It was soon back on course, skirting the island's eastern coast as it continued north. As they passed mile after mile of sunburnt sands, Esme spied a flight of riderless dragons, the same blue and white Pelorusian dragons she had seen at the Esperance dragon festival. They played amongst the waves, far off in the distance.

Daniel grabbed his spyglass and trained it on them.

'Spinners! Looks like they've found themselves a feast.'

He handed Esme the spyglass, and she squinted through it, just as one of the dragons flew up from the water, swinging a ray by its tail. For just a split second, the full length of the ray came into view. It was much larger than a usual ray, and its head was flared. It looked almost like a hooded grey ghost—

She almost dropped the spyglass in surprise.

'That's the same kind of ray that attacked us in the lake!'

They ran to the ship's stern to see more, but by then the dragons were too far away. Everyone watched in uneasy silence as the island of Palmina receded into the distance.

An hour later, the boat sailed on to another patch of eerie calm. The sea and sky grew so still so quickly, it was as if they had sailed into the eye of a cyclone. The ship adjusted its sails partway through the passageway, and this time, when they came out the other side, the temperature dropped.

A flock of seagulls awaited them at the portal's edge, squawking for scraps. They trailed the boat all the way into shore.

Asha, the largest island in the Rowana archipelago, came into view. Clouds hovered around the volcanic mountain at its peak. Beneath it spread a town, around a wide harbour.

Esme, Daniel, and Lillian disembarked to the notes of a wind harp, set on the shore where the grass met the sand. They flung their bags down beside the stringed instrument, and gradually their legs grew accustomed to being back on land.

A family was picnicking nearby, and children chased each other along the beach. One of them, a little girl, raced past the wind harp and then doubled back. She stopped before Esme and fixed her with an unsettling stare.

'I thought people were only supposed to have one shadow,' said the girl.

Filled with dread, Esme twisted around. All she could see was her own silhouette, stretching out behind her in the afternoon sun. 'What did you say?'

The child had already skipped away.

Lillian blanched. 'Did that *thing* follow us here?'

Esme hadn't seen the shadow since they had confronted it in the arts quarter. Along with Lillian, she looked for it amongst the grass, by the wind harp, even on the trunks of trees. A deep hollow scarred one tree and Esme peered into its depths.

'What are you two doing?' asked Daniel, coming up behind them.

'There was a shadow,' answered Esme, 'following us at the dragon festival. It must have come with us on the boat, all the way here.'

Daniel frowned. 'A shadow?'

Esme hitched her gear up on to her back. 'It's weird ... it's not attached to anything. Just a shadow, on its own. I think it might have something to do with the pearl.'

Daniel circled around, searching the ground and trees, shielding his eyes from the sun. 'I can't see it.'

'We can't catch it, or trap it,' said Lillian. 'All we can do is ignore it, I guess.'

Daniel took up his bag. 'Rhys said to skip the town and head west. There's a path along the shore.'

Following Rhys's instructions, they skirted the town and traipsed along a well-worn path toward the western side of the island. The track followed a gradual incline up to the headland. Closer to the point, Esme noticed the first signs of habitation: half a dozen small boats idling by a shed, tucked into the rocks beside the headland.

The headland itself afforded an impressive view to the west. Waves broke beside the point, foaming white on to a black, volcanic beach. Low clouds raced across the skies above, mirroring the ocean's frenetic energy.

'Look!' Daniel pointed further out. 'We must be almost there!'

Far out at sea flew a pair of bright orange serpentine shapes, with small figures astride them. Over the crest of the next hill, the Rowana den came into view. Dozens of dragons glided in and out of an immense stone barn, set back from the beach. A house with a steep-pitched roof stood further along the cinder sand.

They hurried down the hill, following the smell of sulphur and smoke to the entrance of the den. The roof, like the Esperance den, was open to the sky, and the floor inside was black, permanently charred by dragons' breath.

Majestic orange-scaled dragons moved amongst the detritus. Rangers, garbed in dark grey tunics, strode amongst them, separating any dragons that began to spar with one another, and leading others outside for a break from the confines of the den. A thrill raced through Esme at seeing the dragons again in such close quarters. She was still taking in the spectacle when Tango glided in from above, Rhys on her back.

Rhys spotted them at once and waved, but before they could respond, Tristan's bristled face blocked their view. He welcomed them with his usual low growl.

'Good trip? Rhys has been looking out for you. I'm busy with a sick dragon, so I'll leave it to him to show you around.'

Rhys appeared before them just as Tristan departed.

'Was that you out there?' asked Daniel. 'We saw you from the point.'

Rhys nodded, about to reply, but a snort from Tango interrupted him. He turned to stroke her neck, eliciting a low, satisfied thrum from the dragon.

'Feeling left out, are you? Remember Esme?'

The dragon's eyes met Esme's own, and she was lost again in their fire, before being brought back by Rhys's voice.

'Come on. I'll show you all around.'

Esme and Lillian stowed their gear in a room to the side of the den, where they would be spending their nights. On occasion, Esme looked around for the shadow, but it had hidden itself well. The rest of the afternoon rushed by, and they ended their day on the beach of black sand, where the setting sun tinged the waves with red and gold. They watched the flame-coloured Rows dip in and out of the fiery sea until the horizon grew dark, and night fell.

Chapter Twenty-Seven

Dinner that night was served in the dragonmaster's house, in a dining hall large enough to accommodate every last ranger who worked inside the den. Rough-hewn wooden tables crowded the space, and a treasure trove of trophies, paintings, and tapestries covered the walls.

After dinner, Esme went up to examine some of the pieces, and Tristan and Daniel joined her there, pausing in front of a large banner that depicted Rowana's regional emblem: a coiling dragon, wreathed in smoke. Beneath it hung a painting of another venerable dragon, fast asleep in a vast subterranean space. Rock walls glowed red around the scarlet-scaled beast.

'That's Kendra, Rowana's oldest dragon,' said Tristan. 'Older dragons often end up retreating to caves under the sea or in mountains, where they slumber on for hundreds of years. Sometimes they never see a human ever again, and never seek them out. This one's meant to be living deep in Mt Asha, right here on our own island.'

'I've heard of her,' said Daniel. 'Esperance has a similar legend, about an ancient dragon called Amaris, said to sleep underneath the city. She's so old that people say she fought in the wars.'

Later that evening, Esme, Daniel, Lillian, and Rhys returned to the beach, loaded up with firewood and kindling. The moon was almost full, the stars so bright it was like someone had dusted the sky with glitter. Once the bonfire was roaring, Esme brought out Ariane's shell from her pocket and showed it to Rhys.

'Have a listen.'

He put the shell to his ear, and then lowered it again, surprised. 'That's a siren's song, isn't it?'

'You recognise it?' asked Lillian.

'We do training runs near their caves sometimes, although they usually stop singing once they realise we're there. Sirens and dragons don't mix so well.'

'The dragons probably mistake them for food,' Daniel said, laughing.

Rhys leaned forward and poked at the fire. 'I think that's exactly the case.' He returned the shell. 'Where did you get this?'

'It's my mother's. We were hoping to visit the sirens' caves while we're here.'

He shrugged. 'They live at the far edge of the Scryers' Sea, but I doubt they'll let you in, since you're not of their kind. They're very ... antisocial.'

While Lillian peppered Rhys with questions about the caves, the hiss of the fire and the rhythmic sigh of the waves had a soporific effect on Esme. The snarls in her mind smoothed out as she meditated upon the flames, sparks spraying into the sky.

Daniel was bent over the fire, rearranging the logs. From where she sat, it looked as though he was submersed in flame. He seemed older, for an instant—more mature.

'There's something different about you tonight,' she said to him. 'But I can't put my finger on what it is.'

'He looks like the same old Daniel to me,' said Lillian.

'Or maybe Esme's picked up on something you haven't.' Daniel smirked. 'Watch this.'

He reached toward the fire, and immersed his whole hand in the flames.

Esme stared at him in shock, waiting for him to take it out, but he didn't. He just stood there, hand outstretched, watching the flames shift and flicker over his fingers. His face bore no signs of pain or discomfort.

A feeling of disconnectedness—the same disengagement with

reality that Esme had struggled with on her very first day in Aeolia—came over her once more. She switched her gaze from Daniel to the fire, then back to Daniel.

'Wait … is this your Gift?'

Daniel withdrew his hand. She flinched—but it was completely unharmed.

'Yep. It's an uncommon one, like yours.' He could barely contain his grin. 'I'm impervious to fire. To burning of any sort.'

He picked up a flaming piece of wood and held it aloft like a torch.

'How long have you been able to do this?' Lillian cried out. 'Why didn't you tell us straight away?'

His face shone. 'It only happened this afternoon. While you and Esme were off unpacking. One of the younger dragons breathed fire right next to me, close enough to burn. But I couldn't feel it at all, and then I remembered Rhys had mentioned there have been fewer problems with Gifts over this way. So I picked up some hot cinders. The same thing happened.'

'I was right there beside him,' said Rhys. 'Daniel's fireproof. All over. We haven't told Dad yet.'

While Esme and Lillian struggled to absorb the news, Rhys produced a paper bag full of marshmallows. He skewered them on to sticks, and held them out to Esme and Lillian. Daniel simply took a handful from the bag, and held them out over the embers to toast them.

Esme fought the urge to grab his arm and pull it back. She couldn't get used to it.

'I thought Gifts didn't run much in your family,' said Lillian.

'They don't. There's an old family story, though: a ranger on my mother's side, decades ago, had the same Gift. He could stand in front of a dragon, command it to breathe fire on him, and come out completely unharmed. I didn't think it would happen to me, so I never said anything.'

He turned to Rhys, and laughed. 'Unlike Lillian. She never shuts up about what Gift she wants.'

Esme couldn't see Lillian very well in the flicker of the firelight, but she could sense her distress.

'Your marshmallows are burning,' said Lillian, and stalked off toward the water.

'Hnf!' Daniel called out through a mouthful of marshmallow. 'Cm bckph.' He swallowed. 'I was only joking!'

Esme followed Lillian down to the water. Moonlight caught the edge of the waves as they washed into shore.

'Are you okay? Daniel didn't mean anything by it.'

'Yeah ... I'm fine.' Lillian kicked up a cloud of sand. 'I'm just being silly. I'm happy for him. It's the best thing he could have hoped for. If he's impervious to fire, now his parents probably won't be so against him becoming a ranger. It's what he's always wanted.'

They looked back at Daniel. The flames cast a red glow on him, and from a distance he looked again as though he was part of the fire.

'Don't worry about your Gift, Lillian,' Esme said. 'I'm sure it will come when you least expect it.'

As Lillian knelt down toward the water, tiny crabs scuttled away underfoot. 'Is it wrong to want something so badly?'

Esme closed her eyes. The light of the pearl burned behind her eyelids.

'I guess that depends on what it is.'

Chapter Twenty-Eight

Daniel, armed with his new Gift, spent the greater part of the next day badgering Tristan to let him ride one of the dragons. All afternoon, Lillian, Esme, and Rhys observed the debate from the corner of the den, listening to Daniel mount one argument after another.

'I'm getting sick of hearing his voice,' muttered Lillian.

'It'll be much safer with my Gift,' Daniel pleaded. 'And I have ridden before. Back in Esperance.'

Tristan snorted. 'Riding as a passenger doesn't count. It's totally different, being up there on your own. There's a lot more to it than you think.'

'I can sort of see his point, Dad,' Rhys interrupted. 'With a Gift like that, I'd say he'd be a very valuable member of any den.

Tristan threw his son a long, solicitous look, his eyes lingering on Rhys's scars.

'How about Argus?' said Rhys. 'We could start Daniel on him.'

'Fine,' Tristan growled. 'Go rig up Argus. But no flying where I can't see you. Double-check everything, then check it again.'

Daniel's mouth was moving again, but this time no words were coming out.

'I don't think he expected this to work,' whispered Esme to Lillian.

Finally, he stuttered, 'I—I can't thank you enough.'

'Then don't. Thank me by not getting yourself hurt.' Tristan strode off to get the gear.

Argus, an old, regal-looking dragon, rested beside the doors of the den. His scales had a dull gleam to them, like beaten copper. A long, jagged scar twisted down one side of his long body.

'All the new riders start on Argus,' said Rhys, slapping the dragon's flank. 'He knew my grandfather, and my great grandfather. He's a good, steady dragon, and forgiving of beginners. More forgiving than my dad, at least.'

Tristan arrived, jangling with gear. Rhys proceeded to strap a series of ropes and clips on to Argus, before leading the dragon outside to the sand. A chorus of other rangers joined them, adding their own advice to Tristan's barrage of instructions.

'Follow Argus's lead. He knows what he's doing.'

'Except when he doesn't. He's quite old, you know—'

'Listen to him. He'll teach you more than we ever can.'

'Stay loose. But not too loose, or—'

'Don't lose your focus.'

'Use the ridge to steady yourself. Don't lose your grip.'

'But don't grip too tightly.'

'And above all, the most important thing is—'

'Okay, okay,' said Rhys. 'Let's get going.'

Tristan had the last word. 'If all else fails, remember to breathe.'

Roused by shouts and cheers, Argus rose into the air and began to cruise back and forth along the shore. The old stalwart's wings were so immense that Argus only had to beat them twice to every four of Tango's. The dragons rose higher and higher, until Daniel looked like an insect, clinging to a branch in a wild storm.

Over the next few days, Daniel undertook a series of rigorous drills, designed by Tristan and administered by Rhys, until he began to shed his raw beginner status. By the end of the week, he was already starting to show signs of the disciplined bearing of the other riders in the den. In contrast to his awkward stance on the first day of riding, he now sat naturally on the dragon's back, his posture relaxed, his body moulded to the creature beneath him. Rhys, beside him, on Tango, held a similar pose.

'What's it like, riding?' asked Esme, over dinner one night.

Daniel laughed. 'You'll find out soon enough. Rhys has agreed to take us to the sirens' caves, first thing in the morning.'

Rhys nodded. 'Only if you're still keen to go. Daniel's improved enough to take one of you on Argus. The other can ride with me on Tango. What do you think?'

For days, Esme had been envying Daniel's newfound wings. 'I'd love to.'

'What about you, Lillian?' asked Rhys. 'We'll be clipping you both into a passenger's rig. It's perfectly safe.'

'I've ridden once before—'

'Good then, it's settled,' Daniel interjected.

'—it was terrifying.'

'Great. We'll leave straight after breakfast,' said Daniel, standing up to clear his plate.

After breakfast the next morning, Daniel and Rhys strapped extra rigs onto Tango and Argus, under Tristan's close supervision. The dragonmaster passed two packs to Esme and Lillian, identical to the ones Daniel and Rhys already wore.

'Standard issue for rangers. It's waterproof. You'll find a knife in there—careful, it's just been sharpened—a net, a sea-silk blanket for emergencies, ashlight, first-aid kit, a compass, and some food and water.'

Esme held the knife up to the light. It resembled a diver's knife, something used back home to help people escape from tangled nets, seaweed, and other underwater obstacles. This one, though, had a twisting dragon etched into its hilt.

'The caves are about an hour's flight from here,' said Tristan. 'Stay low. And at any sign of bad weather, head right back. No buts.'

'Thanks Dad,' said Rhys. 'We can take it from here.'

'So, who's going to ride with me?' asked Daniel, once Tristan had left.

Esme and Lillian, without realising it, were both edging toward the more experienced rider.

Rhys chuckled. 'How about we toss a coin?'

'Good idea.' Daniel pulled a merle out of his pocket. 'Heads, you ride with me, Lillian.'

The coin spun high in the air, before falling back into Daniel's palm, heads up. Lillian reluctantly moved over to Argus.

Rhys knelt to help Esme strap the diver's knife around her ankle. Her palms, slick with sweat, kept slipping.

'Steady there. You okay?'

Esme had forgotten, in all of her excitement about flying, that she had never been any higher in the sky than the platform of the Keeper's Tower, or the top of the lighthouse back home. 'I can do it,' she said firmly, finally managing to fasten the buckle.

Rhys stood back up. 'Don't worry. First time's the best.'

'No, it's not,' Lillian called out from a few feet away.

Rhys showed Esme how to clip in, emphasising the importance of checking everything twice. Lillian was already astride Argus, shifting about in her saddle and sounding increasingly agitated. Esme could hear every word of her conversation with Daniel.

'You might be fireproof, but remember, I'm not! It's so high up here. How do you—are you sure you know what you're doing—how do you keep yourself on this thing again?'

Daniel kept repeating the same thing, over and over again. 'Keep your feet in the cleats. It'll help you with your balance when he moves around.'

Rhys issued the same instructions, after helping Esme mount Tango. 'Got it?'

'Got it,' said Esme.

Tristan's advice sounded in her head. *If all else fails, remember to breathe.*

Argus took off first, disappearing through the open roof, followed by Tango. Esme hung on, white-knuckled, to the ridge before her, as Tango rose and fell alarmingly with each wing-beat. With each motion, she was flung up in the air, only to come crashing back down again. The sensation was akin to being thrown about in the dizzying heights of a ship's swaying crow's nest, while the vessel beneath ploughed the sea.

As Esme grew used to Tango's rhythm, she gradually loosened

her stranglehold on the dragon's ridge. Her apprehension swiftly turned to exhilaration, as she gave in to the joy of flight. Nothing mattered anymore, except the surge of Tango's body beneath her, the beat of the dragon's wings, the wind against her face, and the waves rushing by below. Now she knew why Daniel's face was fixed in a permanent smile.

Once they had passed by the volcano, garlanded by Asha's green hills and black beaches, they soared east, across the ocean. The dragons slowly dropped in height, until they were skimming the waves below. Before her stretched the boundless plains of the ocean: a vast, silky carpet rolling out over the edge of the world.

Their journey passed far too quickly. Soon, a tiny crescent-shaped islet appeared ahead. The dragons circled it, before making a bumpy landing onto the grassy verge that topped the cliffs.

Esme climbed down from Tango, and leaned against the dragon's side to catch her breath, glassy-eyed. 'That was amazing.'

'When Daniel improves,' Rhys said, 'we'll take you *under* the water.' They advanced to the edge of the cliffs, just in time to see the brown, whiskered heads of seals disappearing into the water. Half a mile out to sea, a circle of craggy outcrops rose up out of the blue.

'There,' said Rhys, pointing out across the water.

At her first sight of the sirens' home, only one thought ran through Esme's head.

I'm sure I've seen these caves somewhere before.

In her mind's eye, she was cast back to one of the paintings she had discovered the night of her father's wedding. It had depicted the exact same arrangement of rocks—and there had been a creature in the canvas, too. An elusive finned creature, half-submerged in the water.

A siren.

Maybe Mum really has been here.

Chapter Twenty-Nine

'I'll take the dragons for a run and a feed, and then meet you back here,' said Rhys, waving them off.

From the pebbled beach, the swim to the caves looked more challenging than it had from the top of the cliffs. The water was awash with whitecaps.

Daniel faltered. 'Are you sure about this?'

Lillian splashed into the sea after Esme. 'Having second thoughts?'

'Well, we don't exactly have an invitation, do we? And Rhys said that if they smell dragon on you—hey, wait!'

Daniel struck out for the caves along with the others. The current was running against them and they soon descended to make the rest of the trip underwater.

Esme kept an eye out for sirens, nudging Lillian when she thought she saw one in the distance. It turned out to be just a fish, flashing silver in the wavering light. When they resurfaced, the caves were less than a hundred yards away.

'They look deserted,' said Esme.

'Just because you can't see anybody, doesn't mean—'

Daniel's words disappeared in a gurgle. Fear registered on Lillian's face. A second later she was gone, too.

Only Esme was left, treading water, panic-stricken.

A silvery fin broke through the surface, before submerging again.

'Lillian! Daniel!' she cried out.

An icy hand grabbed her ankle, dragging her beneath the water's surface. Spiked tails flickered in the half-light. She reached down for the diver's knife strapped to her leg, and another hand pushed hers away. An arm encircled her waist, so tightly she could barely breathe.

A ghostly face peered into Esme's, before the three trespassers were pushed back up to the surface.

Esme and the others trod water, ringed by a circle of pale androgynous beings, with icy green eyes and hair as rough and choppy as the surface of the sea. Their sculpted cheekbones fell away like the curve of a perfect wave; their translucent skin was honed to a marbled beauty, their faces as mutable as the ocean itself. As they moved their heads, the light fell on their faces in different ways, and their features shifted between masculine and feminine with a hypnotising fluidity.

Lillian whispered urgently to Esme. 'The shell. Show them the shell.'

Esme scrabbled around in her pocket and offered Ariane's shell to the nearest siren. It produced an immediate effect, but not the one she had hoped for. Chill Arctic eyes bored into her. Tails slapped in the water and the sirens closed in, herding them away from the caves, back toward the islet.

'Wait!' Lillian called out.

She glanced at Esme and Daniel in desperation, then began to sing. Her voice, tremulous at first, soon rang out over the water. The song was in lilting siren language, and each note was filled with hope and longing. The sirens slowed and then stopped completely, turning their heads toward her.

As soon as the song ended, another took its place, floating over the waves from the direction of the sirens' caves.

This new music was eerie and beguiling, the kind of song that would have led Odysseus to a watery grave, had his crew not secured him to the mast of his ship. However, it bore no malice or evil intent. A soliloquy of the sea, it spoke of the ocean, of its many moods, of its towering rages and quiet reveries. The song spoke, too, of the rise and fall of tides, of the cycle of time, of the beginning and the end of all things. As it told its story, the sirens' hostile glances evaporated. They drew back and allowed Esme, Daniel, and Lillian safe passage.

The singer, another siren, rested on one of the rocks by the entrance to the caves. The siren's skin was so pale it was almost luminous, with scales that glittered like shards of frosted glass. Esme produced the shell; the siren took it and gazed down at the patterns on its surface.

'You presume to enter our sanctuary? Very few have crossed our threshold who are not of our kind.' The siren's eyes drifted back down to the shell. 'I am Melisande, a guardian of the songspells.'

'*The* Melisande? I—I just sang one of your songs,' Lillian stuttered.

The siren's face took on the semblance of a queen, imperiously choosing whom she would allow to enter her domain. She inclined her head toward Lillian. 'You may enter.'

She inspected Esme next. 'And you.'

Daniel looked up hopefully, but when Melisande turned her gaze upon him, her nostrils flared.

'You … you reek of dragons. You may wait out here.'

Esme and Lillian followed Melisande into a vaulted cavern where watery paths wound around rocks and into hidden crevices. A low hum throbbed through the space. As Esme's eyes adjusted to the dim interior, she saw that the cave's inhabitants were observing her with considerable interest, from a distance.

Melisande led them to the back of the long cave. A cluster of rocks formed a barrier before them, and the siren bid them climb before vanishing under the water. On the other side of the rocks lay a large pool, wreathed in light, which moved and twisted in myriad patterns, like a quilt of quicksilver. Magic saturated the air.

Melisande emerged from within the pool and came to rest on a rocky ledge. As she did, the luminescence from the pool crept further up the walls, and the hum grew louder. It rose and fell, transporting Esme to a distant past where the seas brimmed with stars and light and music.

Melisande's voice fell on Esme and Lillian like soft rain. 'In the beginning, when these islands were first formed, the waters of Aeolia looked much like this pool—for a time. We keep the old ways alive, but sadly, our songspells grow weaker with each passing day.'

She held up the shell toward Esme. The dots were now glowing, the way they had in Ariane's painting.

'Your name, child?'

'Esme. Esme Silver.'

'Tell me, Esme Silver, how did this come to you?'

'It was among my mother's things. She—Ariane—disappeared several years ago.'

'Your arrival in our waters, bearing a shell from the Isle of Mists, raised great suspicion in my kin. Others, too, have travelled here in the past, seeking knowledge of our home. Few have ever been granted entry.'

'It's a great honour,' said Lillian, dipping her head. Esme dipped hers, too.

Melisande's tone turned reverent. 'The Isle of Mists was our ancient home, the story of its decline so old that it has passed into legend. However, it still exists, hidden from all. It remains a desolate place, unfit for habitation. This shell is found only on its shores. It contains within it a songspell of restoration, of healing, and is one of many left there by our forebears. We no longer visit the isle, having lost all hope of its rebirth. From time to time, however, we receive news of its continued decline.'

Melisande dipped a cupped hand into the pool and drew out a palm full of water. It glowed like liquid silver.

'This Ariane of whom you speak was the most recent bearer of such news. Some years ago, she visited here in the company of a siren, one from another cave. Both had come directly from the isle. We were at first suspicious of your mother's motives, but she had gone there only to study it, to document its sad decline, to honour and preserve our history. Something we value greatly.'

She paused.

'Your mother's health had been badly affected by the poison on the isle. She lingered here for some days in order to recover. Fortunately for you, we count her, and her kin, amongst our few friends.'

Esme met the siren's gaze. 'I ... I need to go there. To the Isle of Mists.'

'After hearing how she fared, you still wish to visit this place of despair?'

'If it holds a clue as to what might have happened to her, then ... yes. With your permission, of course.'

The siren regarded her for a long while, and as she did her features shifted. She became a he—a regal king. This new persona studied her gravely. Esme's face grew hot. The longer the silence stretched, the more worried she grew. The siren, Esme was sure, could see inside her, see that deep down she was looking for more than just her mother. Any moment now Melisande would banish her from the cave, forbid her from ever visiting the Isle of Mists.

After what seemed an eternity, the siren spoke, inclining his head toward her.

'Very well.'

Esme sighed in relief. She was thankful when the siren turned his penetrating gaze away, toward Lillian.

'Your name?'

'Lillian, Lillian Lovell.'

When the siren next spoke, it was in another language. The syllables ran together like a stream. The pool's aura brightened again, and the siren shimmered along with it, less flesh and fin than pure light. For a moment, it was like Esme could see inside his soul. What she saw there was pure song, wrapped around pure song, in a never-ending litany.

'Your Gift, so close now, speaks to me of what might be.'

'My Gift?' asked Lillian.

'Use it wisely, if you wish to be counted amongst our kin. If you do, you will always be welcomed here ... songstress-in-waiting.'

Lillian, too mesmerised to speak, only managed a nod.

On the way back to the cave's entrance, Melisande returned the shell to Esme. The speckle of dots on the shell continued to fade and then gleam into life again. Outside, he bid them farewell.

'West from the Isle of Asha you will come across a vast rock, one carved by the ocean into the shape of a cresting wave.' He turned to Lillian. 'Sing the song from your companion's shell, and the isle will appear. It need not be sung by a songstress, it need only be sung well.'

Melisande's clear, tenor voice, so different from the soprano pitch of the first song, followed them back to the islet. The current was no longer against them, and a gentle wind—perhaps a gift of nature, or perhaps Melisande's parting gift—sped them back to shore.

Chapter Thirty

In her dreams, Esme wandered through a desolate cave, searching for her mother—and the pearl. Water dripped ceaselessly down the walls. In the stale air she heard a voice, as if the rocks themselves were speaking.

You should not have come here. This is an ancient place, not for mortals. Here you will perish.

The pearl, and her mother, called out to her, but as she drew closer, they receded into the darkness. Shadows pressed down on her until she could hardly breathe. She fought her fear, raising a hand to shine some ashlight. There *was* no ashlight. She leaned against the rock wall. There was no weight to her. She no longer had a body.

There was nothing left of her but shadow.

A sharp tap on her shoulder roused her from the dream.

'Esme, are you awake?' asked Lillian.

She shot up, almost cracking her head on the bunk above, before stumbling out of bed. 'I am now. Let's go.'

The cold, pre-dawn air chilled Esme's lungs as she hurried along the beach with the others, toward Asha's headland. Every one of her muscles ached, taut with anxiety; her nerves were frayed from broken sleep.

The black boulders of the point reminded her of the day she had chased the sea eagle around the cliffs, back at Spindrift, the day when everything had been set into motion. Whatever happened today, she could be sure of one thing. After all the efforts that others had made to shut her out of the investigation into her mother's disappearance, she had made it further than anyone.

A strip of wet sand led around the point, ending at the boatshed that Esme had noticed on their first day here. Daniel disappeared inside and emerged with a lantern, which he hung on the prow of one of the vessels. Esme could just make out the name *Kendra*, lettered on the boat's side.

'Got everything?' asked Daniel.

Esme and Lillian patted the packs slung over their shoulders. Daniel, along with his own pack, had brought with him a soft case, about five feet in length.

'What's that?' asked Esme.

'A spear, from the den. Just in case. Yes, I know how to use it,' he said, in response to their raised brows. 'Dad sometimes takes me spear-fishing on his work trips.'

They scrambled into the boat.

'Er, head west, *Kendra*,' said Esme.

The waves were more subdued around this side of the island, and the process of launching the boat to sea easily accomplished. Once they were settled on their voyage, Daniel groaned.

'I hardly slept at all. What about you?'

'Barely,' said Lillian. 'I couldn't get the song from the shell out of my head. I know it so well now, I could sing it in my sleep.'

'You *were* singing it in your sleep,' said Esme.

Daniel looked up from his compass. 'West north-west now, *Kendra*.' The boat changed course accordingly. 'Rhys muttered something about the rock being more north than west of the den, before going back to sleep,' Daniel explained. 'He wanted to come, too, but he's working today.'

Everyone fell quiet for a while, the silence of the journey broken only by the creak of the vessel, and the slap of the water against its sides. Clouds hid the moon, and the lantern did little to illuminate the inky water either side of the boat.

'It's so dark,' said Daniel. 'I can't see a thing.'

'Do you think that shadow could still be following us?' asked Lillian.

Esme didn't answer, but a cold tremor ran though her. She was sure that the shadow was with them. She was sure it had been watching her all night, concealed in the eaves of their room in the dragons' den.

The skies gradually lightened with the pink of dawn. A smudge of dark grey had appeared on the horizon.

'Is that the rock?' she asked the others.

Everyone strained forward to see.

'I don't think so,' said Daniel. 'It's moving, too. Here, have a look.' He handed her the spyglass.

'Oh, it's just another boat. What's it doing out here so early?'

'Fishing, I'd guess.'

Esme twisted back round to see how far they had come. Asha had fallen out of sight. Several orange specks wavered in the distance. They rapidly grew in size, and moments later, a flight of riderless Rows passed overhead.

The dragons stopped by the other boat, plunging in and out of the water around it.

'Must be a feed out there,' said Daniel, training his spyglass on them.

He was interrupted by a triumphant cry from Lillian.

'There! Look. To the left!'

A solitary extrusion of rock curved up out of the water, a curling wave forever on the brink of breaking into the sea. Daniel directed *Kendra* around the back of the islet, and they left her there, idling in the water. It was a short but steep climb to the top of the rock formation, where they stood on the lip and surveyed the empty expanse of sea. The ocean stretched out before them, formless and grey. Water lapped on to a small stretch of sand below the rock.

A slight movement, about fifty yards out, caught her eye. 'Look—what's that?'

It was the leathery head of an enormous turtle, bobbing up and down in the water. Meanwhile, Lillian was pacing nervously up and down the narrow ridge, holding the shell to her ear.

'Do you think it matters where I sing? Do you think the isle is really here? Maybe I should warm up—'

Daniel groaned. 'Just sing, before you fall off the edge.'

After a short while, she stepped forward, and began.

There was an authority to Lillian's voice that Esme hadn't heard before. The notes rang out like a clarion call, commanding the elements to obey, and bending the airs and waters to her will. The song rang out once, twice, and then a third time. The wind gusted the first round away, but the subsequent ones gathered power. On the third round, it was like a key had turned in a lock. The air grew muggy around them.

Goose bumps broke out on Esme's arms.

About a hundred yards from the rock, the air began to condense into a white mist. It spread outwards, creeping up and over the water, until it reached an invisible barrier, rising upward to form a great white wall. There was no end to it; the wall curved off to the left and right before disappearing out of sight.

'The isle,' Lillian whispered. 'It's really here.'

Tall, thin shapes loomed ominously behind the haze, like crooked giants' fingers, but the mist itself seemed oddly benign. Esme had assumed it would be dank and listless, weighed down with poison, but instead it resembled a fine morning mist, the kind that could lift with the first rays of the sun.

Lillian passed Esme the shell, her eyes wide. It was glowing again, the way it had in the sirens' caves.

'Maybe it knows it's close to home,' said Esme.

They made their way down to the base of the wave-shaped rock, and swam out toward the island, stopping a few yards short of the wall.

'I don't get it,' said Lillian, eyeing the mist. 'It doesn't look poisonous at all.'

'We could swim under,' suggested Esme. 'See how far we get. The island can't be that far off.'

Something bumped up against her from below: the mottled

head of the turtle. It was the biggest turtle Esme had ever seen: at least five feet long from head to tail, its grey back ridged with white dots. As its rheumy eyes blinked up at her, Professor Sage's wizened face came to mind. The old leatherback nudged her again, as if telling her to pay attention, and then paddled directly into the mist.

It reappeared almost at once, and floated beside them, showing no ill effects from its trip through the barrier.

Encouraged, Esme swam up and touched her fingers to the white wall. To her astonishment, a stream of revitalising energy ran through her.

'It's okay ... I think. It feels exactly like the songspell in the shell.'

After testing for themselves, Daniel and Lillian came to the same conclusion.

They swam into the mist, ready to dive down under the water if the vapour turned toxic. Instead, it continued to caress them with its fine fingers, its effect invigorating, like the spray of a waterfall.

The foreboding shapes that Esme had spied earlier turned out to be a series of soaring limestone rock formations, crowned with luxuriant greenery. The mist cleared beyond the last of the pinnacles, and the isle came into view.

Lillian gasped at the sight; Daniel gawked; Esme simply gazed, struck with awe.

The emerald sea lapped onto an idyllic isle, embroidered with crystal-clear waterways. The beach was strewn with the same shells Ariane had painted, the same kind of shell Esme held tight in her hand.

For a moment, Esme thought it had to be a mirage, but then she stepped onto the shore and felt solid ground beneath her feet.

Along the shore lay thousands of almost identical, smooth, patterned shells. She picked one up and cradled it in her hand. When she put it to her ear, the songspell flowed out at once. The sprinkles of dots on the indigo whorls pulsed with faint light. At night, this beach would shine like a galaxy of stars.

Lillian's eyes were as starry as the shells below.

'I don't know how this could have happened. All I can think is—maybe that last songspell the sirens left here finally worked.'

The isle was riven with streams, and hollowed out with pools: more of it lay under the water than above it. Where there was land, cycads, ferns, and velvet-green mosses thrived; insects buzzed, and brightly hued butterflies flitted through the sky. Tiny red-breasted birds winked in and out of wisps of trailing mist, or perched on the branches of twisted, vine-covered trees. There was no trace anywhere of the devastation that had once wracked the sirens' home.

'Can anyone else hear that?' asked Lillian.

Something else had joined the song of the birds, a familiar hum in the air. A pool, wreathed in life-giving mist, came into view. The heart of the island pulsed before them: an enormous pool, thick with magic. Traces of siren song emanated from the water; hundreds of tiny lights flickered across the surface in a mesmerising dance. Tiny rivulets streamed away from the pool, threading across the island like the living roots of an ancient tree.

Lillian leaned down beside the water. Her face, when she looked up again, was radiant. Esme couldn't tell whether the light was coming from within her, or from the pool.

'We must be the first people to ever see the island like this,' she whispered. 'The first to see it restored.'

Daniel grinned. 'And here I am, leaving dragon-stink all over the place.'

Nothing blighted the isle now—nothing except for their uninvited companion, the shadow that had followed them all the way here.

Esme had glimpsed it in the water on their way through the mist, and again when they had made it ashore. As they resumed their search for something—anything—that Ariane may have left behind, the shadow tracked them all over the island, settling under cover of leaves, darkening the edges of streams, and disappearing amongst the mosses and ferns.

Esme, Daniel, and Lillian combed the island for signs of Ariane's presence, and found nothing. They soon reached the island's northern end, where chalky limestone cliffs fell from a high plateau, and waterfalls shimmered off rocky inclines.

Up on the plateau, tendrils of mist drifted over the mossy rocks. From every side, cliffs dropped straight down into the sea, plumbing its depths. A sense of isolation pervaded this silent eyrie, and it infected Esme, too. She slumped down on one of the rocks.

'What's the matter?' asked Lillian.

'I'm glad the island's back to the way it was. But there's nothing of Mum here. I know it's been a long time since her visit, but I don't know. I just … had a feeling we were finally getting closer.'

Together, they ventured to the precipice and peered over it. The cliff's edge stretched out too far to see what might lie at its base.

'The only place left to look is down there,' she muttered.

'Then let's go see,' said Daniel, leading the way back down the cliffs.

When they reached the beach, Esme called out for the others to wait. She took out her mother's shell, and placed it reverently amongst its sisters and brothers.

It was like Ariane had left a part of herself here. Her mother had been a friend of the sirens, and their home had been restored since her visit. Maybe, somehow, these two things were connected; maybe something good had come of Ariane's visit here. The shell's patterns merged with the others on the beach, and when Esme stepped back, she couldn't make hers out anymore.

Her heart heavy, she made her way down to the water.

They swum round, staying close to the shore. By the time they arrived at the base of northern cliffs, the landscape had dramatically changed. Mist clung to the ribbed cliff-faces that joined the island with the sea. Daniel, who had stroked ahead, stopped and called back to them.

'There are caves around here!'

They caught up to him and dipped their hands in ashlight before entering the first cave's interior. The roof was lost in darkness, and stalagmites and stalactites crowded the space. The cave stretched a long way back, and Lillian and Daniel swam ahead. They called for Esme to join them, but she lingered at the entrance instead.

Something in her had quickened since their arrival at the cliffs: a flutter in her chest, replacing the dead weight of earlier. She couldn't articulate it, only follow a sudden impulse to keep going around the shoreline. She slipped outside the cave, and swam on.

Soon, Esme spied one more opening: a dark scar, cut deep into the rock. Shadows closed around her as she entered a long, narrow, cathedral-like space.

This was a place frozen in time, a palace of endless winter. Limestone turrets thrust up toward needled columns hanging from the heights. Countless helictites sprayed out in circlets, next to regal, fringed curtains of limestone. Shallow pools along the water's edge brimmed with calcified cave pearls. Water wound through it all, a royal carpet leading to the palace's inner sanctum.

A light beckoned her forward.

Further in, a thick limestone shelf ran around the interior of the cave. Daylight filtered on to part of it, from a gap high above in the rock.

The light shafted down onto a huddled figure: a woman, cocooned on the dais. Esme could feel a power radiating from her—a power she had felt before. As she drew closer, she could make out the figure's features—features she recognised, features she knew well. The power was emanating from something clasped in the woman's hand: a pearl, pulsing with soft light.

Hunger in her heart, words formed noiselessly on her lips, Esme flew toward her mother.

Chapter Thirty-One

Esme scaled the rocks to the platform, sprinted across the wide limestone shelf, and bent over the figure. It *was* her mother: dark-haired Ariane, her skin as pale and waxen as the alabaster cave in which she lay, as if she herself had become part of its endless tableaux of sculptured shapes.

The Pearl of Esperance glowed in her mother's hand, but all Esme had eyes for was the figure curled up around it. Fearing the worst, she put her head to Ariane's breast.

The faintest of heartbeats reached her ear.

Relief coursed through her. A dam burst inside, unleashing a flood of tears. Soon she was awash in great heaving sobs, clinging to her mother like a life raft.

By some miracle, her mother was still alive.

Her lips brushed against her ear; with trembling fingers, she smoothed a strand of Ariane's hair away.

'Mum! It's Esme. I found you. I'm here.'

She scrambled to open her pack and shook out the sea-silk blanket. She laid it over Ariane, gently, the way a mother covers a sleeping child. Then she called out to Daniel and Lillian. Their names echoed back at her, bouncing off the innumerable spires and tapers between her and the cavern's entrance.

Through her tears, her eyes alighted on the luminous pearl in Ariane's hand.

It was as if someone had taken all the beauty of the world and condensed it into one precious drop of light, reducing the universe to a singularity once more. Her face was reflected in its iridescent surface, shifting and shimmering, like Narcissus staring into the pool.

It sung out to her, calling her more strongly than ever. The pearl felt so much a part of her that—surely—it was hers already. She reached out toward it, but the splash of water at the cave's entrance brought her back to her senses.

'Lillian! Daniel! I'm over here—with Mum!'

The splashing grew louder, but instead of Daniel and Lillian, two strangers were climbing the rocks.

The first of them was a tall, silver-haired man, whom Esme recognised at once. Dr Nathan Mare's face was gaunter than in his photograph, the shadows of the cave filling in the hollows, but he still wore the same air of nonchalance.

The other person with him was less at ease: a boy around Esme's age, his eyes downcast. The boy's slouched posture suggested that he'd rather be anywhere than here. He hung back, skulking in the shadows, while Mare came closer.

'Esme? You've found Ariane. Thank the gods.' Mare's voice carried no malice, only relief and genuine concern.

'You're Nathan Mare ... aren't you?' she said uncertainly.

She cast a worried glance back at the cave entrance. Daniel and Lillian were nowhere to be seen.

'My friends ...'

'They're fine. The most important thing is that your mother is safe.'

Mare's tone was so reassuring that she found herself wanting to believe—despite all she knew—that he only had good intentions. Now that the doctor was fully illuminated by the skylight, the guile and cunning she had expected to see in him simply wasn't there.

It wasn't a spell, like the one in Celia's brooch. It went deeper than that. An instinct was rising in her that he would look after her, the way a child trusts implicitly that her parents have her best interests at heart. Esme fought against it, but there was an aura about Mare that was rapidly subsuming her own.

Hadn't Professor Sage said that he'd saved people in the past? After all, he *was* a doctor. He'd know what to do.

She'd never seen such kind eyes.

'Let me examine her,' he said. 'See if she's still with us.'

'She is—sort of.'

He smiled a smile so intimate that it made Esme feel like she had known him all her life.

'If she is alive, then it can only be the pearl that has kept her alive. I imagine that the pearl's influence is what has restored the isle, too. I was so surprised to find it the way it is. I read all about its devastation in your mother's compendium.'

Still uncertain what to do, Esme strained for a sight of Daniel and Lillian. The cave's surreal, water-sculpted shapes pressed in all around her. All she wanted was to get her mother somewhere safe, even if that meant trusting Dr Mare.

She gazed down at Ariane's sleeping form. The sight of her—so pale and vulnerable—set off warning bells in her head. Something inside her whispered that this was a trap: the same trap her mother had fallen into. She stared at Mare, trying to assess him with some objectivity. Then he fastened his eyes on the pearl for the first time.

It was like someone had flicked a switch, and plunged everything into darkness.

Mare's true intentions were laid bare, every artifice stripped away. There was something else in his eyes, along there with avarice. Deadly intent. Bloodlust. This was a man who would stop at nothing to get his prize.

'I can see now,' he said softly, 'why she would have wanted it for herself.'

His next words were muttered to himself, but Esme heard every one of them in the amplified chamber.

'I've searched for it so long … for half my life.'

Half his life.

Her fists clenched. Everything clicked into place. Until now, Esme hadn't been able to fathom why her mother would take the pearl to this unreachable hiding place. Now she knew. The last piece of the puzzle slotted in.

It was Mare's bond with Ariane that had led to all this in the first place. He must have befriended Ariane, encouraged her to work with the professor, and supported her research into Aeolia's past. All so that he could find the pearl—the real object of his desire.

She flung herself at her mother, pushing Mare away. 'No. Stay away from her!'

It made sense now, what Ariane had written in her notebook, the line in it about Nathan haunting her dreams. And the strange sketch, too, of the pearl, in the diary at her studio. The pearl, held up in triumph, surrounded by the sinking islands of Aeolia.

Ariane hadn't just been afraid for herself. She'd been afraid for everyone.

Mare stepped back, his voice silky-smooth. 'You're mistaken. I'm only trying to help.'

Esme's voice cut through the air, sharp like steel. 'I'm not mistaken. Not at all. I know what you really want: the Pearl of Esperance.'

'Nonsense,' said the doctor. 'Ariane coveted the pearl as much as everyone else. She used to talk endlessly about it.' His voice dropped to a whisper. 'She's had you fooled all along.'

Esme glanced down at her defenceless mother, at the dark hair curling over her pale neck.

'I don't believe you. I saw the way you looked at it. Mum brought the pearl here, where nobody would be able to find it—to hide it from *you.*'

Mare stepped back until he was half in shadow, half in light, like a nocturnal animal glancing away from a searching beam. A cry from outside penetrated the cave, followed by a scream, cut off abruptly.

It sounded like Lillian's voice.

'What's going on out there?' Esme cried out.

Mare shrugged. 'One of your friends may have gotten in the way of one of Quigley's rays.'

His voice had lost all of its warmth. Now, he sounded clinical and cold, like a surgeon dressed for theatre, ready to slice into skin.

'Call it off!'

'There's not much I can do. They've all gone quite mad, like their creator. Not many people survive being mauled by stygians. Quigley's demise, I suppose, was inevitable.'

He glanced at the scar on Esme's leg, and she covered it instinctively.

Quigley. He had been a colleague of Mare's at the university—the same man who looked as though he had been infected by stygians, the same man who had mistaken her for Ariane, the same man who had died in hospital, demented and delirious.

'Those creatures—they're *his*? How—how do you know so much?'

Mare remained in the shadows, like a silver wolf on the perimeter of night. 'I have plenty of friends in the city who keep an eye on things for me.'

Friends? Celia had said that Mare had many friends in Esperance.

Esme's retort was spiked with bitterness. 'People don't treat their friends the way you do. When Mum was pregnant with me, you experimented with her Gift—and mine.'

He stepped closer, and his eyes fixed on the pearl again. 'I don't understand,' he crooned. 'I saved your life once, but now you seem to value it so little.' His careless glance brushed over her, as if she and her mother were mere specks of dust on a wall. 'I see that you have made up your mind. I just wish we could have met in better circumstances.'

He held out his hand.

'Give me the pearl, and I can save your mother.'

Mare was only a few feet away. He could easily have stepped forward and taken it. So why hadn't he?

'Take the pearl from her,' he repeated. 'She would let you have it. Take it, and give it to me.'

Then she remembered the lines in the Compendium. *The pearl can only change hands safely when it is gifted from one guardian to the next.*

She glared at him. 'The pearl isn't mine to give. And it isn't yours. It doesn't belong to one person. It belongs to Aeolia.'

Outwardly, she sounded so certain, but inside, there was little conviction to her words. She still wanted the pearl for herself, wanted to feel its power course through her veins. It was right there; she would just have to disentangle Ariane's fingers, and then—

'Very well.'

Mare retreated toward the boy, and returned with him a moment later. In the light, the boy's face appeared wan and unfocused. Mare's companion extended a hand, directing a thin blue stream of vapour toward Esme and her mother. The air around them turned cold.

'Stop it!' Esme cried out.

Slivers of frost had already begun to form in Ariane's hair.

'You can give me the pearl now,' said Mare, 'and save your mother—or what's left of her—or we can extract it from her frozen digits. A pity. You were such perfect subjects. A matching set.'

Chapter Thirty-Two

Esme shivered uncontrollably. Her fingers were clammy; her toes were going numb. Ariane's face was turning blue. Then she heard Mare's voice cry out, and the flow of freezing air stopped.

She looked up to see a shadow spreading throughout the cave; the same shadow that had warned her about the pearl, the same shadow that had followed her here, all the way from Esperance. It grew quickly, blackening the already dim interior, swallowing the limestone shapes around it. In the gloom, it thickened, until it was neither shadow nor form, but somehow both.

As it shifted and swayed, a figure became recognisable within its folds: a woman, her form indistinct, as if she could dissolve back into the blackness at any moment.

Mare drew up to his full height, and tentatively addressed the spectre. 'Ariane?'

Every muscle seized up in fear. Esme hadn't considered the possibility that the body lying beside her might merely be a husk— Ariane's real consciousness torn from it, wrapped up in darkness, warped by possession of the pearl. She searched the figure's face for some trace of her mother, but it was impossible to tell.

The wraith swivelled around to face Mare and the boy.

'How *dare* you try to take what is rightfully mine?' she shrieked. 'How *dare* you come between me and my beloved pearl?'

Shadowy ropes snaked out from her palms, trussing the two of them together. With another gesture, she flung the parcel of bodies up into the air, and then, with a final flick of the hand, turned the cave's contents into her personal arsenal. While they screamed, she raged above them, her words as cutting as the piercing shards of limestone.

With every word the woman spoke, her features became more distinct.

This wasn't Ariane.

Esme had seen this woman's divining rod in the keeper's clinic, read about her in the compendium, and witnessed the grief of the king and queen over their long-lost daughter. The spectre resembled Queen Sofia in almost every aspect.

It was Anna Agapios, the first Keeper of Ephyra, and the first person to succumb to the allure of the pearl.

Esme shielded her mother as best she could from the violent storm unleashed by Anna. Eventually her rage subsided, and she sent Mare and the boy crashing to the ground. She flew toward Esme and her mother, drawing the darkness with her.

'For thousands of years, fools like you have tried to abscond with my jewel, not knowing or caring that the pearl's power is already spoken for! This *woman*,' she pointed a long finger at Ariane and spat out the words, as if addressing a piece of vermin, 'is merely another in a long line of them.'

Anna's spiteful utterances echoed around the cave, but Esme didn't shrink or cower. With each word, she grew more and more angry, until finally, raw fury propelled her to her feet. It blazed through her, and with it came a momentary flash of claws and scales and dragons' breath, as if Tango had lent her some of her fiery heart.

'This *woman* is my mother, and she doesn't want the pearl for herself. She's protecting it—for all of Aeolia. She's keeping it safe from people like *you!*'

'People like *me*? *My* mother—*my* parents—*tricked* me into giving them my pearl. They took all I had, all that was mine, and then they abandoned me!' The shadows around Anna's figure writhed and contorted, and she began to glow red. 'All the knowledge in the world was mine. All knowledge—'

Apoplectic now, Anna flew to the top of the cave and erupted in volcanic rage. She spewed forth a stream of fire—cinders and flames and jets of lava—until the interior of the cave, filled with fire and brimstone, turned into the very image of the underworld.

When the fire abated, Anna flew forward, but Esme, her own heart still ablaze, balled her hands up into fists. 'They took the pearl from you for a reason. It's not yours—it's never been yours!'

'Enough!'

Esme flinched as an invisible hand slid down her lower leg, a hand that burned her when she tried to push it away. The strap on her ankle unbuckled by itself, and the diver's knife loosed itself from its sheath. It rose up and glided over to Ariane, where it hung directly over her heart.

Esme flung herself at Ariane. Her fingers grasped at her mother's, and closed over the pearl.

Esme was swept away, cast into the vast web of creation.

The pearl's power seared through her, quickening every part of her, transporting her to the realm of the gods. Every atom burned with possibility. She tasted eternity and supped at time immortal. She was an eye, a vast eye in which the world was reflected. She was the thread that ran through all things, unravelling the world at will. She could create, or destroy, at her whim. Time had no meaning here. Death was merely an abstraction.

The pearl floated in the air before her, crowding every corner of her vision. Queen Sofia appeared within it, incorporeal, crowned, sceptre in hand. Her voice betrayed no emotion.

'For what do you wish?'

Countless visions flashed before Esme. She saw herself enthroned as queen, the citizens of Aeolia bowing before her. Then, as a renowned enchantress, whose very thoughts could make and unmake the fabric of the world. If she wanted, she could wear the mantle of a great seer, possessing all knowledge of all things to come. If she wished, she could rise as a mighty conqueror, waging and winning wars across Aeolia. More and more images paraded before her, each more spellbinding than the one before.

'Search your heart. What do you truly desire?'

Search my heart?

As the images flickered within the pearl, she heard a quiet whisper from within. The voice plucked at her, gently and insistently. She pulled herself away from the pearl's potent power, and listened to her heart.

Then she gave her answer.

'All I've ever wished for is my mother to come back to me.'

The queen smiled: a sad smile, as if she was thinking of her own daughter. The pearl grew more luminous than ever before. Now it held no seer, nor queen, nor enchantress: only Esme's sleeping, dark-haired mother, whom she had sought for so long.

The visions faded. The figures vanished. An unearthly voice began to sing. It sung of the wonders of the world: of islands rising up from the depths of the ocean, of gods travelling across the far face of the briny seas, of a sea eagle soaring in the clouds. And as it sang, the bonds that had tied the pearl to Esme loosened and fell away.

Esme's eyes opened. Nothing had changed. The knife still hung over her mother's heart. The pearl still lay in her palm. Above her head, Anna curved over her and her mother, like a giant vulture about to feast.

'Give it to me!' Anna shrieked. 'Give me the pearl!'

Esme sprung to her feet. With one hand, she knocked the suspended knife away from her mother's heart. With the other, she held the pearl out before her, like she was wielding a weapon.

Anna's avaricious features froze in place.

Light burst from the pearl, converging into a beam as strong and searching as the eye of the lighthouse back home. The beam formed the blade of a sword, a sword of brilliant light. The pearl itself was embedded in its hilt.

Esme raised the blade high, and struck at the wraith again and again.

Screams filled the cave as the ethereal blade tore through the shadowy remains of the first keeper. Her shrieks turned to moans, and her moans turned to whimpers, until she was in tatters. Esme wrapped both hands around the sword's hilt, and with a forceful thrust, delivered the final blow.

Anna howled, then disintegrated into a thousand tiny wisps of darkness, fragments fine as ash. What was left of her swirled through the air, blowing across the length of the cave.

Her final whisper was like the last whistle of a dying wind: 'Thank you.'

As Anna dissolved into the ether, so did the bonds around Mare and the boy.

The sword vanished, and the pearl's light grew, illuminating the crystalline palace, animating its endless phantasmic forms and reflecting them in the water below. Nebulous figures appeared before Esme, becoming more and more corporeal as light continued to stream out from the pearl. Rulers of old, come to defend the pearl, appeared first; keepers too, armed with their divining rods; and warriors from ages past, dressed for battle, swords at the ready.

King Michail and Queen Sofia were amongst them.

Mare and his companion staggered to their feet. The remaining spirits raised their swords, sceptres, and divining rods, and charged toward them.

Mare and the boy cowered before the guardians of the pearl. Their faces were frozen in shock, white, apart from the bloody marks inflicted by Anna's spears. The boy recovered his senses first. He grabbed at Mare's arm and dragged him toward the water. Esme looked on as they swam away as fast as their injuries could allow.

When Mare was out of sight, the spirits gathered around Esme, bowing their heads in acknowledgment.

Then they, too, were gone.

Esme, unsteady on her feet, staggered back to her mother. She gazed around, bleary-eyed. Everything was still a blur: the attack by Mare, the fury of the first keeper, the beneficence of the pearl.

The pearl.

It still pulsed gently in her palm. She stared down at the lustrous gem. Its beauty no longer beguiled her the way it once had; her feverish, maddening desire to possess it was gone. All she felt was an urgent desire to return the pearl to its home, in the centre of Esperance.

She was roused by a splash in the water below. It was Lillian, swimming toward her, climbing up the steps. She quickly slipped the pearl into her pocket before Lillian could see it.

'Esme!'

Something was wrong. Someone was missing. The haze in her head began to clear. 'Daniel! Where is he? I heard—'

'Daniel's fine. He's gone back to Asha, to get Tristan and Rhys. Some of those rays attacked us again, but we managed to get up on the rocks. He got one of them with his spear. Wait, is that—'

Lillian had noticed Ariane's inert form. She hovered over Esme's mother, her eyes bright with tears. 'Oh, Esme. You found her.'

'She's alive. But I don't know what's wrong with her.' Esme's voice trembled. 'She won't wake up.'

As Esme buried her face in her hands, something warm fell over her shoulders: another blanket, followed by Lillian's arm.

Together they sat silently, surveying the remains of the battle. The diver's knife lay on the ground beside Ariane, shining in the light that spilled down from above. Blackened limestone spears were scattered around the edges of the shelf, like the remains of a bonfire. The cave reeked of smoke.

Lillian's brows lifted. 'What *happened* in here?'

'I thought it was you and Daniel coming in here, but ... it was

Mare.' Esme hugged the blanket to herself as she told Lillian all that had happened, pausing every so often to collect herself. From time to time she stole glances at her mother, reassuring herself that her presence wasn't some fleeting delusion, that she wouldn't dissolve into nothingness, the way Anna had.

Some time later, a voice called out: 'Esme! Lillian!'

Their names echoed through the cave. A pair of fiery orange wings flashed before them. It was Daniel, piloting Argus through the curtains of stone. As soon as the dragon landed on the limestone shelf, Daniel slid off and wrapped Esme in a hug so tight she could barely breathe.

'Sorry I took so long. That blasted song—took us eight tries to get it right.'

More commotion at the cave entrance signalled the arrival of Tango, ridden by Tristan and Rhys. She came to rest on the stone platform, landing right beside Esme. After checking Ariane's condition, Tristan and Rhys worked silently and efficiently to secure her on Argus, the bigger dragon. Esme, worried at the journey ahead, couldn't help pulling at one of the ropes.

'It'll hold, won't it?'

'Of course,' said Rhys. 'This is what we do. She'll be fine. How are *you* doing?'

Esme bit her lip. 'The cave—we only found it right at the end. We almost left without her.'

'Come on,' he said, offering her a hand up on to Argus. 'Let's get her out of here.'

The dragons beat up the cliffs and pierced through the veil of mist. Once they had settled into flight over the open sea, Esme glanced back, but the island was nowhere in sight. It had vanished back into the ether. The Scryers' Sea stretched back behind her, as blue and smooth as slate. Nothing disturbed the surface of the water except for a wave-shaped rock, forever on the brink of breaking into the waiting sea.

Chapter Thirty-Three

Pale curtains fluttered at the window, beyond which beckoned the lagoon and the winding waterways of Esperance. Ariane lay motionless, in silent repose. Only the slight rise and fall of her breast, beneath the covers, signified her tenuous hold on life. She had been back in Esperance a few days now, lodged in a clinic just off Keepers' Row.

In the time that had passed since her mother's rescue, Esme had hardly left her side. Each moment together was like a warm salve to Esme's heart. She bent over, smoothing Ariane's dark tresses, and adjusting the blanket under which she lay. Her mother looked no older than she had seven years ago; it was as if time had stopped for her during her extended sojourn on the Isle of Mists.

Ariane's eyelids curved downward, dark lashes kissing porcelain skin. Even in sleep, she still wore a hint of the enigmatic smile Esme knew so well.

She drank in her mother's presence, the way a parched heartland drinks in rain after a drought. Her eyes misted over. She had shed so many tears in the past few days that she didn't know how there could be any left. So much had happened in the years that Ariane had lost, so much of which she was unaware. How would Esme break the news about Penelope—if her mother woke up?

When she wakes up, she told herself.

The door cracked open.

'How is she?'

Augustine entered, dressed in his usual black attire, his blond hair tied back in its long ponytail.

'The same as she was yesterday,' said Esme, looking up. 'And the day before.'

'I thought it might be time for me to give her a full examination, now that the healers have concluded theirs. Willow's come with me to assist.'

The keeper unbuckled the case in his hand, and the diviner sprung out. She shook off her confinement by flitting around and inspecting the room, before settling on the windowsill. Augustine bent over Ariane solicitously, his eyes ranging over her inert form.

'Back on the isle ... I can't believe I almost trusted Mare,' said Esme. 'He said he only wanted to help, and for a moment I really believed him. He was so persuasive. It was like ... he had a Gift for it.'

The keeper sighed. 'Don't let it concern you. You're far from the first to have been drawn into his aura. Mare has always had extraordinary powers of influence, but they come to him naturally, I'm afraid. That's one of the things he *did* inherit from his parents. That, and a dangerous obsession with Gifts.'

Augustine sat down and rubbed at his temple.

'When Mare worked for me, Gifts were all he ever talked about. One day, he told me that he was researching ways to make them more powerful. We ended up in a furious argument. I told him that tampering with Gifts would throw the world out of balance, that magic was something to be treated with caution and respect.'

'*Memento, verentur, secundum,*' murmured Esme.

'Remember, revere, respect.' The keeper nodded. 'I'll never forget the look on his face when I told him that: the sheer disappointment, followed by hatred, pure hatred. He left the clinic that day, and never came back.'

'But he didn't stop researching, did he?' Esme pointed out bitterly. 'He kept on experimenting, just without his patients' knowledge. On people like my mother, and me.' She shook her head. 'I don't even want to think about what he might have done with the power of the pearl.'

'Well, it's thanks to you and your mother that we didn't find out.'

She nodded. 'What I don't understand, though, is why *I* got through all this okay. I wanted the pearl so badly for myself.'

She closed her eyes for a moment, recalling the pearl's beauty, the way it had taken over her senses. The power that ran through the pearl had left an indelible imprint on her. Its beauty still filled her with awe, but her greed to possess it was gone, replaced by a sort of reverence, a wish to safeguard it from all.

'I can see why the queen thought it was sent as a test,' she said.

The humour lines on Augustine's face creased. 'Or some sort of cruel cosmic joke, played on us for the gods' amusement.'

He regarded her thoughtfully.

'If the pearl *was* a test, then it's one you clearly passed. I cannot say for sure, but it is my theory that your love for your mother was strong enough for you to overcome your lust for the pearl.' He paused. 'A lust that Anna, Mare, and countless others were never able to conquer. I am glad that the first keeper, at least, has found peace. Anna's diviner disappeared from its glass case in my clinic a few days ago.'

Willow stirred and tapped at his hand impatiently.

'Yes, let us proceed.'

With a wave of Willow over Ariane's slumbering form, Augustine began his examination. Esme gripped the sides of her chair, anxiously awaiting his verdict. When the examination was complete, Augustine lay Willow across his lap. A troubled expression clouded his face.

'Your mother appears to still be whole in both body and mind. I was afraid for her, now that she no longer has the pearl's power to sustain her, but she is very much still with us.'

Esme let out a long, shaky breath. 'But will she wake up?'

'I don't know. From what I can ascertain, something has gone wrong with her Gift.'

'Her *Gift*?'

The keeper nodded. 'Ariane's Gift is the same as yours: the ability to travel through Aeolia's waters into the past.'

Of course, Esme thought. If she and her mother shared the same Gift, it explained so much: how Ariane seemed to know even more about Aeolia's past than the professor did; how she had discovered the pearl's hiding place; and, above all, Mare's abiding interest in her.

'From what I can tell,' the keeper continued, 'your mother's Gift is active right now—in constant use. Ariane isn't with us, because she's trapped somewhere in Aeolia's past. I doubt she even knows she's left the isle.'

Esme stared blankly at Augustine. His words were muffled, like he was speaking from far away. She struggled to make sense of things.

'Trapped? But how? When she was in the cave, she wasn't even in contact with water.'

'True enough. But you are forgetting what she had in her possession. The pearl is the very last essence of the most powerful substance in Aeolia: the water-drop that formed this world. A royal road into the past.'

Willow drifted from the keeper's lap and wandered around the room. 'I suspect your mother's plight is directly related to Mare's handiwork,' he continued. 'I spied the same thread of darkness in her Gift that I saw in yours. Travelling through Aeolia's past for so long, while under the influence of something as powerful as the pearl, by way of a Gift made even more unstable by Mare's tampering ... I'm afraid it's impossible to predict what will become of her.'

He laid a hand on hers.

'Rest assured, though, that we will do everything in our power to keep her safe. This clinic is staffed by the finest healers in the city.'

He wrestled Willow back into her case, and before leaving, put his hand to Ariane's brow. His brilliant royal-blue eyes, unchanged over generations, looked deep into Esme's.

'Don't despair. Your mother has made it this far, despite all odds. If she has half the mettle of her daughter, I'm sure she'll pull through.'

⚘

Esme paced the room incessantly after the keeper left, struggling to absorb the news. At least now she knew what was going on. No physical infirmity was keeping her mother asleep. Ariane's ailment was a magical one. All she could do, Esme decided in the end, was take the keeper's parting words to heart.

Somehow, her mother had made it through: survived her flight with the pearl, her years on the Isle of Mists, Mare's best efforts to extinguish her, and Anna's rage. Surely, she would make it through this trial, too.

She had to get back home and tell her dad the news. But would he even listen to her? She glanced down at her mother's sleeping form. The last time her father had been told of other worlds, he'd almost had her mother committed to a sanatorium. How would she convince him not only of the existence of another world, but that his long-lost wife awaited him there?

Ex-wife, she reminded herself, grimacing.

But all that could wait. She left the clinic and headed for the Merle Fountain to meet up with her friends. The citizens of Esperance were out in full force, celebrating the return of their good fortune. Groups of water-walkers, ecstatic that they could use their Gifts again without fear of sinking beneath the water's surface, glided across the canals, obstructing the flow of traffic. A few streets on, children shrieked with delight as they frolicked amongst the waves on a stretch of normally placid water. On the shore, a smiling group of water-weavers were busy stirring up the canal with expert gestures of their hands. The waves chased the children, the children chased the waves, and their joy infected Esme, too.

Daniel was waiting for her by the fountain. 'Hi! How's your mum? Any news?'

His smile slid off his face as she told him what had transpired that afternoon.

'Mare,' he said, disgust curling his lip. 'I'd like to have speared him as well as that ray.'

'I think he suffered plenty in the cave … after Anna showed up.'

For a short while, the two of them stood in silence, watching the water cascade over the marbled sea dragons, on its way to the coins below. The stygians were doubtless still in there, cannibalising each other in their hidden chamber, but the pearl the king had set them to guard was not.

'Thanks for helping me hide the pearl,' she said to Daniel, keeping her voice low. It was barely audible amongst the rush and burble of the fountain. 'Bringing it back here would never have worked. Too many people know about the hidden chamber. But your idea was perfect.'

'Thanks for hiding it from *me*,' he replied. 'If you hadn't kept it wrapped up the whole time, I doubt I'd have been able to resist using it to tell the gods off for leaving the pearl hanging around in the first place. Yeah, yeah, I get it, it's vital to the world's survival, but why torment us poor humans with it? I swear to Poseidon, that pearl—'

Lillian sprinted into view, puffing and panting. 'Stop,' she said, cutting Daniel off. 'I don't want to hear about the pearl. I don't want to know where you two hid it. I just want to forget about it.'

'We weren't going to tell you anyway,' muttered Daniel.

'How's your mum?' Lillian asked Esme.

When Esme repeated what she had told Daniel, Lillian's eyes narrowed. 'Ugh. I know a songspell for people like Mare. If I ever get to cast it, he'll wish he'd never been born at all.'

'Maybe you'll get your chance one day,' said Esme.

'So when are you going to tell your dad the news?' asked Daniel.

'I'm leaving tomorrow. I'll try and convince him to come here with me, but if I can't, I'll be back with or without him.' She paused. 'Do you think both of you could visit Mum while I'm gone? I know you've both done so much already, but … I trust you two more than anyone in the whole world.'

Trust. The word had left a strange taste in her mouth, but somehow, when it came to her friends, it sounded right.

'This world, anyway,' quipped Daniel.

'Of course we'll visit her,' said Lillian. 'Every day—at least until school starts up again. But you'll be back before then, won't you?'

'I hope so.'

Faint strains of music floated toward them from the direction of the plaza, and they decided to join in on the celebrations.

'If only they knew what you'd done, Esme,' said Daniel. 'Why the city's back to normal. You'd be a hero.'

'I hope they never find out,' she replied. 'The fewer people who know about the pearl, the better.'

Only a close circle of people knew the full story of Ariane and the pearl: Daniel and Lillian, Tristan and Rhys, Miranda, the professor, and the keeper. Celia and the mayor knew parts of the story, but nothing involving the pearl.

The citizens of Esperance, in the absence of another explanation, had just assumed that the earth had finally wearied of its long tantrum. Not a single tremor had affected Esperance since the pearl's return, and all over the city people's Gifts were blossoming back into life. Lord Mayor Trevelli revelled in the restoration of his city's fortunes; although, when interviewed about his role in it, he fell unusually silent.

'You'd get the key to the city,' Daniel went on. 'Free dragons-breath buns for life. Free everything.'

'Is that what the key to the city gives you?'

'I've got no idea. But you must get something, apart from a big fat golden key.'

'I'm pretty sure it's just honorary,' said Lillian.

Suddenly, Esme remembered a picture of two people holding the key to the city—an old photograph, in an old newspaper. Eleanor and Jules Mare. The glint of such a prize was instantly tarnished.

An honour I can do without, she thought.

'Fame's overrated,' she said to the others. 'Friendship's not.'

An impromptu choir had formed in the plaza, spilling over the steps that led to the entrance of the town hall. Hundreds of songstresses and bards sang songspells together, filling the air with magic. Tension fell away from the faces of the crowd as they swayed and danced and lost themselves in the music. The city was still in shambles, buildings were still in ruin, but the fear that had once stalked Esperance's streets had dissolved. Hope had been restored at last.

When the songspells ended, Esme and the others headed over to the palace bridge. High above, dragon riders and their steeds put on their own jubilant display, sending fireballs streaking through the night sky. The lake rippled red with dragon fire, reflected from above. For Esme, each sight and sound was sweeter for being the last.

When there was a break in the action, Daniel lowered his gaze. 'I told my parents about my Gift.'

'How did they take it?' asked Lillian.

'Still in shock. But they'll come round.' He smiled. 'I went to see the dragonmaster this afternoon, with a letter from Tristan. She offered me a job on the spot. One day a week in the Esperance den. I start tomorrow.'

'That's great,' said Esme.

'What about your Gift, Lillian?' Daniel asked. 'Has it come through yet?'

Lillian gave him an impish smile. 'No. But don't worry, you'll be the last to know when it does. Oh, look!' she cried.

Countless wisps of light were drifting toward them across the water. Soon the lake looked like it was floating amongst the stars, reminding Esme of the sirens' light filled pools, and the beach on the Isle of Mists. The sirens had already been told about the restoration of their home; Lillian had gone to deliver the news before their return to Esperance.

The sirens' ancestral home had been reborn. The citizens of Esperance, and the people of Aeolia, no longer had to endure endless calamity. As the three of them made their way home, hope flickered inside Esme. Surely, health could be restored to her mother, too.

She didn't mind so much indulging in wishful thinking these days.

The following day, Esme stood beside the rock pool on Laertes Island to say her goodbyes. The tide was turning. These pools would soon disappear, absorbed into the wider ocean as if they'd never been there at all. Above her soared Ariane's faithful companion: the sea eagle from Picton. The majestic bird arced over them, as if bidding farewell, before gliding back toward the city.

'Thank you,' she murmured, as it disappeared out of sight.

Daniel had given Esme a waterproof satchel, in which she had already stowed the compendium, as well as a roll of film, filled with photographs of her mother in the clinic.

Miranda handed her a wrapped bundle. 'Some breyberry bread for you—and your dad.'

She wiped away a tear, before enfolding Esme in a long hug. 'Don't worry about your mum. You've been so brave. She would be—will be—so proud of you.'

Lillian produced a shell she had brought back from the Isle of Mists, and slipped it into Esme's hand.

'Let me know if you can still hear the song when you get back home. If you can, maybe you can get your dad to listen, too. Good luck!'

Lillian made way for Daniel, who shifted from foot to foot.

'This is where we first met,' he said.

She nodded. 'You had your spyglass—you were watching for dragons. And now you're up there riding them.'

He enveloped Esme in a long hug. He had just returned from his first day in the den, and smelled of ash and fire and smoke.

'Melisande was right,' said Esme with a laugh when they broke apart. 'You do smell like dragon.'

They lingered there for a moment. Esme wasn't quite ready to go.

Tears pricked at her eyes, but she held them back. She didn't know what awaited her back on Picton, but she felt stronger than ever: more than ready to go and face Mavis, Penelope, and her father. Reuben, at least, would be glad to see her—she hoped.

She tightened the straps of her bag and waded into the pool.

'I'll be back in a few days, with or without my dad. Promise.'

Her friends returned her last wave. Daniel's voice followed her as she dived down to touch the enchanted shell at the bottom of the pool.

'Remember to breathe!'

Immediately, the water began to spin, but this time, Esme knew what to do. She flew down through the bottom of the pool, and back up the other side, toward Spindrift—and home.

In a cavern far below Esperance winds the sinuous coils of an ancient dragon, a creature so old that she has almost passed from the annals of history. Her name is Amaris. She slumbers on, dreaming of past conquests and vanquished foes, her sleep no longer disturbed by the travails of the earth. She guards the Pearl of Esperance, the luminous stone of the gods, and she guards it well, for the future of all Aeolia depends on it. The Pearl of Promise, in turn, dreams its own dreams: of those who have sought to possess it, those who have helped to protect it, and the enchanted drop of water whence it came.